BLOODLIST

▼

The man's heart and lungs were thundering in my ears like a train. All my senses were sharp and new and wonderful. I could even smell the blood, an exciting scent when mixed with the sour tang of fear. On his thick, rough neck the skin seemed oddly transparent where the large vein pulsed. First it disturbed, then it tantalized. My mouth sagged open, dry and aching with sudden thirst.

I felt drawn to it like a cat to milk . . .

THE VAMPIRE FILES

Don't miss Jack Fleming's continuing search for the woman he loves—the woman whose blood curse will haunt him for all eternity.

Book Two: *Lifeblood*—While Jack seeks the elusive Maureen, a determined vampire-hunter is stalking Jack.

Book Three: *Bloodcircle* (coming in October 1990)— Jack discovers others of his own kind.

THE ADVENTURE NEVER DIES!

Ace Books by P. N. Elrod

The Vampire Files

BLOODLIST
LIFEBLOOD
BLOODCIRCLE
ART IN THE BLOOD
FIRE IN THE BLOOD

The Vampire Files

— BOOK ONE —

BLOODLIST

P. N. ELROD

ACE BOOKS, NEW YORK

This book is an Ace original edition,
and has never been previously published.

BLOODLIST

An Ace Book/published by arrangement with
the author

PRINTING HISTORY
Ace edition/March 1990

ISBN: 0-441-06795-6

Ace Books are published by The Berkley Publishing Group,
200 Madison Avenue, New York, New York 10016.
The name ''ACE'' and ''A'' logo are trademarks
belonging to Charter Communications, Inc.

PRINTED IN THE UNITED STATES OF AMERICA

10 9 8 7 6 5 4 3

For Mark and Ben.

With special thanks to:
Walter B. Gibson,
Michael J. Stackpole,
Roger E. Moore, and Barbara G. Young,
the terrific people who cast
Dark Shadows *upon my childhood.*

And a very special thanks to
Mr. Jonathan Frid.

Throughout the whole vast, shadowy world of ghosts and demons there is no figure so terrible, no figure so dreadful and abhorred, yet dight with such fearful fascination, as the vampire, who is himself neither ghost nor demon, but yet who partakes the dark natures and possesses the mysterious and terrible qualities of both.

—*Montague Summers*
The Vampire: His Kith and Kin

THE CAR WAS doing at least forty when the right front fender smashed against my left hip and sent me spinning off the road to flop bonelessly into a mass of thick, windblown grass.

It was a well-engineered accident, involving no small skill on the part of the driver. A body, depending on its size and weight in relation to the speed and position of the car usually does two things: it either goes under the car or bounces over it. Going under, it can get dragged, leaving a lot of bloody physical evidence all over the road and vehicle. If it gets flipped up and over, the driver risks a dented hood and roof or a broken windshield or all three. The professional hit-and-run artist knows how to avoid such risks and will try to clip the target with just the front bumper or fender; that way he has only some scratched paint to touch up or at most a broken headlight to replace.

I had been hit by such an expert. There was minimal pain, though, and that was swiftly receding. The idea my spine had been broken was the first real thought to surface in my cobweb-clogged brain since I woke up on the beach. I'd been groggy then, with only enough stuff working in my head to shakily stand and blink down at my soaked clothes. It never occurred to me to question why I was on a beach and in such a condition, and I was still in a thought-numbing state of shock when I climbed a short, sandy rise and found the road. There was no rational decision on what direction to go in, my legs took me left and walked. When I heard a car motor rumbling up behind me I stuck out a thumb and walked sideways.

The small dot down the road swelled into a dark green Ford with a big lumpy-looking man at the wheel. While still a little distance off, the car slowed abruptly, its headlights raking painfully into my eyes. I shaded them, blinking stupidly as the motor gunned, gears shifted, and the thing shot forward. The driver held a straight course, as though he'd changed his mind about picking up a hitchhiker, then he swerved at the last possible second. If my brain had been running on more than one cylinder, I might have been able to jump away in time.

The landscape stopped spinning and I lay belly-up, staring at an unnaturally brilliant Milky Way a few feet from my nose, wondering what the hell was going on. I tried moving a little, the initial pain of the impact was gone, but I was cautious of broken bones. Everything worked perfectly, though—I'd been incredibly lucky. Twisting onto my stomach, I stared down the road.

The Ford stopped, the motor cut, and the lump behind the wheel was just levering himself out the door.

The only cover for fifty yards was long grass. The beach was just across the road, but this particular stretch was clear of concealing rocks. Except for the car, the only option left was a stand of trees on my side of the road, which was much too far away.

The man was coming up fast and had a gun in one hand.

Anything was better than waiting for it. My feet dug into the ground and I bolted for the trees like a frightened rabbit. He spotted me, changed course, and yelled for me to stop. After hitting me with the car, he couldn't have really expected me to do him any convenient favors.

In an open space a gunshot doesn't sound like a gunshot, not like the ones you hear at the movies. All I heard was a flat, unimpressive crack, then the impact sent me sprawling.

It'd been a lucky hit; we were at a slight angle to one another and the narrow part of my body was toward him. The bullet entered my lower right back, just above the pelvic bone, traced through my vitals and out the front, just above the belt buckle. I doubled up and instinctively tried to hold things in, but there was nothing. The sharp, hot pain was already vanishing and my hands came away clean from what should have been a bloody mess.

My would-be killer trotted up, turned me over, and stopped short as I stared accusingly at his stupefied face. He was puffing hard and looked ready to say something but gulped it back. He quickly leveled the gun with my eyes. The business end looked as big as an open manhole. His finger was ready on the trigger; orders were being sent from his brain to the tiny muscles, telling them to contract. Before they could respond I grabbed the gun and twisted it out of his hand. His finger was caught in the trigger guard, there was a soft pop, and he yelped with surprise and pain as one of the bones snapped.

He fell back, trying to get away, and I seized an ankle, jerked, and pulled him down. His left fist swung up and slammed into my face, but with little effect. I managed a weak, backhanded swat and left him half-stunned. In another second his arms were pinned to the ground and he was utterly unable to break free. It was easy to hold him still even though he was built and muscled like a wrestler and outweighed me by a good eighty pounds. He looked up at my face hovering inches from his own and whimpered.

The man's heart and lungs were thundering in my ears like a train. All my senses were sharp and new and wonderful. I could even smell the blood, an exciting scent when mixed with the sour tang of fear. On his thick, rough neck the skin seemed oddly transparent where the large vein pulsed. First it disturbed, then it tantalized. My mouth sagged open, dry and aching with sudden thirst. I felt drawn to it like a cat to milk.

He gagged and his bladder let go as my lips brushed his throat, then he passed out.

I jerked back, wondering what the hell I was trying to do. Pushing away until I no longer touched him, I lay facedown in the spiky grass, shaking like a fever victim until the thirst faded.

With a hand under each arm, I dragged him backward over the irregular clumps of grass and sand to his car. I felt strong enough to carry him, but didn't relish coming into contact with his wet pants. Fortunately the key was in the ignition, so I was spared a search of his lower pockets. I opened the passenger door and stuffed him inside.

My mind was more or less functioning again and full of questions. Who this stranger was and why he wanted to kill me seemed like good ones to start with, so I picked his coat pocket and went through his wallet.

The driver's license was issued to a Fred Sanderson of Cicero.

The name might have been fake, it meant nothing to me, but the town struck a sour note in my general memory. A bare ten years had passed since the Capone gang invaded the place and took over. Big Al was in jail now, gone but not forgotten if Sanderson was any example.

Except for five dollars and the phone number of someone named Elsie, there was nothing informative in the wallet. I unbuckled Sanderson's belt and slipped it from his well-muscled waist. He was heavy, but in solid condition. As I'd thought, the leather strip had been specially constructed to overlap on the inside. Working it open, I took careful count and transferred the five hundred dollars hidden there into my own pants pocket without a single pang of conscience. After what he'd put me through he owed me, and I needed the operating funds.

I looked long and hard at his face. The heavy jaw and thick lips were frustratingly familiar, but nothing clicked in my memory.

It was very bright now, the sky all strange with the sun and stars shining improbably together. It was confusing until I realized it was the moon that was flooding the place with such brilliance. Like icewater, fear spread out in my guts and left me shaking at the edges. The night was too bright, it was wrong, totally *wrong*.

Distraction. I needed distraction. Where was I?

East of us were tall buildings in the distance. I was still more or less in Chicago. The last thing I recalled was some phone call launching me out of the hotel I'd just checked into. I'd left at midafternoon to do something and ended up that night soaking wet on a deserted patch of Lake Michigan shoreline with some crazy trying to kill me. Wonderful.

I felt my head for lumps, found a swelling behind one ear, and smiled with relief. A concussion of some kind; that would account for the initial disorientation, the memory loss, maybe even make my eyes overly sensitive. I'd only imagined the gunshot and had taken care of Sanderson on adrenaline alone.

Almost as an afterthought I checked my wallet and was surprised to find it in place and intact. I thought I'd been mugged. The papers were out of order and damp, but everything was there, including the money and change left over from the precious twenty I'd used to pay for the hotel room. It was when I returned the wallet to its inside pocket that I noticed my shirt front. A big burn hole was in it just over my heart, surrounded by water-diluted red stains. There was a smaller hole lower down, next to my belt buckle.

I tore the shirt open and found an ugly round scar just left of the breastbone. It was large, but looked freshly healed.

The lapping of water on the shore sounded loudly in my ears. Far out on the silver lake, the streamlined shape of a rich man's yacht glided slowly east and disappeared behind an intervening point of land. My left hand twitched and clenched. I made it open again. The palm had more than a dozen puckered réd circles on it. More scars, and I couldn't think of how I'd acquired them or what might have caused them. At least they didn't hurt. My right hand was also damaged with a narrow pink welt like a nearly healed cut just above the knuckles. It, too, was painless. Cautiously I spread a hand over my heart. It should have been banging away like a trapped bird, but there was nothing, nothing but the scar and still night-cool flesh.

I rebuttoned the shirt, not wanting to look or speculate anymore and stared helplessly at the lake. It gave no answers or comfort so I opened the driver's door and slid behind the wheel. I rubbed my face and was surprised at the heaviness of the beard there. Reaching over, I swiveled the rearview mirror around and stared with an icy shock of comprehension at the empty glass.

No.

Please, God, *no*.

Death had come to me that night, unexpected and unfair. Death had changed me, then left, taking with it the memory of that supreme moment we all must face. Eyes shut, I hung on to the steering wheel and vainly tried to adjust emotionally to what had once been a distant and purely intellectual concept. In a way I was more frightened by the idea that someone had wanted to kill me than by the fact that they'd succeeded. It was too much to take in, the best thing was to shut down the feelings for the moment. I'd get used to things soon enough, not that there was much choice about it now. In a larger sense it was what animals and mankind had faced since old Adam found himself outside the garden: adapt or die.

Having died already, there was only one alternative left, even if it was mentally distressing.

For something to do I tied Sanderson's arms behind his back

with the belt and used his flowered necktie on his ankles. Rooting around in the glove compartment turned up several road maps, so I was able to make a good guess about our present location and figure out how to get back to my hotel.

It was a tight fit behind the wheel, we were about the same height, but my legs were longer. I didn't bother adjusting the seat, that was always more trouble than it was worth. The starter started, the engine kicked and caught, and I eased it into first. Thirty minutes later I stopped in what looked like a safe, secluded place and cut the motor. We were about a mile from my hotel according to the maps; an easy walk through the sleeping neighborhoods. This was a dead-looking business district, with a few tired stores, some dusty warehouses and empty lots decorated with weeds and broken glass. From the look of things, the Depression hadn't been kind to the place.

Sanderson was awake, but playing possum, the altered rhythm of his heart and lungs betraying his condition. He was either very controlled or too scared to flinch when I plucked his yellow silk handkerchief from his front pocket. I used it to rub my prints from the steering wheel, dashboard and gearshift, and stuffed it back in his pocket. His gun was weighing heavily in my own pocket as I leaned across the seat and gave his cheek a solid pat.

"You can open your eyes now, I know you're awake." My tongue played over teeth which had receded to their normal length. At least I'd be able to talk without lisping. "I said you can open your eyes." I gave him a hard shake.

They popped wide.

"Name?"

"F-Fred Sanderson."

"Sure it is. What are you doing in town, Fred?"

"Visiting friends."

"They got a boat?"

He shut up until shaken again. "Yeah, so what?"

"Why'd you run me down?"

"Wha—"

"You heard me, why did you try to kill me?"

The heavy jaw snapped shut again, his eyes rolled toward the door, and he struggled against his bonds. I lost my patience then, and for the first time took a great deal of pleasure hitting a man. I pulled the punches, though. I wanted to persuade, not kill him, and it took surprisingly few blows to soften him up. Despite his tough looks, he had no tolerance for pain.

"Frank Paco—said—I—just a job—" he burbled through a bloody nose.

"He your boss?"

"Yeah." Sniff.

"He wanted me dead? Why?"

He coughed messily.

"Why?"

"You wouldn't talk."

I got the handkerchief again and wiped his nose. "Neither are you."

"He wanted the list, you wouldn't tell him where, so he—" He froze. "How did you—it was right in the heart—"

"I got a bulletproof vest. Come on, keep talking."

Sanderson looked anything but convinced. "You *know* all this." His voice was rising with panic. "Why do you ask, you *know* all—"

"What's the boat's name?"

"Elvira."

"What's the list? What's on it?"

"I dunno—honest, I don't. *You* got it, you know what's—"

"How did I get it?"

"I dunno."

"Answer."

"It was Benny Galligar. You got it from him. *You* got it! I dunno nothing, I swear! Just lemme go!" He was all but screaming, and the panic had him rolling around, trying to break free. I tapped him again, did it too hard, and that ended the questioning for the night. Shoving the exasperation to one side, I went over the car again for prints and found it was registered to International Freshwater Transport, Inc. It might not be of much use, but I filed the name away for future reference.

Outside the car, I wiped the handles clean with the bottom of my coat and repeated the action on the passenger side. Sanderson's head was lolled over, leaving his neck taut and vulnerable, with the blood-smell rising from his body like perfume. I stepped back quickly before something regrettable happened, and hurried down the street.

Sooner or later, God help me, I would have to feed.

* * *

The hotel night clerk was half-asleep when I asked for my key.

"That's two-oh-two?" he mumbled, groping for it, but there was no key hanging next to the number. "Hey, you're not Mr. Ross."

"No, I'm Jack Fleming and I want my key."

"Fleming? Oh, yeah, we had to move your things out. Don't worry, I got them right back here."

One thing after another. "Why'd you move them out?"

"Well, you only paid for the one night and when you didn't come back, we couldn't leave the room go empty. There's a convention in town an' we gotta rent the room while there's business. You know how it is."

"Yeah, I know. Can I have my stuff?"

"Sure, no problem." He hauled out a battered suitcase and a smaller, but no less battered case that held the means of my livelihood, a typewriter. I found my clothes intact, if sloppily folded, and my portable seemed to be in working order. While I checked my things, the clerk had woken up and was checking me.

"Been having some trouble?" he asked cautiously. His eyes trailed with open curiosity from my unshaved face to my damp, grubby clothes.

"Something like that." I pulled out another coat from the suitcase, turned my back to the clerk, and changed the old for new.

"Jesus Christ, are you all right? There's a big hole and blood all over your back!"

It was annoying. In sparing the guy the sight of my punctured shirtfront, I'd given him the full benefit of the back, where the bullet that killed me had exited. I buttoned up the fresh coat and tried to bluff it through.

"Hey, you shoulda seen the *other* guy."

"No kiddin', there's—"

"Yeah, well, don't worry about it," I snapped. "The less you know, the better for both of us, if you know what I mean."

"Yeah, sure." He backed off unhappily. Perhaps as a long-time resident of Chicago he knew exactly what I meant.

"Do I owe any on my bill?"

"Just for one more day, that's all."

"You could have left things alone for another day, couldn't you?"

"Huh?"

"Couldn't you have left my stuff up there for one more day?"

"Mr. Fleming, you were *gone*—"

The man's tone alerted me. "Gone for how long?"

He looked in his book. "It was right here, you checked in Monday, then left your key with the day clerk—"

"Did I get any phone calls?"

"I dunno, we don't keep records of that. The switchboard girl might know. Anyway, when you didn't come back by checkout time Wednesday, we packed your things up. It's Friday now and we couldn't keep the room not knowing if you were coming back or not, not for no three days we couldn't."

Friday morning.

I paid up and left the hotel on shaking legs.

I wandered around for a couple hours, unhappy and frustrated by the lapse of memory. Perhaps it was the shock of being killed. Some people could block out horrible experiences in that way, and being murdered had to rank pretty high up on the horrible-experience list.

List. Whatever the hell that was.

Benny Galligar. I might have known him from New York.

It was getting brighter, the added light hurt.

The moon was long gone, the stars were fading, and things were brilliant enough right now that if I were still out when the sun came up, my eyeballs would fry in their sockets. I spotted a hand-painted hotel sign at the end of the block and hurried for it.

At the cost of fifty cents, and that was a severe overcharge, I got a monk's cell with a single dirty window overlooking a narrow alley. I locked the door, the lock a piece of bent wire that slipped through a metal eyelet screwed into the frame. The door still sagged open, so I shoved a rickety chair under the knob, but it was even money it'd all give way the first time someone breathed on it wrong.

Despite the limited view, the sunlight might still find a chink in the dirt and come in. I thought of sleeping under the bed, but one look at the floor changed my mind. I had joined the ranks of the Undead, but still retained firm ideas about basic sanitation. A thin blanket hung over the window dimmed things, but not by much.

I dragged my clothes off, poured water into the washbowl, and splashed my face and neck. Shaving would have to wait till tomorrow, there was no time tonight. It was creepy, anyway, not being able to see my face peering out from the mirror. I examined myself without one. Purple and black bruises were all over my stomach and flanks, with many short rows of small crescent marks that had cut the skin. I could guess they had come from brass knuckles. My wrists were encircled with raw-looking weals, indications I'd been tied down. Large crescents overlay the smaller ones, probably the result of some well-placed kicks.

I'd seen bodies like this before, but only in the morgue when I'd been covering a gang killing. The sight was always sickening. Considering the amount of damage I'd taken, the shot in the heart might have been an act of mercy. The bullet mark was still there, but looked less ugly than before. I felt for the exit hole and found a large rough depression on my back. Both were painless. The small circles on my left palm were still a puzzle, but they were quickly healing as well, the angry red softening to pink.

The sheer violence that had been directed so personally at me was more than enough to leave me emotionally stunned. *Why* it had happened was a total blank and overwhelmingly disturbing on every level.

I rubbed down with a wet towel and pulled on clean underwear and threw out the old. Of the bullet Sanderson had fired, there was no sign, except for the holes it left in my clothes. For some reason I thought about what my mom once told me concerning underwear and accidents and smiled, then my limbs went all stiff and sluggish. The sun had just come up.

Pulling the pillow and spread from the bed, I walked into the closet and shut the door. I dropped the linen on the floor to foil any light leaks and to put something between me and the dirt, then I dove headfirst into the pillow and didn't come up.

Maybe I expected something like sleep or straight black oblivion, but it wasn't that good. Frozen in place for the day, the body was utterly still, but occasionally it sent a sensory message along to the brain.

Hard floor.

Footsteps somewhere in the building.

Something crawling on the right hand.

The brain noted it all, but wouldn't or couldn't respond. It was busy dreaming.

Water, floating, darkness, pressure, blinding light. Cheap birth symbolism, but the midwife had brass knuckles and a gun. She had Sanderson's grinning face and stood aside so the doctor could aim his own gun and blast me back into the dark forever.

Heat, bad air, clothes soaked with a thousand years of sweat. Voices, yelling, wanting something. Where is it? Where did you put it?

Fighting them, but no control.

Her hair was a dark nest on the pillow, soft and thick in my fingers. Sky blue eyes flushing deep red as I gave her blood and she gave me heaven on earth in return. Where are you? Where—

—did you put it? Just tell us, we'll let you go.

Liar, I forget. I don't know. I'm dying.

I'd always bring her flowers. She didn't eat candy. She never ate. Our private joke.

Leave me alone, I don't have it, but they kept at me, killing an inch at a time.

Books tumbled open, the words clear and sharp and utterly false. Thousands of books lined up in uneven rows like an army before the uniforms are issued. One thick black book, almost, but not quite true. Her thick dark hair—forget the books, just love her, that's all she really wants. Give her—

—the list, where did you put it?

Where did you go? Why did you leave me?

A boat, a big one, but the water still closes over us all, pulling us down into the cold—

—and stiff, I've got to move. If I can just move I'll stop dreaming. God, let me sleep or wake, but not this.

No control.

A man screaming.

Falling.

Dying.

No control.

Sunset.

Release.

▲
2
▼

I PUSHED THE pillow away and forced air into the dormant lungs. The dream dance whirled away into nothing, leaving a cold, stiff, frightened man to deal with the memory. Why hadn't she told me about the dreams? She told me what to do when death-time came, but never mentioned this. Maybe it was just trauma, maybe it would fade eventually, for now there was nothing I could do but try to shrug it off and get dressed.

It was something of a trick to shave without looking, but if I got nicked I never felt it. It'd be interesting when it came time for a haircut, I'd yet to see a barbershop without a mirror.

My other suit was too heavy for the weather, but the heat didn't seem to be bothering me. In a way it was disturbing not to be sweating. I took down the blanket, tossed it on the bed and cracked the window for the sake of appearance. The spread and pillow joined the blanket, and I shut the closet door.

My shoes squeaked coming downstairs. The dip in the lake hadn't done them any good. I dropped the useless room key at the front desk and went outside.

The first trash can I found became home for my bullet-ridden, bloodstained clothes. The labels and laundry marks got thrown into a storm drain farther down the street.

A mercenary street kid charged me a nickel for directions to a district full of pawnshops. Most of them were closed by now, the ones still open didn't have what I needed. I leaned against a doorway, tired and restless. My senses were painfully sharp, matching my teeth. I pushed the canines back in their sockets with shaking fingers. I'd have to feed soon or drop in my tracks.

The last open shop looked no more promising than the rest, but the first thing I saw inside was the big steamer trunk in the middle aisle. It was a good three by five feet and solid looking. Except for some travel stickers and dust, it was almost new. My satisfaction was apparent to the sharp-eyed owner and it took ten minutes to haggle the price down to a reasonable level. Once in agreement, money changed hands and I was hauling the trunk out the door.

No cabs were in sight so I was resigned to walking the six blocks back to the hotel. The trunk was awkward with its bulk, but oddly lightweight because of my new strength. I went as quickly as I dared, hoping other pedestrians would be alert enough to get out of the way in time.

"Hey, buddy, c'mere a minute."

Startled at being addressed, I paused, then cursed myself. Just like any hick fresh off the farm, I was about to be mugged. The man in the alley was in deep shadow except where his gun poked out; fat lot of good it did him with my night vision.

"Come on, put down the box and get over here. Now." He waved the gun.

I eased the trunk to the pavement. I was fast enough now to take the guy, but the gun might go off and bring the cops, and I had no desire to risk putting bullet holes in my last suit. Wishing hard I were anyplace else, I stepped forward.

The man shimmered, went gray, and vanished. So did the alley.

As though from a long distance, I heard his yelp of surprise and the slap of feet as he ran away. That was of minor concern, though; I was having trouble with my senses again. No weight, no form, and just this side of total panic; I could see nothing, but was aware of shapes and sizes close by. I felt the wind pushing me right through the wall of a building, my body(?) was oozing between the cracks in the bricks. I shoved away hard and launched myself through the wall of the opposite building, and stumbled to my feet in a ladies' clothing store.

It was great to have feet again and legs and all the other things that usually come with a solid body. I leaned on a table, delighted to have hands again. Reality was just wonderful. . . .

I looked around and wondered how I was supposed to get out.

All in all, dematerialization was tough on the nerves, but a hell of a great way to avoid a mugging.

My escape from the dress shop was a reluctant undertaking. Going through the doors the usual way required breaking a lock and perhaps setting off an alarm. At least the place was closed. My sudden appearance out of nowhere might spoil business for the owner though it would have made for an easier exit out a door. I wasn't sure I could repeat the trick. In retrospect it seemed more instinctive than conscious, like trying to swim when thrown into water for the first time. Don't panic and the body would do all the rest.

The third try was successful.

One second I was in the shop, the next, outside with the trunk and making sure my body was all there. Everything was intact, but I was very tired and my throat ached with thirst.

I turned the room light on out of habit, then squeezed the trunk through the door. Between it, the bed, and my belongings, it was beginning to look like a set from a Marx Brothers movie. I sank onto the creaking chair and miserably considered food. There was no way I could cheat around my condition. The mere thought of going out for even the rarest of steaks made me nauseous, but that in turn led to another thought.

Hurrying downstairs, I whistled up a cab. By the time one arrived I was twitching with restlessness. I forced myself to move sedately getting in and remembered to sit close to the door to be out of sight of the rearview mirror.

"Where to, mister?"

"The Stockyards," I lisped around my teeth.

We crossed water twice to get there, the opposing natural force pressing me hard into the seat as the cab lurched forward. The pressure was uncomfortable but bearable. The roaring emptiness inside was far worse.

"You all right, mister?" the driver asked as I paid him.

I nodded without speaking and kept my eyes down, not wanting to frighten him. I felt strange and no doubt looked strange. The last time I was this way a man had fainted, and a repetition of the experience would be inconvenient now.

The air was permeated with the smell of blood. There were

other smells, but this was the one that cut through them all and gave me a direction to follow.

The place was full of people and noise, train whistles shrieked, cattle lowed and bellowed, men shouted and cursed—men were everywhere, including where I wanted to go.

I went in, anyway.

At this point I was challenged only once by a large specimen who, from the size of his shoulders, looked like he swung the sledgehammers that sent the animals on their final journey to the dinner tables. I couldn't understand what he was saying to me, except it was hostile in some way. He was nothing less than an annoying obstacle to walk past, but he stopped me with a slab of a hand.

This kind of behavior irritates me at the best of times, but I was now to the point of physical pain. I swatted his hand away and snarled some threat, a mild enough reaction considering how badly I felt. We locked eyes in anger for an instant and for the first time I became aware of another human mind.

I told him to leave, and from my brief contact with him knew he thought his sudden retreat was his own idea. I wanted to think about this, to examine and test it to make sure it was not just imagination, but something stronger and much more insistent was in charge. All it wanted was to end the desperate, empty agony that was turning me inside out. Clear thought blurred and faded, the body was taking over in order to survive. It needed privacy from the interference of others; sought and found it among the more distant cattle pens. It wanted a quiescent victim and chose the least alarmed animal from the dozen that milled around the enclosure.

Here, too, was a mind; an alien one to my own, with simple dull impulses I could override. It stood rooted as I approached because I wanted it to do so. I drew close and touched one of its big surface veins, nearly sobbing with relief. For what I had to do there was no conscious thought or the least anticipation of revulsion. This was now normal if I wanted to survive. I closed in, intuitively knowing what to do, cutting neatly through the thick flesh with my teeth to open the vein.

Warm and rich with life, it pulsed into my mouth.

No more than a minute passed and I had all I needed. I released the animal; physically, mentally, and gratefully. A little blood dribbled from the wound, but soon stopped and it mingled with others, apparently none the worse for wear. I leaned against a fence rail and wiped my lips clean with a handkerchief. The pain and tunnel vision were gone, it was like waking up from the day's bad dreams. I had only to shake off the memory and start functioning again. My first idea was to leave the Stockyards as discreetly as possible. My newly learned vanishing trick might come in handy, but I'd have to wait awhile on that one and get used to the idea.

Prosaically using my old dependable legs, I left the place and found a taxi, returned to the hotel, and had it wait. Upstairs, I threw my stuff in the trunk, carried it down, and checked out. The driver and I managed to secure the thing to the car. It stuck out the back, but was in no immediate danger of falling into the street.

I hunched down in the backseat and asked to be taken to the same train station that had welcomed me to the city two days ago. Correction, six days ago, but I'd think about the amnesia later, right now I felt like a finalist from a dance marathon. It was not enough to feed and shut out the sunlight, I had to have earth around my body and it would have to be soon. I had to go home.

Once at the station, I booked the trunk on the next train to Cincinnati. By the time a man came for it, I was already inside. To my delight I was able to vanish and reform without trouble and without disturbing the lock or thick leather straps. Gingerly perching on the typewriter case, I braced my arms against the sides and held the suitcase in place with my knees to keep things from rattling too much as I was bumped from one end of the station to the other. Packed in like a living pretzel, the trunk didn't seem nearly so large, but from the grunts and curses outside, the porter disagreed.

The trip, at least at night, was very boring. I initially suffered through a couple bouts of mild claustrophobia, but was far too weary to let the cramped quarters get to me. I kept movement to a minimum, not wanting to alarm the baggage man, but still shifted around, vainly seeking a more comfortable position. It was tempting to get out and take a walk, but I was abnormally tired and unsure of my ability to get back inside again. At least I didn't need air.

The train crawled toward Cincinnati, but the sun came up

before we got there, and I was trapped in the dark with senseless memories for the day. It was just as bad as the last dream bout, but faded sooner, and when the train stopped I'd slipped into a semi-aware trance that brought no rest, but did abridge the passage of time. When night came again I was stationary and correctly guessed from the intrusive sounds that the trunk had been unloaded and was waiting to be claimed.

I felt marginally better just being in Cincinnati, and drifted easily from the trunk to reform in a crouch among the other baggage. When no one was looking I slipped out and blended in with the rest of the travelers, keeping my hat pulled low. This was my hometown and I had a lot of friends, the last thing I wanted was to renew old acquaintances. Once outside, I ducked into a cab and gave directions that took us north of town and down a narrow, unlit rural road. The driver got a little nervous after awhile and asked me if I was sure I knew where I was going. I was sure, as sure as an iron filing knows where the magnet is.

I had him stop and asked if he minded waiting.

"Waiting for what? There's nothing out here."

I took out a dollar bill and told him that was his tip, tore it in two, and gave him half. He still looked apprehensive.

"I'll have to keep the meter running."

That was fine. I left the road and walked up an overgrown private lane.

Grandfather's farm was deserted now and the place seemed smaller than I'd remembered. In truth, the land around had shrunk over the years, sold off a few acres at a time to make the taxes. My father refused to sell the house itself, though, or the immediate acreage, not that there were many buyers these days. Grandfather and Great-Grandfather Fleming and their families were buried here along with a lot of memories. Run down as the place was, I was glad it was still ours.

My parents lived in a smaller, more modern house in the city. Mom treasured her gas stove and indoor plumbing; no one lived out here anymore. I looked up at a corner window on the second floor that marked the room I'd been born in. This was my home as I'd never known it before, the house standing on the living earth I needed to survive.

Searching the barn turned up some old feed sacks in good enough condition to use once the dust and field mice had been shaken out. Taking four sacks, I doubled them one inside the other, making two sturdy bags. Another search turned up a ball of twine and a rusty shovel with a broken handle. It would do. What it lacked in leverage I could make up for in strength.

The cemetery grounds were still cared for, indicating Dad's occasional presence. I cleared a patch under the big oak tree of leaves and acorn husks and began shoveling dirt into the bags, working over a large area so the missing soil would be less noticeable. When the bags were three-quarters full I twisted the ends and tied them up tight with the twine.

Despite the hard work I was no longer tired.

A big stone that hadn't been there on my last visit a few years back was marking Grandfather's grave. I went over to touch the cool gray granite. The previous wood marker had borne the same deeply chiseled letters that spelled out my own name.

In Memory Of
JONATHAN RUSSELL FLEMING
1820–1908

I was glad no sentimental phrase was carved under the date, nothing would have been appropriate. A man like Grandfather or the family's feelings for him could not have been so neatly summed up.

When I was eight, my puppy died. Like me it had been the runt of a litter of seven, and for that reason it was my favorite. With the dreadful practicality to be found on working farms, the body was disposed of in the trash burner. Unable to accept the idea, I hid under the porch all day holding the limp little ball of fur and wishing it back to life again. When the family missed me, I ignored their calls. After all, they'd ignored me and it was only fair.

In the end Mom found me and dragged me out, promising certain doom on my backside as soon as I dropped my britches. Even at that early age I was mulishly stubborn, refusing to participate in my punishment and resisting all efforts to be separated from the puppy.

Grandfather interfered.

"Not this time," he told Mom. "I'll take care of him. I'm not as mad as you are." He took my hand and we walked down to the graveyard and sat under the oak tree.

"You shouldn't have hidden out, Jack," he said at length.

"No, sir. But they were going to burn Pete, and I don't want him to go to Hell." I held my breath; it was the first time I'd used a bad word.

Incredibly, Grandfather nodded. "I see what you mean. Would you feel better if we buried him proper?"

"Yes, sir, but I don't want him dead."

"Neither do I, but there are a lot of things we can't do anything about, and death is one of them."

"Why?"

The old man considered the question awhile, trying to gear the answer for an eight-year-old mind. "You like summer, don't you?"

"Yes, sir, no school."

"But if it lasted all the time you might get tired of it, don't you think?"

"I dunno."

"When school comes along in the fall and you get to see all your friends again, aren't you glad of the change?"

"I guess."

"And when winter comes you do different things because of the snow, and that's a nice change, too."

"Yes, sir."

"Well, now—this is the interesting part, Jack—dying is a change, too, just like the seasons. People live in the spring like you and your brothers and sisters, they grow up to a long summer and autumn like your parents and me, and then sooner or later they die, and that's like winter. It's not a bad thing—it's only a change."

"But don't people go to Heaven?"

"Sure they do, but they have to change, they have to die to get there. Some folks are even glad of the change because it means they'll have no worries and something different to do. When your Grandma was dying years ago she was hurting and tired; she was ready for a change. We were sad when she was gone, but we also knew she wasn't hurting anymore. We knew she's gone to Heaven and was happy."

Grandfather's voice had cracked. I was stunned to see tears rolling down his lined face. He pulled out a bandanna and wiped them away.

"Now, I don't know everything, but I'll just bet you Pete was hurting somehow and knew he needed to die, and when he did, he didn't hurt no more. He didn't want to make you sad, but he just couldn't help it.''

"So he changed?''

"Yes.''

"So he's in Heaven?''

"I don't see why not, but it doesn't really matter what happens to his little body, it's all the same to him. The part of him that you loved isn't here no more—he changed. What really matters is that you know about this and that it's all right to feel sad. It's also good to be happy when you remember how he made you happy while he was around.''

I thought about it hard while we buried the puppy near the oak tree, ringing the small grave with some stones. Halfway through the job I started crying, and Grampy loaned me his bandanna without a word and went on with the work. When he finished, he looked up at the northern horizon and took a deep, cleansing breath.

"I think winter is coming,'' he said, and winked at me. It was only September; I didn't understand. I did the next morning when we found he'd died in his sleep. I was the only one who didn't cry at the funeral.

I couldn't help but think of my own change. "What would you think of me now, Grampy?'' I whispered at the stone. I could almost sense the big bones resting in their pine box, patiently waiting for the Second Coming.

I tossed the broken shovel back in the barn and stalked down the lane, the two thirty-pound bags swinging light in my hands.

The return trip to Chicago was boring, but easier to get through with the earth packed into the trunk with me. Rested and more confident about vanishing, I spent most of the night sitting on top of the baggage reading a dime magazine. I could almost ignore river crossings, and when daylight came I was able to truly sleep, or whatever it was. The dreaming had faded. The presence of the earth even dulled the next night's hunger down to a low-level ache.

It took a good half hour to claim my trunk. The Chicago station was very busy, just as it was when I first arrived. There was a week-old trail to pick up on, but I had a good idea about where to start.

The trunk was laboriously loaded into a cab, and the cab took me to a small hotel the driver knew about that was within walking distance of the Stockyards. It was a cut above the fleabag I'd last stayed in. For ten dollars a week I got heavier curtains, a fan that worked, a radio, and a private bath. Its proximity to the Yards must have had an effect on the price and the presence of luxury extras.

Not bothering to unpack or even drop off the key, I left the hotel to get some dinner. My visit this time was more discreet; I knew the lay of the land better and trusted my disappearing trick to keep me out of trouble. It was taking a little practice to get it just right, but I was catching on fast. Learning to wiggle my ears as a kid had taken a lot longer.

On the way back, I stopped at a newsstand, bought some local papers, a copy of the one I'd worked for in New York, and a street map. The vendor gave me directions to the nearest Western Union office. The place was open with two fresh-faced young clerks in command. I filled out a telegram to my parents saying I'd arrived in the Windy City and managed to land a terrific job at an ad agency and they'd advanced me some money for one of my ideas. Along with the message, I sent twenty-five dollars. They'd been having hard times since the Crash, and hardly a payday passed that I didn't mail them five bucks or so to help out, but this time the amount was conspicuously large. They might think I'd turned to bank robbery, which wasn't too far off the mark, but the truth was hardly something I could tell them about.

I went back to the hotel. While the tub was filling I read the headlines and funnies and jotted notes on the rates for the personal columns. Using the hotel stationery, I printed out my usual message, all seven words of it, then shut off the tub taps and went downstairs.

This place actually had a bellboy on duty. He was reading a comic book in an alcove with his wooden chair tilted back on two legs, making more dents in the floor. I asked him if he wanted to make four bits. He put away the book. It took a minute to straighten things out. His usual type of errand for a guest was to either locate a female companion or a bottle of booze or both, neither of which I had much use for at the moment. I gave him the four bits and enough money for him to place my message in all the papers I'd bought. It would run for two weeks.

He promised to do it first thing tomorrow. I told him to bring me the receipts in the evening and he'd get another tip.

Upstairs, my room had steamed up slightly from the bath water, so I opened the window and turned on the fan the thoughtful management had bolted to a table. It stirred the air around and felt good against my skin as I stripped.

By now the bruising was nearly gone and the scar over my heart was fast disappearing. My body was making good use of the fresh blood I'd imbibed.

I studied the tub warily before stepping in, grimacing at the flash of apprehension it caused. It was only the free-running stuff I had to worry about, really. Nothing happened when I stepped in and soaped up, it just felt like something ought to. I sank back and thought about the beach . . . perhaps with the water around me I could go back . . . the stars had been so bright, the lake stretching on forever . . . silver and black. Before the peace of the beach there had been crushing darkness . . . hard pressure pushing from all sides, weight dragging me down . . . smothering pressure, growing worse—

I was on my back on the bathroom floor along with a lot of water. The pressure was gone, but my left hand twitched as though electricity were running through it. My body trembled uncontrollably. It lasted a moment more, scaring the hell out of me, then abruptly stopped.

If it brought this kind of reaction, I wasn't so sure now I wanted to remember my death. I dressed, nervously tried to push the incident from my mind, and vowed never to relax in a tub again.

It was past midnight when I stepped out into the humid air and turned right. The address I wanted had been in the phone book and the map said it was on the same side of the Chicago River as my hotel. After spending the last two nights cooped up in a trunk I wanted a long walk. At least it would save on cab fare.

Forty minutes later I reached the warehouse offices of International Freshwater Transport, Inc. There was no dark green Ford in the street. I didn't know whether to be disappointed or relieved.

The front door was a thick, no-nonsense steel thing. I tried to go through the metal, but found it to be more dense than building bricks or my trunk and couldn't pass until I slid under the thin gap between the door and threshold. I felt like sand dribbling through the skinny part of an hourglass.

This operation had no budget for extras. The reception office was a small area divided from the warehouse by wood planks nailed to two-by-four framing. There was a steel desk, some broken-in chairs, and a couple file cabinets, suspiciously unlocked. The papers inside were routine and therefore useless.

The desk held the promise of a single locked drawer that I opened with the help of a letter opener. Inside were two ledger books, the last year's and this year's, and a half-full fifth of whiskey. After looking at the books, it became obvious the drawer had been locked because of the whiskey. IFT, Inc. was just what its name suggested: shipments came in, stayed at the warehouse, and then continued to their destinations. Most of the traffic was between the U.S. and Canada, hence "international" in the title. Maybe it looked good on the letterheads. Maybe Sanderson's car was stolen, in which case I was wasting my time.

I flipped through more papers lying on the desktop. Nothing. The blotter on the desk was a giant calendar. It was the last week of the month and covered with old doodles and odd notes. The first Monday was circled in red with an underlined notation. The ink had gotten smeared by something wet, so the specifics were lost, but there was one clear name in the mess.

Mr. Paco. Something or other—Mr. Paco.

Sanderson's boss. At least there was a connection, so I went through all the papers again more carefully, but had to give up. Aside from the single name on the blotter he wasn't mentioned again, but I went through the tried-and-true motions. I noted down names and addresses, anything that might prove useful later on. Taking no chances, I wiped away my fingerprints on the unlikely idea they might call the cops when the broken drawer was discovered. Finished with the office, I checked out the warehouse.

It was big, of course, and despite my now-excellent night vision, gloomy, but that was only an emotional reaction. The actual level of light was more than sufficient. Predictably, it was filled with hundreds of wooden crates, each labeled and neatly stacked. Some were marked as farm equipment, others as spare parts, nothing there was of a perishable nature. I pried open a box and rooted around in the packing material, finding new metal junk that did indeed look like spare parts to something. The operation looked well organized and aboveboard, and nothing, absolutely nothing, was familiar to me.

It was a quarter to four when I got back to my room. I thought I should feel tired, but wasn't, that I should be hungry, but there were no pangs. All the things one usually felt after an extended errand weren't there, and I missed them. I missed being human, even the physical discomforts would have been welcome. I was depressed and couldn't even get drunk to forget it.

My trunk was unlocked.

I stopped being depressed and got scared instead.

The lid flipped up. I was hardly aware of doing it. My eyes vainly tried to focus on something that should have been there but wasn't.

My precious bags of earth were gone.

In their place was a folded piece of hotel paper. I grabbed it up. The paper was covered with cramped, precise handwriting.

Dear Sir:

   You do not know me but, as you may gather, I know something of you. If you would learn more, meet me at the address below. I shall be there until dawn. You should have no difficulty locating the street, as it serves the Stockyards.

                                        Hopefully,

                                        A Friend

▲ 3 ▼

WITH GREAT CARE I refolded the paper, thinking furiously. I knew no one in town, unless I counted Fred Sanderson, and the note sounded too high-tone for his ilk. The writer was certainly aware of my nature since he'd taken my earth. He also had to be crazy. Who else but a complete nut would want to make friends with a vampire?

The map verified the meeting place was indeed only a few blocks from the Stockyards, no more than a ten-minute walk.

I made it in four.

Clearly aware it could be some sort of trap, I wavered awhile, torn between curiosity and caution. Grabbing the trunk and running back to Cincinnati was an attractive option, but the identity of my correspondent would remain a mystery, and probably one I couldn't afford. Somewhere down the line I'd been very careless.

Curiosity and the need to recover my earth won out, but I still checked the area before going in. It was a business district, with small stores at street level and a scattering of offices on the upper floors. Many of them were empty, the rest were struggling hard to reach the prosperity which was supposed to be just around the corner. I circled the entire block of buildings slowly, making sure there were no surprises trying to hide in the shadows. Except for a few parked cars with cold motors, the place was deserted and asleep.

There was one lit window in the building I wanted, up on the second floor. Blinds were drawn over the glass. I could see nothing from the street.

Inside, I climbed the stairs as quietly as possible, but the caution was wasted. Between the odd loose board and my shoes, the squeaks were deafening to my ears. At the landing were two doors facing each other with opaque glass panels set in them and numbers painted on the glass. The one with light shining on the other side was on the left. I went still and listened; in the room beyond a single set of lungs pumped shallowly.

Pressing hard against the wall to present a narrow target, I turned the knob slowly and pushed. The door swung open easily and without a creak. I could hear a heart now and it began beating rapidly. His lungs worked faster to keep pace. Given the circumstances, mine would be, too, if they still worked regularly.

The man's voice was belyingly calm. "I gather you found my note. Good evening to you, sir. Would you care to step into the light so we might better see each other?" He had a very distinct British accent.

I hadn't any better ideas and eased away from the wall. Inside was a small, plain room with a single wooden desk facing the door. The man standing behind it was in his mid-thirties, tall and on the thin side, with a bony face and beaky nose. His sharp gray eyes were fixed on me and gleaming with excitement.

On the floor next to the desk were my two bags of earth. He followed my look and took on an apologetic tone.

"I hope you weren't offended by the theatrics, but it was the one thing I could think of that would guarantee your coming here."

I was angry and let it show. He stiffened and clutched at something on his desk. Whatever it was lay under an open newspaper. It was too big for a handgun and the wrong shape for a rifle. I made myself calm down; he'd gone to considerable trouble and risk to get me here, I'd at least hear him out. A few moments passed with the two of us waiting for the other to make a move. His breathing evened out and I relaxed my posture.

"You seem to know who I am," I ventured.

"I only know the name you gave on the hotel register. However, I do know *what* you are."

"And what do you plan to do about it?"

"That depends entirely upon yourself." He gestured with his

free hand at a chair near the desk. "Perhaps you would like to make yourself more comfortable, Mr. . . . tell me, is it really Robinson?"

"Jack will do for now, and I like it out here well enough." I was acutely aware of the man's scrutiny, as if he were expecting something from me.

"Then it is true."

"About what?"

"That you cannot enter a dwelling without an invitation. I occasionally live here, you see."

I was liking the situation less and less. "Just tell me what you want."

"Yes, I see I'm being unfair, but I don't know you and have no reason to trust you."

"I could say the same thing." No invisible force like the want of an invitation was keeping me outside, only natural caution. I first wanted to know what he was hiding under the paper, and it did no harm to have him underestimating my abilities.

"Indeed, but then you are a much more dangerous person than I am if all the stories are true."

Great, the guy really was crazy. "How dangerous are you?"

"To you, at least during the day, I might prove to be very deadly."

He was perfectly right. He knew my hotel and might have means of finding out where I'd go should I decide to bolt for home, or I could walk in and grab my earth and discover the hard way what he had under the paper.

He watched me thinking it out. "I only said that to keep you here; I'm hoping you'll understand I need not be an enemy."

"What are you, anyway, some kind of—Van Helsing?" I nearly said Renfield and changed it only at the last second.

He was amused. "So you've read *Dracula*?"

"Yes, and seen the movie."

"What did you think of it?"

"They could have done worse."

"Was it very accurate?"

"In what way?"

"Concerning yourself, of course."

"I have yet to stalk around in a cape and tuxedo and drool over feminine throats."

"But you do have to drink blood?"

I found that very difficult to acknowledge.

"Why are you so uncomfortable with that concept?"

"Why are you so damned nosy? What do you want?"

"I apologize. I am being frightfully rude to treat you like a lab specimen. Please don't be offended that I got carried away."

The man seemed genuinely sincere. I shrugged. "I'm a journalist, I know how it is."

"Thank you. What paper do you work for?"

"I don't. I quit the one I worked for in New York and came here."

"And?"

"And nothing. I've been too busy to look for a job."

"How odd you should need one. I would have thought that over the years you would have accumulated sufficient funds to be very comfortable."

"You haven't quite got the right idea about me."

"What do you mean?"

"I mean I'm still new at this; I'm just four days old."

That made him pause. "You've been a vampire for only four days?"

"Nights, if you want to be accurate."

"How utterly fascinating."

"If you say so."

"Could you tell me how you came to be this way? Were you attacked by a vampire?"

The melodramatic question made me smile. I shook my head. "It's kind of a long story. . . ."

He took the hint. "May I have your word that you won't tear me to pieces if I ask you in?"

"It's not worth much since you don't know me."

He shrugged. "You took a chance coming here. I'll risk it."

A crazy man or a brave one. "You got it. Besides, this is my last good suit, I don't want to ruin it."

If the joke was funny, he didn't laugh. "Very well, Jack, enter freely and of your own will."

"Don't you think that sounds a little corny?"

"It does at that, but does it work?"

I walked in slowly, making a show of it. His heart was going like a hammer, but his face was calm; a frightened man, but good at hiding it. The idea that I was the inspiration for all this fear made me uncomfortable and nervous, so I'd have to put us both at ease. I stuck out my hand.

"Jack Fleming."

He carefully switched hands under the paper and gripped mine briefly. "Charles Escott."

"Glad to meet you."

"Please sit down." He again indicated the chair next to his desk. Good Lord, but we were so polite and formal.

I sat and tried to look harmless. After a moment, he sank into his own chair, his eyes never leaving me. Whatever he expected me to be like, he'd apparently overestimated my ferocity. I hadn't been ferocious in years. Escott's heart slowed down and I breathed a mental sigh of relief.

"It must be obvious that I am intensely curious about you," he said. "I would very much like to hear your story, if you don't mind telling it."

I chewed my lower lip and did my own sizing up of him, look for look and his surroundings. There were two doors: the one I used and another behind Escott. The walls were bare of any kind of decoration but white paint. The place gave no clue to his personality, the man himself was the only clue. Piercing, intelligent eyes, thin lips, nervous hands; he reminded me of one of my long-ago college professors. His clothes were neat and nondescript; not expensive, not cheap, ordinary and therefore unnoticeable. I'd already figured he'd been following me around. He must have been good at it since I'd been looking over my shoulder all evening.

"Do you plan to shoot me with whatever you have under the paper?"

"Sorry, I'm just naturally cautious." He drew the paper away to reveal a cocked crossbow.

This time the man knew his stuff. If anything could hurt me, it would be the wooden shaft lying ready in the contraption. I regarded it with some respect. "If it makes you more comfortable, you can keep it, just don't shoot me."

Escott's brows went up, surprised that I had given him such permission. It indicated that I could take the thing away from him if I chose. I was sure I could, but not anxious to force the issue. He took his hand from the trigger, but left the weapon within reach.

Having come to a sort of mutual truce, I felt more like talking.

"It started in New York a couple years ago. There was a big publicity build for the movie *Dracula*. It was quite a hit, women fainting in the aisles and that sort of thing. My editor sent me down to interview people who'd seen the show, and write up about how scared they were. It was all pretty predictable stuff, but then I met this girl who thought the whole thing was terribly funny. She was really beautiful. We got to talking about the supernatural. At first I thought she might be into spiritualism or astrology or some other silliness, but she wasn't. She was like a butterfly collector I once knew."

Escott made an expression indicating he needed that one explained.

"He had hundreds of butterflies, he knew all about them, and was willing to learn more, but he never actually wanted to *be* one. She was like that. She knew a lot, liked to talk, but didn't believe in it for a minute."

"I see. I gather you liked her."

"I fell in love the second I saw her." I left it at that, not knowing if Escott could possibly understand. I drew more air and went on. "We dated, just like a couple of kids, and one night she asked me over to her house. We ate dinner, at least I did. She never ate with me when we were out; I thought she was just kidding me along because of the movie. It was a private joke for us, you know? After dinner we listened to the radio, danced a little . . ." My voice was getting thick, I couldn't help it.

"Mr. Fleming, if this is too personal to you, you needn't go on."

I pulled myself together. "Thanks. You get the idea of what it all led up to, going into details—"

"I understand." He sounded as though he really did.

"After that, we were together all the time, at least at night. It was no joke, she really was a vampire, but it didn't seem to matter much. I was in total possession of my faculties, too. I did research on the subject, of course, and talked to her about it. None of the books I found on vampirism remotely mentioned anything about what we had or felt for each other. They were full of a lot of stories of helpless victims and bloodthirsty attackers; kind of sick stuff, really. If you want to get psychological you could call it symbolic rape. When you get into the Freudian end of things it really gets weird, but none of that had anything to do with the reality we shared."

"During this relationship did you—was there ever an exchange of blood?" He kept his voice carefully neutral.

"Yes," was my brief reply.

"The purpose of this exchange was to eventually make you like her?"

"If it worked."

"Worked?"

"She said it didn't always work or else the world would be hip-deep in vampires. Almost everyone is immune to it, you see. It's like a very rare disease: some people can't catch it even if they want to."

"You wanted to?"

"For us to always be together, yes, and she did what she could toward that end, but it was never certain. We'd have no way of knowing until the day I died, but at least until then we'd always be together."

"But something happened?"

The words were sticking in my throat. "We had a date. I went to her house to pick her up and she wasn't there. She didn't have a lot of possessions, but a few clothes and toiletries were gone and she left the rest of her stuff like she meant to come back. Later I got a card in the mail. She said she was having some trouble, that some people were after her because of what she was, and to look out for them. She'd come back when it was safe. That was five years ago." I left unsaid the weeks of worry, fear, and frustration and the months spent trying to find her. In five years the pain had not faded and the wound was still raw to touch.

He saw it on my face. "I'm very sorry."

"I think . . . maybe they found her." I got up suddenly and paced around the room, trying to work off the build of emotional energy. My back to him, I paused to look through the blinds at the empty street below. "You're the only one I've ever told the whole story to."

"I apologize for forcing the confidence. It shall not be repeated to anyone."

I believed him. "Thanks." After a while I got control again and sat down. "Life went on, I guess. I finally decided to leave

New York. Last Monday I breezed into town, found a flop for the night, got a phone call and walked out. Sometime Thursday night or Friday morning last I woke up dead on a beach just west of the city.''

He took a moment to digest it. ''Who called you?''

''I don't know, it might be someone named Benny Galligar.''

''How did you die?'' He made it sound like an ordinary question.

''I was shot. Before that I was beaten up badly.''

''Who did it? Why?''

''I don't know!''

''You don't—''

''Between Monday afternoon and Friday morning I can't remember a damned thing.''

''How extraordinary.''

''If you say so.'' Then I finished the rest of my story.

''How utterly extraordinary.''

''You're repeating yourself.''

''Yours is a fascinating case.''

''You sound like a doctor. What are you, anyway? It's your turn to talk.''

''Certainly I owe you that. I'm a private agent; people bring me their problems and I try to help them. The vernacular here would be private investigator, but I find that particular label and its attendant connotations can give people the wrong idea about my work.''

''You mean you don't do divorces.''

He stifled a smile and leaned forward clasping his hands together. ''Mr. Fleming, if you have no objections, I'd like very much to help you discover what occurred to you in those missing days—to help you solve your own murder, if you will.''

''Well, I don't know—''

''We could be of great help to one another.''

''I'm listening.''

''For instance, you're a newcomer to the city, but I know it very well. I know the people who run things and the people who control *them*. Capone may be gone now, but the gangs are still active and they are very powerful. Frank Paco heads one of them. If he had you killed he must have had a very good reason.''

He straightened, reaching for the crossbow. I tensed and then relaxed. He'd been looking for a pipe that had gotten shuffled under the paper. "Do you mind?"

"No, go ahead."

"It sometimes helps me to think, mostly it keeps me awake." He tilted the chair back after the pipe was drawing, and stared at the ceiling. I stared at my shoes and thought about getting another pair the next night. These looked like something off a bum, but worse. The pipe smoke gradually added a pungent flavor to the air, but for some reason it made me uncomfortable and I considered pulling the blinds up to improve the air circulation.

He was staring at me with open curiosity, and I was beginning to think it was his favorite expression.

"Excuse me, but are you breathing at all?"

"Only when I talk. I'm afraid it comes with the condition."

"In the winter you shall have to remember to wear a scarf over your mouth or people might notice."

"I hadn't thought of that. Listen, do you mind answering some of my questions?"

"Not at all."

"How did you find me and know what I am?"

"I confess to a lifelong interest in the outré, but never expected to come face-to-face with a living, so to speak, example. I first saw you at the railway station and was instantly struck by the fact that we physically resemble each other, though of course, you're a bit younger."

"I don't think so. How old do I look?"

"No more than twenty-three or -four."

"But I'm thirty-six," I protested.

"Perhaps it's part of your changed condition. That *is* very interesting. But to continue, I enjoy watching people: I note their mannerisms, walks, faces, but I don't like to get caught doing it, that spoils the fun. People draw the wrong conclusions or become offended or both, so I practice covert observation."

"Come again?"

"I don't get caught watching. I follow them, face one direction and look in another—and I study their reflections in mirrors."

"I didn't notice any mirrors."

"True, but there were several panels of glass available that served just as well. Even the window on the door of the cab you took was useful. I saw your trunk and the porter, but could not see you. Something as unusual as that could not be ignored, so I followed you in another cab to your hotel. I listened as you registered and got your room number and the name you gave. When you came back down and went to the Stockyards I lost you there somehow, but by great luck you turned up again at a newsstand that was on your route home. Then you spent some time at a Western Union office, and when you left I tried to find out the nature of the telegrams you sent. To their credit, the employees were quite reticent, though one did mention you'd sent money to your mother. Then I had to leave, lest I lose you. I set up a vigil at your hotel, intending to call on you during the day to see if my suspicions were correct. You left again some time later, so I seized the opportunity to search your room.

"Once inside, I took the liberty of going through your luggage and found those two bags of earth. It gave me quite a turn, because up to then I was still only half believing what my eyes had told me. Of course, you might have had some other reason for carrying them around, but it would hardly explain your lack of a reflection. I wanted to meet you and talk, but had to do it without placing myself in unnecessary danger. It would have to be under controllable conditions. My knowledge of vampires is, at present, limited to Stoker's book and that film. I had to hope they were correct. Leaving you my note, I took your bags to guarantee your coming, and set my defenses."

"Just the crossbow?"

"And the hope that you could not cross the threshold without an invitation."

"That's it?"

He opened the desk drawer and drew out some garlic and a large crucifix. He was puzzled when I didn't flinch away, and his eyes went wide with alarm when I actually picked them up. I wrinkled my nose at the garlic, but then I never did like the stuff. I gave it back to Escott. "You can't win them all."

He fingered the cross with astonishment. "But I thought—"

"Yeah, I did, too, once. Look at it this way: I was basically a decent guy before someone killed me, and I don't feel any different now. Maybe if I were, say, the real Dracula with his life history, I'd twitch if I saw a cross, too. As for the garlic, in the part of Europe where it originated as a weapon against vampires it's a basic cure for just about everything. You got a cold, rheumatism, a headache? Try a little garlic. Troubled by vampires? Use garlic, it can't hurt. It can't help, either. What good is something that smells bad against someone who doesn't have to breathe?''

"That is a good point," he admitted. "Was I at least right about the threshold?"

" 'Fraid not. How do you think I was able to get into the hotel in the first place?"

"Oh."

"How did you get into my room?"

"With the aid of some highly illegal, but very useful lock picks, which also served well for your trunk. I must compliment you on that for a very good idea; a large trunk is certainly less noticeable than a coffin."

"It was the only thing I could think of. Besides, it beats taking a flop in a closet."

"I'm sure a coffin might bar you from the better hotels as well."

I gave him a look. He was joking.

"Why, though? Why get to know me? If you're crazy it doesn't show."

"Thank you, I think." He shook his head. "I'm not sure if I can explain why. Perhaps I suffer from terminal curiosity. If you'd been a different sort of person from what you are, I don't think I'd have taken the chance I did tonight."

"What do you mean?"

"Well, any man who sends money home to his mother can't be all bad."

"Good grief."

"How did you evade me at the Stockyards?"

"Like this." I vanished, floated through the door, reformed and came back inside. Escott hadn't moved a muscle, but his heart was thumping hard and his eyes had gone a bit glassy.

After a long time, he said, "That was very interesting, not to mention unnerving. Would you mind doing that again?"

I didn't mind a bit, it was good practice. He was still unnerved. When I thought I had enough control, I tried a partial disappearance while still sitting in the chair. It was all pure show-off.

"That is absolutely astounding," he said. He looked like a

kid with a new toy. "I can see right through you. It's like a photographic double exposure. Can you talk while in this state?"

I moved my lips, there was still some air left to form words. After a second my reply became audible. Faint and hollow, I said, "Don't know, haven't tried."

"It seems the more solid you are the better the quality of sound." He stood and reached toward me. "May I?"

"Sure."

I was finding it interesting as well, though it was disturbing to see Escott's hand passing right through my midsection. I was certain I could feel it, like a tickling within.

"Rather cold," he commented. "And you have a tendency to drift."

"I have to concentrate when it's like this." I relaxed and materialized completely. "It's draining in a way."

"I should think so. Everything about you vanishes—your clothes and effects, that is—I wonder what your limits are." He held out his pipe. "Would you mind, just once more?"

I didn't. Escott took back the pipe and puffed on it. "Still lit . . . I find that very interesting."

"Why?"

"It means things are unaffected when they go with you. That could prove to be very useful."

I pondered on what he wanted to use it for, disappeared again, and came back. "There may be a weight or size limit. I tried to take the chair with me this time and couldn't."

"Perhaps you need more practice. We can research all this thoroughly, I'm sure. What you do is certainly not covered by the present laws of physics." Another idea struck him. "Are your teeth—may I examine them?"

I shrugged and opened my mouth.

"You're very fortunate; they're perfect."

"Erf-ik?"

"You've never had cavities."

"Uh-Ah-aah—"

"What?" He let go.

"But I've had cavities."

"Then you've no fillings."

"You sure? Check the back on this side."

He did and only found unblemished molars. "Your condition is not without its beneficial side effects."

I moaned, "This is getting strange."

"One more look?" He gently pushed back my upper lip and probed the gum area above the canines. "They would seem to be retractable . . . and very sharp." He tugged at one. "Extends at a slight outward angle . . . mm . . . about half an inch longer than the others." He released the tooth, and I felt it slowly slide back. "Extension probably the result of an involuntary reflex occurring when stimulated by hunger pangs. Is that correct?"

"Yeah, they come out when I need them."

"I might like to see that sometime." He fiddled with his pipe.

I found the man's clinical interest, at least on the subject of my dining habits, to be annoying.

Escott continued to poke and cluck to himself, oblivious to my growing irritation. It was like a medical exam, and I never liked medical exams. In the end, I had to take off my coat and shirt so he could see the bullet scars.

"There's hardly any mark in front at all now, but there *is* a large discoloration on your back . . . very slight, though, and it appears to have shrunk. From your description of the chest wound, I'd say you were shot at close range by a large-caliber bullet, perhaps a dum-dum."

"I took a forty-five auto off Sanderson."

"I'd wondered what you had that was making your coat pocket sag so. It would certainly meet the requirements."

"Here." I dug it out and gave it to him.

"And he shot you that second time without harming you?"

"It *hurt* and did not improve my suit. I didn't like it at all." I buttoned my shirt.

"I should think not." He looked out the window. "Well, well, it is getting rather late for you, and I'm a bit sleepy myself. Could we continue this discussion tomorrow at your convenience?"

"I'd like that, sure."

"In the meantime, I shall begin inquiries into your case."

"Well, go easy, you can see how rough these boys play. You better keep the gun."

"Very well, at least as evidence."

I picked up my bags of earth. "I'll be by a little after sundown."

"That would be perfect. Good night to you, Mr. Fleming."

"Good morning to you, Mr. Escott."

4

NOT MUCH OF the night was left. If I rushed it I could pull out and find another place to stay before the sun caught me. Instead I walked home, dumped the bags of earth back in the trunk, and got undressed. My instincts about people were fairly sharp by now, and I had a good feeling about the man. The question of whether or not to trust him had only been briefly considered. With something close to fear I realized I was alone, I needed a friend badly.

There was no hunger the next night, so I could skip visiting the Stockyards and go straight to Escott's office. The afterglow of the sunset made my eyes burn, though, and I made a mental note to acquire a pair of dark glasses at the first opportunity.

It was only eight. A fair amount of traffic still cluttered the street and my mind was on sunglasses, so I almost didn't notice the dark green Ford parked in front of Escott's stairway until too late. I approached the stair opening and at the last moment continued past without breaking stride. Two men were at the top, just emerging from Escott's door.

I raced around the block to get a good look at them from behind. Peering around the last corner, I was in time to see them stowing a long, heavy bundle of carpeting into the trunk of the Ford. They were red and puffing; their burden seemed overly heavy for its size. The trunk lid slammed down and they dusted their hands off. The one on the left had a bandaged right forefinger. It was Fred Sanderson.

Their backs to me, they opened the doors and got in. Before

those doors shut I was making a beeline for the trunk, crouching low. There was no time to try opening it. The engine was kicking over, giving me a face full of exhaust. Not having any better ideas, I vanished and seeped through the crack between the lid and the car's body before they pulled out. I cautiously resumed form again, making sure there was enough room to do so.

I was on my side, crammed uncomfortably against the rug which smelled of dust, grease, and other less pleasant things. It was difficult to hear well over the rumble of the car, but I was sure I detected muted breathing beneath the layers of nap. Reasonably certain it was Escott, I hoped we'd stop soon before he smothered. Under the present circumstances it was impossible to unwrap him.

After the first few minutes of the ride I lost all sense of direction and had to fight off motion sickness. We crossed water, and soon the sound of the wheels on the road steadied. There were no more stops and turns, and the speed was steady, so I gathered we were on a highway. This was worrying; if the ride were too long, I'd be stuck somewhere without my earth, but long before this could become a problem the car slowed and made a sharp right turn onto a very bumpy dirt road. We slid to a stop and the motor was cut.

I pressed an ear to the bundle and was reassured by the sound of working lungs, though I didn't think their owner was conscious yet. Outside, crickets and other small creatures made their little noises. Awkwardly close at hand, the two men lurched out of the car. Not wanting to be discovered in such a tactically poor position, I floated from the trunk and reformed where I hoped I wouldn't be seen.

Trees were all around, but too sparse to offer adequate cover. When I turned to face the car I thought the game was up, Sanderson was looking right at me, then his eyes skipped blindly past. He didn't have my night vision. His friend even gave him a flashlight to facilitate their work.

They opened the trunk and with a none-too-gentle wrench, hauled the bundle out, and dropped it on the ground. From their movements, I'd have to interfere soon, but dark or no dark, I didn't want to risk being recognized by Sanderson. I tied a handkerchief cowboy-fashion over my lower face, feeling foolish about the melodramatics, then turned up my coat collar and pulled down my hat.

The men were professionally matter-of-fact about their task. They yanked one end of the rug up and Escott's unconscious body rolled out onto the leaves and dirt.

"You want to do it here?" the other, younger man asked Sanderson.

"Nah, we might get blood all over us takin' him to the river."

"We could carry him in the rug."

"Georgie," came the patient reply, "we would then have to throw it in with him. The boss don't like wasting a good gimmick, he'll want to use the rug again someday, and then where would we be? Come on and get the legs."

They grunted and lifted their burden. Before they'd gotten ten feet, I darted in and punched Sanderson for all I was worth. I felt and heard bones give under my fist. The big man's head snapped back, and he shot straight away from me and smashed against a tree.

His partner had little time to react, but he was fast. He dropped Escott's legs and clawing for his gun when I knocked the wind out of him with a gut punch. He doubled over with a *whoosh* and was made unconscious by a more restrained tap on the head.

I tore my mask away and knelt by Escott, checking him over. There was a swelling behind his left ear and a little blood from a cut lip, but he seemed otherwise uninjured. On a hunch, I searched Georgie and found a whiskey flask. I sniffed to make sure it was drinkable and dribbled a little into Escott's sagging mouth. I was surprised at my own enormous relief when he coughed violently and opened his eyes. He was understandably dazed; it took a few more minutes and another swallow before he was up to asking questions.

"Dear me, how ever did we get out here?"

"By way of the Fred Sanderson taxi service."

"They caught me like a bloody amateur," he complained, painfully probing his lump. "Did they get you, too?"

"Hardly. I hitched a ride when I saw them load you into the car. Neither of them looked like carpet layers." I indicated the discarded rug.

Escott was unsteady, but made a game effort to get to his feet. I helped him. "I am very much in your debt, Mr. Fleming. I hope that I may somehow—"

"Don't worry about it," I interrupted. "You could have aced

me with a hammer and stake anytime today, but you didn't. We're even."

"But, my dear fellow, such an action never occurred to me." Escott was truly shocked.

"But *I* thought of it. The way I am now I gotta be careful who I trust, but I know you're gonna be square with me. Now before we get all maudlin, let's pack these two mugs in the car and get back home."

I left the flashlight with Escott and got busy manhandling Georgie into the backseat. Having had some practice at it, I removed his tie and secured his hands together behind him, then went back for Sanderson.

Neither of us had to venture very close to know something was seriously wrong. Sanderson's utterly loose posture was enough to alert Escott, who gingerly felt for a pulse. I already knew that to be a futile effort.

Escott turned the body face up into the light and his breath hissed sharply. I looked quickly away, sickened by what I'd done.

Twenty minutes later we were almost back in Chicago. Sanderson's body was in the trunk, wrapped in the rug. Occassionally Escott would check the backseat to make sure the now-blindfolded Georgie was quiet. I'd been silent, driving carefully to avoid the unwelcome attention of any cop with a quota to fill.

"You've got to understand," I finally said, "this is scaring the hell out of me."

"I do understand. A healthy dose of fear will certainly temper your actions from now on."

"That's not it. I'm afraid of what I've become. What I did back there—I knew what would happen if I hit him like that, and I did it anyway."

"Good."

I glanced at him, surprised. His face showed a dour expression that must have matched my own. "Good?"

"Mm. Do you honestly think I harbor any regret or pity for a man who would have been the agent of my death and was by your own guess responsible for yours? Your feeling of guilt is misplaced. Were our positions reversed I should give no more thought to the matter than a soldier does when he must shoot at the enemy."

Half a lifetime ago I had shot at the enemy. I hadn't liked it then, either.

"He would have met his death sooner or later, for such was his life, and then at the hands of someone with far less conscience. If it is any comfort to you, I'm sure he never knew what hit him."

"*What* is the magic word. What have I become? I'm no longer human."

"That is utter nonsense and for your own good I suggest you put it from your head as quickly as possible. Do you in all truth really believe the biological changes within you have stripped you of humanity? You still possess your mortal clay, you still have emotional needs. I think you are giving far too much credence to a fictional character created out of the imagination of an actor's manager."

I gave him a sharp look.

"No, I'm no mind reader, but I can follow your line of reasoning. The character Dracula was a monster. He was also a vampire. You are now a vampire, ergo, you are a monster."

"What makes you think I'm not? Maybe I should pull over and strangle the kid in the back."

"If you feel it's necessary, but you won't."

He was right, it'd been a stupid thing to say and said in anger.

"You're feeling guilty, hence this black reaction. Feel guilty if you must, but leave self-pity out of it, for it is the most destructive of all emotions."

"What makes you so smart?"

"I read a lot." He bowed his head in weariness, looking green at the edges.

"You still want to go on after this?" I said, meaning the investigation.

"Oh, yes, but not just this moment."

I heard something in the back and checked our prisoner from the mirror. "He's waking up," I whispered.

Escott nodded, tapping his lips with a finger. We kept silent for the rest of the trip while Georgie played possum in the backseat.

Following gestured directions, I negotiated the streets and pulled into a no-parking zone. We rubbed the interior down for fingerprints, got out, and Escott lifted the hood. He fiddled briefly with something as I kept a nervous lookout. We both jumped as the street was filled with the earsplitting blare of the car's horn. Escott dropped the hood, swiped at it with his handkerchief, then grabbed my arm, and we hustled out of sight around a corner.

"What was that for?" I asked as we left the area.

"There's a police station not a hundred feet from the car. Once that horn gets their attention they can take Georgie in at least for disturbing the peace. After they find Sanderson they can become more creative in their charges."

"Why didn't you want to question Georgie about this?"

"He wouldn't have known anything useful. I'm already certain Paco ordered my untimely demise because I was clumsy somewhere in my investigations. I did quite a lot of poking around today and he must have got the wind up, and can only expect more of the same until one or the other of us has been eliminated."

"You're pretty cool about it."

"Only because my head hurts too much at the moment for me to be overly concerned about the future."

"You can't go back to your office, they might be watching."

"I have other places to . . . uh . . . lay low for the time being. However, I do have to return to my office to fetch some paperwork; it's too important to leave. I'd be most obliged if you accompanied me. I don't feel well at all."

"Be glad to, but what if some of Paco's men are there?"

"I'm inclined to think only Sanderson and Georgie were involved with this job, but we won't know until we get there, which we won't do unless we find a cab."

Taking the hint, I left Escott resting on a bench outside a barbershop and went looking, turned up a cab near a hotel, and returned to pick him up. He gave directions and paid the driver off some two blocks away from our goal. We walked the rest of the way, eyes peeled, and turned onto the street that ran behind his office. He approached the door of a modest tobacco shop, produced a key, and went in, motioning me to follow. It was full of crowded shelves and fragrant smells, the second floor was devoted to storage and full of dusty crates. Escott pulled one away from the back wall and made something go click. A three-foot-tall section fitted between the wall studs popped open like a door. Two inches beyond this opening was another apparent wall. He put his ear to it and listened.

I made a reassuring gesture, then realized he couldn't see it, for we were in almost total darkness. "There's no one on the other side or I'd hear them," I murmured.

"Oh," he said. He pushed on the wall, opening another narrow door, and eased himself through. I followed. We were standing in a small washroom, but only for a moment. Escott went on to the room beyond.

I correctly guessed it to be Escott's living quarters behind the office. Except for a radio acting as a nightstand next to an army cot and the window blinds, the place was depressingly bare; even a hotel room had more personality. I found myself fidgeting as Escott moved smoothly around in the semidarkness. He'd pulled a suitcase from under the cot, opened a tiny closet, and was busily packing.

"You dropped a sock," I observed.

"On purpose. Should they send anyone here later I want them to draw the conclusion that I've departed in a great hurry, which is what I am no doubt doing. Besides, it was developing a hole."

He went to the office. His desk had been searched. He paused and grimaced at the mess, then stopped and grabbed up some scattered papers. "I'll have to sort this lot out later," he muttered. The crossbow was still on the desk; he picked it up and took it back to the bedroom. I wondered what his attackers had thought of it.

"This will hardly fit in my bag, I'll have to leave it in the tobacco shop for the time being. It is a bit too conspicuous to carry right now."

"How did you happen to have it in the first place?"

"It's a working prop left over from my acting days. I made it for a small part I had in the Scottish Play."

"The what?"

"*Macbeth*," he said sotto voce. "As a weapon these days it's a little bulky, but it is powerful, lethal, and silent. I have smaller ones, but thought you might be more impressed with something large."

"You thought right."

"Then you're certain wood can harm you?"

"The lady I knew in New York mentioned it."

"Ah." Escott returned to the washroom and shoved the suitcase through the doors, along with the crossbow. He paused at the medicine cabinet, dropped some shaving items into his pockets, and then, to my puzzlement, tugged at the frame of the cabinet itself. It swung out, revealing a flat metal box standing on edge in the space behind. He opened it, making sure the papers inside were still intact before taking them away.

"Who did your carpentry?"

"Oh, I did it all myself," he said with some pride. "I love this sort of thing, don't you?"

As Escott locked the tobacco shop door, I asked, "Do you own this place?"

"Half of it. The other owner actually runs it. I help him financially through these hard times and he helps me by maintaining a good hiding place and, if necessary, escape route with twenty-four-hour access and egress."

"Are you rich?"

"Sometimes." He swayed a little. "Sorry, that bash on the head is making itself felt."

"Lemme take your bag."

"Only if you insist."

"Where to now?"

"I'm not sure. Not knowing just where I slipped up on my investigations, I can't be certain which of my other places would be safe."

"Then stay away from them and get a hotel."

"Mr. Fleming, I don't think you have grasped the tremendous influence the gangs have on this city. If I show my face at the wrong hostel I am very likely to get it blown off, putting to naught your efforts tonight on my behalf. Within hours, if not already, Paco and his men are going to know of my miraculous escape and be looking for me. It's very bad for their image when someone thwarts them, you see."

"Then you'll leave town?"

"I'm . . . not sure." Beads of sweat had popped out on his forehead and his face was gray. He was having some kind of delayed reaction. I caught his arm to support him.

"Hey, you're really sick. Come on, we'll sneak you up the backstairs of my hotel, you can flop there."

"But I really shouldn't—"

"You can't think in the shape you're in now. You'll be safe enough there under my name."

He protested mildly once more, but now and then everybody needs a keeper. I appointed myself his and dragged him off.

Once back at the hotel, Escott collapsed with a groan on the bed while I ordered up some ice and poured out a double from Georgie's permanently borrowed flask. With the whiskey on the inside and the ice on the bump outside, he went into an exhausted but healing sleep. I was stuck with the whole rest of the night and wondering what to do with it when someone knocked at the door. It was the bellhop returning with my change and receipts.

"You wasn't here when I came on, or I'da brought 'em sooner."

"That's all right, I was busy. You got them all?"

He held up a few pounds of newsprint. "Sure do."

I tipped him and told him I'd want copies of each paper every night and to put it on my bill. He grinned, knowing I'd have to tip him each time he brought them up. I winked back and took the papers inside.

I spent the rest of the evening reading. My notice appeared in the personal columns of them all and by some miracle the wording and spelling was correct.

DEAREST MAUREEN, ARE YOU SAFE YET? JACK

It was the same notice I'd been putting in the papers without a break for the last five years. If she were alive, if she only glanced once at it, she would let me know. After all this time I'd little hope left. Checking the papers for a reply each day and getting none had eroded most of it away. I fended off the inevitable depression of disappointment by sifting through the rest of the pages.

The war in Spain was heating up, FDR was confident the economic crisis was over, and there was an encouraging rumor on the fashion pages that hemlines were going up. The shoe ads reminded me it was high time I did something about my footwear, so I squeaked downstairs to look for my friend the bellhop. I gave him a picture of what I wanted with my size scribbled next to it, five bucks, and a silent blessing for not asking questions.

It was a longer night than usual, with nothing to do but listen to Escott sleep. The papers filled the time up, though, and I kept my eyes and brain focused on them or else I'd be seeing Sanderson's mangled face instead. Before turning in I wrote a note for Escott, telling him he was welcome to stay as long as he wanted and to put any meals on my tab. I opened the window wide, turned on the fan, and took to my trunk for the day.

He was gone when I woke up, but there was a note on the radio stating his intention to return after dark. I was uneasy but let it go and went through my nightly ablutions, dressed, and strolled downstairs to buy something to read. The bellhop had my shoes, and I let him keep the change for his tip. He was making a fortune off his oddball guest, but I didn't mind; he was honest, incurious, and the shoes more or less fit. We got on so well he loaned me his own copy of *Shadow Magazine*. When Escott let himself in later, he found me comfortably engrossed in something called "Terror Island."

"An intriguing title," he observed. "Here, I borrowed your key."

"Anytime, I've got other ways of getting in." I marked my place and put the magazine to one side. He cocked an amused eye at it. "I know the writer; I like to keep up with his work," I said, trying not to sound defensive.

"I have serious doubts that anyone can, he turns them out at an astonishing rate."

"Well, they usually have more than one guy working on the stuff."

"Not for this one so far. Certain elements of his style have been constant."

"You don't seem the type to go for stuff like this."

"You are the first person who ever thought so."

"I take it you're feeling better?"

"Apart from the slight headache and some bruising, I am quite myself again, thank you."

"What were you doing out in broad daylight?"

"I was safe enough after I retraced my steps by making a few calls on the phone downstairs—"

"Have a seat"—I dragged a pile of newsprint from the chair—"and tell me all."

"Thank you, I will. Yesterday I paid a visit to International Freshwater Transport and while enquiring about their rates, took a good look around, especially at the faces of their help. At least three of them had no obvious duties other than to watch me, and the names of the daily work schedule were suspiciously neutral.''

''Neutral?''

''John Smith, John Jones, John—''

''I get it, go on.''

''As I was leaving the warehouse, I spotted Sanderson. With your description of him in mind and the fact that his index finger was still well bandaged, he was impossible to miss. He looked twice at me as well, perhaps for a moment he thought I was you. I left and then spent time researching the business. Several hours and false trails later, I determined that Frank Paco does own the business, but is overly modest about it. IFT is not a growing concern, they seem to make only enough to keep their heads above water—excuse the pun—but not much more. They also do not appear too interested in improving things, either. They were not at all anxious to do business with me, and the rates they quoted were discouragingly high.''

''So you think they have only a few select customers?''

''Yes, and to me that indicates smuggling.''

''What kind?''

''Almost anything: stolen goods, drugs, people wanting in or out of the country . . . Such business can be most profitable if properly organized. Perhaps if we returned to their warehouse and opened a few crates we could discover the source of their profits.''

''I'd be happy to try again.''

''Anyway, after all these labors I was quite starved and stopped in at a little cafe I like, and there made my downfall. It was pure carelessness on my part; that and the fact that Mr. Sanderson was a man very skilled at following people. His young partner Georgie was with him and sat nearby nursing some coffee, while the more noticeable Sanderson remained discreetly in his car. Georgie heard me order my meal sans the American accent I'd used at IFT. He must have mentioned it to Sanderson, then they followed me to my office.''

''How did you find this out?''

He coughed slightly. ''One of the waitresses there is somewhat fond of me, I can't imagine why, and she happened to notice their car tagging behind me when I drove off, and didn't like the looks of it. From there I can deduce their later movements. Having found my office, Sanderson probably called his boss to inform him of my suspicious activities at the warehouse. Paco is not known for his tolerant attitude toward the curious, so he sent them after me. I think it was Georgie who did the actual violence to my person. His shoes were rubber soled."

"How could he sneak up behind you in that small area?"

"Sanderson was using his car for a distraction. He was racing the motor with the bonnet up as though there were some problem with it. When I went to the window to see what the noise was about, Georgie coshed me. They went through my desk, as you saw, and fortunately for me, waited for darkness before taking me downstairs in the rug. You know the rest."

"Except what you did today."

"With that out of the way I went home for a change of clothes and to make more calls. Georgie is still in jail and his friend Paco has never heard of him. I've also found out Paco is no longer actively seeking me."

"Why not?"

"That is a good question. Perhaps he's under someone else's orders or something else has him busy."

"Who or what?"

He shrugged. "It or they have my gratitude in the meantime. I think I may have turned up an interesting possibility for you. If you've nothing better to do we can look into it more closely tonight."

"Are you kidding? I'll get my hat."

We went down and got into a black Nash that had been a luxury model a few years ago. The outside had some dimples in the metal running in an almost straight line from front to back, but the finish had been well polished and the interior was as clean and blank as his office.

"What are those marks? They look like bullet holes."

"They're bullet holes. I had them repaired, as they ruined the paint job."

"Bullet holes?"

"Bullet dents, actually."

"How'd they get there?"

"I understand someone took a few shots at the previous owner with a machine gun." He busied himself starting the motor.

On the front seat between us was a hat, a brown derby with

a red satin band. On one side of the band was a miniature stick-pin in the shape of a diamond-trimmed horseshoe. He took his own hat off and put this one on. He was wearing dark gray so it figured he had some good reason to look so mismatched. He saw the question forming on my face and smiled.

"It's our passport," he explained, which explained nothing. He liked his mystery game, so I let him enjoy it. He was working on my case and whatever he wanted was fine with me.

We drove to an area he said was called the Bronze Belt, which was Chicago's version of Harlem. Once there, he cruised the streets slowly, scanning them for something or someone. I asked him which.

"Oh, definitely a person. One has only to make the right contact and one is in."

I nearly asked in what, but that would have been too obvious, and I'd been thinking of something else, anyway. "Have you turned up anything on this Benny Galligar?"

"From my local sources I learned he is considered to be only 'small time,' though he specializes in safe-cracking and lately some bodyguard work. No one has seen him for a week or more, but I have several inquiries going. He should turn up soon."

"Hope so, I'd like to know why he called me, if he did call me."

"He is originally from New York. The logical inference is that he knows you from there. If you can recall anyone with that name—"

"He'll be changing his name like other people change socks. I did know one or two Bennys, though. In New York you practically trip over them; maybe if and when I see him—"

"He was described as a small man, graying hair, lined and lived-in face, forty to forty-five, nervous manner, sometimes affects an Irish accent when he's in the mood—"

That rang a bell. "Wait, Benny O'Hara, sometimes he'd sell me a tip, you know, where to go to see something interesting."

"For a story?"

"That's how it usually worked. I knew him as Benny O'Hara. How could he have known I was in town?"

"Perhaps he was staying at your hotel. I'll check on it. I've been there once, the night clerk remembers your last visit quite clearly, perhaps I can persuade him to go back a little further in his memory."

"Yeah, between him and the day clerk there must be something useful."

"Be assured, I shall try."

We paused for a red light and a skinny brown kid suddenly poked his face into my window.

"I thought this buggy looked familiar," he said, grinning at us. "You up here lookin' for a shine, Mr. Escott?"

"Hello, Cal. Actually I'm looking for a shoe. How are you?"

"Same old stuff, a day late an' a dollar short."

"I cannot overcome your time difficulties, but I can possibly aid your monetary problems." He passed a dollar over to Cal, who made it disappear.

"You're a real friend. Next time you need a shine, you look me up, it's on the house."

"Where will you be?"

"I could be anyplace, but if you go down three blocks and turn right one, the gents on the corner can tell you proper. You just say I sent you." He flashed his teeth, pushed away from the car, and went off with a quick, pavement-eating stride.

The light changed and Escott followed the directions, easing the big car into an empty space on the curb and letting it idle.

A group of dark men were standing just outside the cone of light from a streetlamp on the corner ahead. Escott told me to stay put and got out. The men had been talking and continued to do so, but their posture had subtly changed. It was apparent they were fully alert to our presence, but content to wait and let us make the first move. Two of them dropped their cigarettes and stood a little straighter, their arms hanging free so they could more easily get to the angular bulges their tight-fitting coats were unable to hide. Two more shifted their weight to the balls of their feet. They moved out and bracketed Escott when he got close enough.

His head moved slightly as he acknowledged them and there was some low conversation I couldn't quite hear because of the noise of the car. He said something to the armed men; the one on the left shot back a suspicious question. Escott touched his hat and looked reasonable. The man was dissatisfied with the situation, but Escott kept talking and once gestured back to the car, presumably about me. I had half a mind to get out and come over, but this was his show and he didn't look to be in any immediate danger, despite their belligerent attitudes. I sat and stewed and unsuccessfully tried to read lips.

The man on the left made a decision and sent one of the brackets into the building they were guarding. He came out after a minute with a report even more dissatisfying to the leader, but he nodded grudgingly to Escott. Escott came back and opened my door.

"We're in."

"What, the frying pan?"

"The Shoe Box."

"Is it a speak?"

"It used to be. Now it's a respectable nightclub."

"Just how sticky are things?" I gestured with my eyebrows at the men.

"Not very, nothing to worry about now. The gentleman we will see is a cautious fellow, but will welcome us as long as he has sufficient notice. He has a very strong dislike for surprises."

"Gang boss?"

"What a colorful way you have of phrasing things, no doubt due to your journalistic training."

"And the fact we're in Chicago, it seems to be a major industry here."

"For only a fractional percentage of the population, I assure you. Not everyone here is a boss, someone has to do the support work."

"Like him?" One of the brackets was walking toward us.

"Yes, well, let's go."

I shut off the engine, pulled the keys, and got out. He closed the door and walked away. "Aren't you going to lock it?"

"There's no need, no one would dare touch it now."

I made a casual glance around and noted a few dozen faces watching us from windows and doorways up and down the street; men, women, and even a few kids. They all had the same attentive look about them as the door guards. The Shoe Box was a well-surveyed fortress. I felt like a target in a shooting gallery, which led me to speculate if any of them were armed. Escott seemed comfortable, though, and he was nowhere near as bulletproof, so I told myself to relax. We followed the bracket into the building.

There was a small entry hall and then a long passage with a wood floor that acted like a drum to our footsteps. I heard loud and fast music vibrating through the right hand wall, mixed in with the thrum of conversation, clinking glassware, and laughter. We passed by a closed double door that led to the fun and went on to the back of the building, stopping outside another door. Our bracket said he could let Escott in, but he'd have to search me. If it would speed things along, I had no objections and held my arms out. He was efficient and had the quick, light touch of a pickpocket, which might have been his usual occupation when he wasn't pulling guard duty. He found my pencil, notebook, and wallet and nothing more lethal in my pockets than some change. He tapped my shoe heels, checked my hat, decided everything was harmless, and opened the door and stepped to one side.

It was a big room, furnished with sofas, overstuffed chairs, and low tables. One of the tables was really a fancy model of radio that cost more than I'd made in a year. It was playing softly, just loud enough to mask off the sounds coming from the nightclub. At the far end of the room was a small bar near a long dining table where a man was seated alone, eating what appeared to be his dessert. As we came in he tapped a napkin to his lips and turned to look at us.

His skin was sooty black, his hair cut close to the scalp with a short beard edging his jawline and elaborately trimming the mouth and chin. Dressed in light brown with a deep red silk shirt and tie, he looked almost foppish, but was easily getting away with it. He stood up, a big man and not one you could ignore.

Escott spoke first and in a voice rather louder than required to carry across the room. His tone was a mixture of anger and pity. "O thou Othello, that wert once so good/ Fall'n in the practice of a damned slave/ What shall be said to thee?"

Our host was still for a moment, staring at Escott, whom I was sure had need of a straitjacket and gag, then he responded in a rich voice: "Why anything/ An honourable murderer if you will/ For naught I did in hate, but all in honour." Then he barked out a short, delighted laugh and came over to wring Escott's outstretched hand. Both men were grinning.

"Charles, you s.o.b., what do you mean showing up like this with the derby? You could have mentioned your name to the boys! How the hell are you?"

"I am in good health and only wanted to see if it still worked.

I would have called, but you'd moved and left no forwarding number or address I could acquire.''

"Then it's your own fault. You should come around more often. You gave my men a start with that old-hat routine.''

"As I had intended—it keeps them on their toes.''

"Well, it doesn't go with the suit, so dump it. Have you eaten yet? Dessert, then; we've still got some pie and coffee.''

"That would be fine, but please allow me to make some introductions. This is a friend of mine, Jack Fleming. Jack, you have the honor of meeting the best Othello I've ever had the pleasure of working with; Shoe Coldfield.''

Coldfield stuck out his hand. "Any friend of Charles—and that's short for Shoe Box. I got no bones to pick on how I started out. Just watch my smoke, I'm going to be mayor of this town someday.''

"Really now, you can do better than that,'' Escott said dryly.

"All right, governor then, but only if they raise the pay. How did you find the place?''

"We saw Cal, or rather he saw us.''

"Smart kid, that.''

"He's grown.''

"He's eating regular.''

We sat down at the table and coffee was brought in by a kid in a busboy jacket who was also doing duty in the nightclub. Through the walls I could still hear music, which made an uneasy counterpoint with the radio.

"What brings you here, Charles? Working on a revival?''

"I heartily wish. Should I return to the boards, you will certainly be the first to know. In truth, I need a favor.''

"These days who doesn't? What's on your mind?''

"I'm working on a little problem for Mr. Fleming, and since yesterday, for myself, in which Frank Paco is involved.''

Our host sobered up, taking a cautious tone. "Just how involved is he?''

"Yesterday two of his men tried to kill me, and were it not for Mr. Fleming's timely intervention, they would certainly have succeeded. He survived an attempt on his life only last week from the same source and has been laying low ever since.''

"Can't say as I blame you. What do you need? Smuggling out of town?''

"Nothing quite so drastic. Let me apprise you of the whole

situation." Escott told him the basic truth, but said I sought him out and wisely omitted all the facts concerning my condition. ". . . so until Mr. Fleming knows what occurred during those missing four days he will always have this rather nasty problem."

"How do you think I can help? He needs a head-doctor."

"I was hoping you could help us get into Paco's house."

Coldfield shut right up, from sheer disbelief I suppose, since I was feeling the same way. "My mistake," he finally said. "*You* are the one who wants a head-doctor."

"Shoe, I am quite serious."

"If Paco is after you, you oughta be. Why get into his place?"

"For a good look around and to find out what he's up to."

"Hell, I can do that from here. What do you want to know?"

"Some information on International Freshwater Transport might be useful."

"It's just his smuggling operation, everyone knows that."

"But what does he smuggle?"

"It used to be booze and he still brings in some of the fancy foreign stuff. If the price is right he'll take most anything, including people in or out of the country. Lately it's been machine parts and chemicals coming in."

"Is it possible to find out whom they go to and for what purpose?"

"I can try tomorrow, but can't guarantee anything. I generally keep my people away from his territory. I suppose you want specific names for the chemicals, p'fesser?"

"It could help identify what he's up to, but please do not expose your people to undue risk. Yesterday I only made casual inquiries and his reaction was most violent."

"Don't worry. You gonna put him out of business?"

"That would be nice."

"Yeah, we can dream, but he's got friends. Word has it he's been dealing with Slick Morelli out of New York."

"Is that name familiar to you?" Escott asked me.

"Sure, he's a big nightclub owner there, ran a lot of speaks, then fancied them up into top spots after Repeal. He sold a few and concentrated on one or two of the biggest. He always had the best acts and the prettiest girls. Of course, this is only what I've heard, I never had the chance to take a look." Or the money, I silently added.

"He hasn't changed much," said Coldfield. "He's done the same thing for one of the biggest clubs in town up on the north side; he's got a half-interest in it."

"The Nightcrawler?" asked Escott.

"Yeah, maybe he likes fishin' or something."

"Does he own a yacht?"

He nodded. "A nice one, too, if you can have any other kind. The *Elvira*."

I stirred in my chair at the mention of a ship.

Escott noticed, but continued. "Who is the other owner of the club?"

"A fat guy named Lucky Lebredo. He oversees the gambling there."

Escott glanced at me. I thought about the name, then shook my head. He turned back to Coldfield. "Do you know of any connection between Paco and Morelli?"

He shrugged. "If there is, it's probably money. Paco likes to spread it around and always needs more, Morelli keeps his in a mattress and the Good Lord help you if you borrow from him. He takes his loan interest right out of your hide."

"Do you think Lebredo is involved with them?"

"I don't know. Maybe not, all he seems to do is gamble. He's got an adding machine for a brain, and a deck of cards is just another part of his body." He paused. Escott was looking at something we couldn't see, hovering just over the table centerpiece. We waited him out in silence until his eyes blinked a few times.

"You back?" Coldfield asked casually.

"Yes, just thinking, but I need more information."

"Then you're still serious 'bout going in?"

"Very serious."

"What did you have in mind?"

"Have you read the social columns?"

"Never miss 'em," he said with a trace of sarcasm.

"Then you may have noticed Frank Paco is hosting a reception at his estate this Friday. The place is going to be filled with politicians, hangers-on, and the man Paco plans to support in the next gubernatorial election."

"Yes . . ."

"The whole thing is certainly going to be catered."

Coldfield thought it out and smiled. "You mean you can cook, too?"

"No, but I can pass as a waiter."

"Not on this one you can't. You know damn well one of my joints is doing the food and service, and face it, Charles, you're just too white for this job."

"Then I can work as a white waiter."

"And stand out like a sore thumb. No sir, Paco likes his staff well done. Besides, what white man would be working for me? Whites work for white caterers, and once in a while they take on a colored kid 'cause he works cheap, but it just ain't done the other way around."

Escott's pride had been piqued. "Am I or am I not a character actor?"

"The best, but no blackface makeup is going to pass a close look, and your nose is all wrong, anyway. If you were me, would you want to take the chance?"

"I agree," I said. "Paco might know your face, Georgie could be out on bail by now, and if either of 'em spots you, you're scragged and so are the caterers."

Escott's eyes snapped at me a second, then he visibly calmed and shrugged it off. "Of course, you're both right. We'll have to think of something else. Perhaps I could get hold of an invitation or forge one."

"Not easy, they check 'em against their guest list. You'd have to be in someone else's party to sneak past, and then you still have your face to consider. Look, why does it have to be this Friday? Try some other night when Paco is gone and just break in. I can stick one of my boys on the catering staff to case the place for you."

"That is most kind."

"Great, anything to save your ass. Listen, how 'bout we all have dinner tomorrow night, right here."

"Dinner, yes, but it's on me—to make up for too long an absence. Hallman's, I think."

"You're joking, Charles. I couldn't get past the door."

"You most certainly will if it's my party. If you plan to run for governor you'll have to get used to breaking open some doors."

"When I do that, the cops get nervous."

"And well they should. Eight o'clock?"

"That's early for me, but I'll be there, and try to have some dope on the warehouse from my boys."

"Please advise them to use all caution; that thump on the head they gave me was nearly fatal."

"Your skull is too thick. I heard something was fatal to Paco's chief gun, Sanderson. They found him in a trunk the other day. That anything to do with your problem? The papers are saying Georgie Reamer hit him with a sledgehammer." He was looking at me with interest.

I was careful not to look at Escott for a clue. How much Coldfield knew or guessed about last night would be my affair. I shrugged. "Hey, I used to be a reporter—don't believe everything you read."

We left without hindrance from Coldfield's men, one of them even nodded and smiled as we went out to the untouched Nash. I gave the keys back to Escott and we got in. The watching faces were still around, but were not as interested in us as before. Word must have been passed that we were welcome in the neighborhood.

"He's some guy," I commented.

"Yes, I met him in Canada when we were both young and hungry. I was already in an acting company when he walked into the theater with his shoe shine box and asked for work. We got to be friends and with a great deal of argument, persuaded the manager to hire him on permanently. He worked at moving scenery and in wardrobe at half-salary. Occasionally, I'd do him up in white-face so he could carry a spear in the background when we were short of players, but he was being wasted. If you could have seen us in *Hamlet* as Rosencrantz and Guildenstern, he nearly sweated his makeup off and gave the game away. At least it showed the other actors in the company that he was more than capable, but our manager was a pigheaded old reprobate. He refused to even consider Shoe for the obvious part of Othello."

"But he did play it?"

"Oh yes, but it was a bit of a challenge for me to arrange it. The one thing I did manage was getting him the part of understudy to the lead. The manager allowed that much."

"Then the lead got sick?"

"Not precisely . . . I had to help him along. Between the

chloral hydrate the company Iago slipped him and the ipecacu-anha I provided to treat his symptoms, he was in no condition to play the Moor of Venice, and Shoe had his chance. I must say he brought the house down with his performance."

"What about the lead?"

"He recovered in a week or so and no harm was done. By then he had received a telegram offering him a radio announcing job in New York and he left. I'm afraid we didn't miss him much, a very unpleasant ham, he was."

"Was the telegram genuine?"

"Why, what a suspicious mind you have, Mr. Fleming."

5

I GOT MY trip to the Stockyards out of the way and was ready and waiting at a quarter to eight when Escott picked me up. He was in an ordinary suit, which was a relief to me because Hallman's sounded like a white-tie-and-tails joint and I was fresh out of tuxedos.

"I may have a problem at this place," I said.

"What would that be?"

"Let's just say that I have a very restricted diet."

He opened and shut his mouth. "Dear me, I'm afraid I never even thought of that."

"Neither did I. Doing business over food is a very normal thing. We take it for granted.

Escott considered it. "Yes, I can see—you must have a tremendous amount of free time to be unfettered with having to stop and eat every four or five hours."

"I'd gladly go back to it if I could."

"Would you rather skip this evening, then?"

"No, I'll just say it's stomach trouble and nurse a coffee. As long as we're on my case I want to be along every inch of the way, if it's all right with you."

"I've no objections. I made more inquiries after Benny Galligar/O'Hara today, but with negative results."

"If he was in trouble with Paco, he's probably blown town by now."

"I agree. He's set a very sensible example for us."

"Yeah, too bad I ain't got any sense."

* * *

Hallman's was a white-tie place, after all. Escott must have noticed my lack when he went through my room last Monday, and I silently blessed him for his consideration in wearing a regular suit. Like many swank places in Chicago, Hallman's was cheek-and-jowl with less savory neighborhoods. The street it faced was a high-tax area with bright lights, expensive shops, and other classy restaurants, but cross the alley behind it and you were gambling with your skin. Sometimes it was a gang, sometimes a loan operator, but both types shared an avid interest in acquiring someone else's money. The cops had regular beats in the area, but could hardly prevent the odd out-of-towner from getting picked off by local hunters. When Escott got out of the car this time, he made a point of locking it.

A uniformed man at the canopied entrance guarded some potted palms and a red carpet that ran out to the curb. He held the door for us and bowed slightly.

"Good to see you again, Mr. Escott."

"Thank you, Mr. Burdge. Can you recommend anything tonight?"

"Any of the veal dishes, but stay away from the fish. Our regular fish chef is off tonight and his replacement did his training in the army."

"An inland army, no doubt."

"You got it."

We went in and checked our hats, telling the maître d' we were still expecting one more and would wait by the door. It wasn't a long wait; at eight a gleaming new black Nash drove up and stopped next to the red carpet.

"I see you have similar tastes in cars," I commented.

"Well, he did give me such a good deal on my present transport a few years ago that I couldn't turn him down. I must say he still knows how to make an entrance, a natural talent. The stage lost a very fine actor in him."

The chauffeur was out and opening the rear door of the Nash; Burdge, the doorman, stood a little straighter and held the door to the restaurant. It was some credit to his self-control that he wilted only a little when Coldfield emerged into the light. He was postcard perfect in a custom-tailored tuxedo with a satin-lined cape and a silver-headed stick. He carried the clothes comfortably, like Fred Astaire, albeit a much larger-sized Astaire

with coal black skin and a beard. He sauntered up to the doorman, who was looking a bit confused as to how to handle the
situation. Coldfield gave Burdge a look that banished any inclinations of refusing him entry, and then came in.

Escott tapped his hands together in soft applause. "Well
played, sir. A pity it could not have been preserved on film."

Coldfield was pleased. "You said it, history is being made
tonight." He nodded to me. "Ready to get tossed out with the
best?"

"I'd like to see anyone try."

The maître d' was well trained; his eyebrows only bounced
up an eighth of an inch and back down again before he got hold
of himself.

"Your usual table, Mr. Escott?" he asked. In a minute I
understood why. Escott's usual table was in a discreet alcove off
to one side of the main dining area. The man was only remind-
ing Escott he wasn't trying to shuffle our dark companion out of
sight. Whether he wanted to or not, I'd never know.

We sat and went through the business of ordering drinks and
studying the menu. Playing my part, I read through it and shook
my head.

"Anything wrong, Mr. Fleming?" Escott asked.

"I'm not up to eating anything yet. I got a bad burger for
lunch and the thought of more food—" I made a queasy face
and shrugged.

"What a pity, perhaps a little broth to recover? No?"

"No, thanks, I just gotta let things run their course so to
speak. Don't mind me, you two go ahead and enjoy yourselves."

They did. Escott had veal, Coldfield a steak, and I watched
the other patrons between our bouts of conversation. The smell
of food did make me feel a little sick, but it was the memory of
eating that really nettled me. I'd finally made it into a fancy
place with someone else paying the bill, and all I could enjoy
was the decor.

We got our share of looks. One group quite obviously cut
short their meal and left, their backs stiff with indignation. They
wouldn't have minded or even noticed him if Coldfield had been
part of the cleanup staff, but being a fellow customer was too
much for their tender sensibilities. The maître d' would have
caught their verbal wrath had he been by the door as they left,
but being an alert man he'd removed himself from the area in

time. This graceless show was not lost on the other diners, who had been wondering what to do themselves. Happily, they had the good taste to mind their own business, and the conversation buzz soon returned to normal levels.

"You may have pulled this off, after all, Charles," Coldfield murmured.

"So it would seem. I should like to live to see the day—"

"Yeah, I know, I know. Well, you at least got me in here—"

"No, you got yourself."

"I'm hell on doormen," he agreed. "But you're just lucky."

"How so?"

"He had a pretty good idea I wasn't Jewish."

Halfway through the meal a waiter came up with a telephone. "An important call for you, Mr. Escott."

Escott said hello into the mouthpiece and scowled a lot. I couldn't quite hear what was being said on the other end, even if I had any business in doing so.

He shook his head. "No, I couldn't possibly, this is a very bad time. . . . What? All right, then, but hurry." He hung up and the phone was taken away.

"What's the problem?" I asked.

"I shall have to absent myself for a few minutes. One of my sources of information wants to talk and will only do so face-to-face. He's coming by to pick me up."

"Can't he come in?"

"Not this one. He likes to keep on the move, so we have to go through this little comedy now and then. We drive around the block a few times, then he drops me off. Strange fellow, but often useful. If you gentlemen will excuse me, I should be back in time for dessert." He stood up with a quaint little bow that only the English can get away with, and left. Coldfield watched his departing back with an indulgent smile.

"How long have you known him?"

"Off 'n on, about fourteen years. Haven't seen much of him since he took up this private-agent stuff, but then I've been busy, too."

"Do you mind his kind of work?"

"Why should I? He doesn't seem to mind mine."

"What do you do?"

He gave me a look of mock surprise. "Why, I run a night-club."

"At a considerable profit?"

"No point being in business if you don't make a profit."

"How long has he been a private agent?"

"Awhile."

"You play it close to the chest."

"That's how you survive in this town."

He never gave a direct answer to any questions that were too probing, and I asked quite a few before catching on. It must have been the reporter in me. After I figured things out, we stuck to neutral subjects and watched the place slowly empty. Then we watched the staff cleaning up. Our waiter hovered just within sight, broadcasting polite but clear signals that he thought it was time we left.

"Think he stiffed us for the check?" I said jokingly, looking at the clock on the wall. He'd been gone nearly forty minutes.

"No, they'll just put it on his account. He's been coming here for years."

I worried anyway. The phone call could have been a trick to get him outside. Coldfield read my face and told me to relax.

"Charles can take care of himself."

"I hope so."

We waited. A lone busboy in thick glasses shuffled around cleaning the tables. His walk and movements bothered me for some reason, and when I caught a glimpse of his blank face I knew why. His was the careful heavy-heeled, loose-limbed walk of the mentally retarded. He moved from table to table, cleaning up and wiping down, then looked at us and wondered why we hadn't left yet. He was about fifty, with overlong gray hair, a thrusting box-shaped forehead, and thick gray brows that grew across the bridge of his nose. His mouth was open slightly as he stared at us and then at the waiter, undecided on what to do.

"Maybe we should wait outside," Coldfield said.

The waiter came up and said something to the man, pointing to the kitchen. He nodded and went away.

"Yeah, we can do that."

We got up, much to the staff's relief, and went out into the warm, muggy air. The potted palms were inside by now and the doorman locked up behind us.

"Have you any idea who called him?"

He shook his head. "Come on, let's get my car."

Coldfield told his chauffeur to wait by the restaurant door in case Escott turned up, and got into the driver's seat and turned the key. He opened the other door for me and I barely shut it before we were moving. He swung sharply around the block, his lips tight. He was worried, too.

We made a futile figure-eight circuit of the two facing blocks, so he pulled up and parked next to the canopy and cut the engine. Tension was coming off of him like heat, but he kept it controlled. His door wasn't slammed shut in frustration as he got out, and I tried to follow his example.

We hung around awhile longer. There was an alley between the restaurant and another building and I heard noise coming from it, but it was only the staff leaving for the night. They filtered out the side door one by one and the manager locked up. I spotted the doorman and went after him. He'd seen Escott get into an old car with someone and they drove off, but I couldn't get him to be more specific. He hurried off to his ride home and I went back to Coldfield with the negative news.

His eyes were scanning up and down the street, his hands clenched tight on the silver knob of his stick. "Damn him and his work," he growled.

I silently agreed. A car cruised past but didn't stop. Each new set of headlights put our necks to swiveling, but in vain.

Another sound came from the alley—footsteps—but it was only the middle-aged busboy. He carried a box, which I remembered seeing him fiddling with in the alley while the other workers left. He walked past us, staring at Coldfield either in recognition or because of his color, and went on to the parking lot, disappearing around the corner. Almost immediately after, we heard a brief cutoff noise coming from a surprised human throat. Coldfield, the chauffeur, and I exchanged looks and hurried to investigate.

The busboy had his back to the brick wall of the restaurant, protectively clutching his box. In a semicircle around him were three young men still in their teens. Clustered by Escott's Nash were four more of the same type: hard-faced and hard-muscled street kids with all the social conscience of wharf rats. It didn't take a genius to figure they'd been trying to steal the last car in the lot, and the poor busboy had interrupted them.

For a few seconds we were all frozen and staring in a sort of tableau, each side summing up the other, then the chauffeur smoothly pulled out a .38 and held it at ready. He started to say something, but a long, thin shape arced out and smashed down on his thick arm. He swallowed his scream as his knees buckled and fell on top of his dropped gun. One more kid lurched out from his hiding place behind us, swinging an iron pipe down on the man's bowed head.

The time it took to raise the pipe up and down *must* have been brief, but to me he looked like he was moving through cold molasses. Without really thinking, I stepped in, plucked the pipe away from the kid, and hit him in the stomach with my free hand. I remembered in time to pull my punch, though. I didn't want to rupture his internal organs.

The other boys took this as a signal to attack, three of them going straight for Coldfield, who defended himself with his stick, giving as good an example of dirty street fighting as I'd ever seen. He was big and holding out well enough, but we were still badly outnumbered. Two kids rushed in on me with knives, which I simply took away from them since they seemed so slow to me. I shoved them away and sent them staggering into a third kid, and the whole group went down. I used the breathing space to lift the chauffeur to one side, and grabbed his gun.

The three shots I fired at the sky did the trick. The punks disappeared like water into dry ground before the last echoes faded.

Coldfield was a little winded but none the worse for wear, except his tux would need some repair work. He came over and knelt by the chauffeur.

"Is it broken?"

The man felt the arm carefully and shook his head. "Nah, he caught me too high. Cracked maybe, be a hell of a bruise."

"We'll get the doc to look at it. I'll finish driving tonight. You okay?" he asked me.

I pretended to be breathless and nodded. "No problems."

"Goddamn punks. The streets just ain't safe anymore."

I was about to ask him if the streets in this town had ever been safe when I noticed the busboy cowering against the wall. "Hey! You all right?"

He hunched over his box, too shaken to move, the eyes behind his thick glasses were bugged halfway out of their sockets. I walked over slowly, trying to say reassuring things so as not to frighten him more. He let himself be led out into the glow from the street lights. His teeth were chattering. I asked him where he lived.

He moved his head vaguely around. "Bad boys . . . hurt."

"Did they hurt you?"

"No." He stared at the chauffeur's arm. "Hurt?"

"Where do you live?"

"Number five." He held up five fingers and counted them off.

"That's very good. Where is number five?"

He counted again, this time going to ten in one rush and waited for my approval.

Coldfield sighed. "I hate to say it, but maybe we should just look for a cop who knows where he belongs."

"He might have an address on him. Have you got any papers?"

He looked blank.

"Wallet?" I tried. Another blank look. I pulled my own wallet out and showed him. "You got one, too?"

He fumbled in his pockets after putting his box down and found one. I opened mine and showed him the papers inside, but instead of following suit, he just stared at it. Impatiently, Coldfield took it from him, and the man instantly burst into tears of protest.

"Mine," he said feebly, and looked at me for help, his face streaming. "Mine—"

Coldfield had backed away so he could get a better light on the wallet, then he folded it, stalked over, and punched the busboy in the face, knocking him flat. His eyes were blazing. "You goddamn son of a bitch!"

The chauffeur and I gaped, then looked at the busboy who was just coming to his feet, holding one side of his head. What we were seeing didn't clearly register at first, but it looked like part of the man's forehead had peeled bloodlessly away from the skull. He put his thumb under the loose flap and tore it completely away and rubbed gingerly at what would soon be a black eye.

"Do I get that catering job now?" Escott asked.

It took us all awhile to get on speaking terms again. I felt like punching him myself, but Escott apologized profusely, especially to the chauffeur. His original plan had been to get into his car and drive up to us, but the punks had interfered. Once the explanations were out Coldfield settled down.

"But I ain't sorry I hit you, 'cause I'd have done it anyway," he said, still annoyed. I remembered he hated surprises.

"I don't blame you for it, old man." Escott opened his trunk and stowed away the box which contained his clothes and makeup equipment. He brought out a flask and passed it around, which did a lot to improve the general atmosphere. "My question still stands: do I go in with the caterers?"

Coldfield sighed. "Yeah, why the hell not? If you get killed it'll even us up for tonight."

We went to the Shoe Box and Coldfield got busy arranging a doctor for his chauffeur. In the end one of his other men was summoned to drive him to the hospital, where the arm could be properly examined. He laid no blame on Escott for it, saying the car thieves would have been there anyway, and went off with his friend. As they walked down the hall I heard him giving a highly dramatic account of how he came by his injury and how the boss had stepped in and single-handedly saved the day. He'd probably get a lot of drinks out of that story, and Coldfield's reputation wouldn't suffer, either.

Drinks were waiting for us when our host had finished his business. He drained his own and sank into one of the over-stuffed chairs. The radio was off and the club band apparently on break. The only noises now were the customers a few rooms away and someone banging around in a nearby kitchen.

"Hey, Jack." He jerked me back from wherever I'd drifted.

"Come on and have a drink. You deserve it after all that rumpus."

I joined them. Escott was perched on the edge of a couch, a sheet of paper in his hand and his forehead wrinkled.

"What's that?"

"A list of the stuff Paco has been shipping in and keeping, but don't ask me what they add up to; that's Charles's specialty." He went to the bar and made another drink. Returning, he nodded at my untouched glass. "Don't you like my booze?"

"It's fine, I'm just not much of a drinker."

"You're more a fighter. I was busy, but saw some, and I've never seen anyone move that fast in my life."

"It's amazing what you can do when you're scared."

He snorted and raised his glass. "Here's to being scared."

I was going to pretend to sip, but it was no good, he was watching me too closely. I braced myself and gulped. The stuff dropped down my throat and hit my guts like hot lead.

Coldfield read my face all too clearly. "I guess you really aren't much of a drinker."

"Bad stomach is all, always had it." I kept gulping at nothing, trying to keep the stuff down, feeling like a balloon about to burst. Escott provided some distraction as he shook his head over the paper.

"There is definitely something to this, but I need more information. Tomorrow I shall have to find out who actually ordered this and where it ends up after removal from the warehouse."

"All right, but just make sure you're at the caterers by six, or they leave without you. I'll let them know what you're trying to pull and tell them not to make a fuss. You goin' to do this act again?"

"Oh, yes."

"What about Jack? You said you wanted him in, too."

"Not exactly. I shall ask Mr. Fleming to remain nearby with the car. If things get too warm for me, I'll slip out and he can drive us away." He looked at me. "Are you all right?" He'd been too absorbed to pay attention earlier, but now his eyes darted from the empty glass to my face and he understood what had happened.

I tried a weak smile, but kept my lips firmly together, telegraphing to him that I had an urgent problem.

Escott thanked Coldfield, said that we had to get moving, and hustled me out of the Shoe Box and into the car in record time. After a short block I asked him to pull over. I couldn't stand it any longer. He did, I opened the door and leaned out for the explosion. The booze shot into the gutter like a burst from a firehose. I spat out the last drops, blinked at the dirty street below, and forgot to clutch the doorframe when the dizziness hit. Escott grabbed my arm to stop—

"Mr. Fleming?"

—me going over the rail into endless black water. A heavy hand on my neck forced my head down—

"Fleming?"

—retching, no air, blood pounding behind my eyes—

"Fleming!"

He yanked me upright and kept me from sliding under the dashboard. "What's wrong? Fleming?"

"A dream . . . on the boat."

"You remembered something—what?"

He had to wait a long minute for the shaking to pass, and my left hand was still trembling while I told him what I could. He looked at it, then up a me.

"Touched a nerve, has it?"

"It's almost over."

"Then you've had this kind of seizure before?"

"Seizure?"

"When I see someone going all boneless as you did, I call it a seizure, and you seem familiar with it."

"Yeah, I had one a few days ago when I tried to remember what happened before I woke up on the beach. It's like I'm not here anymore. I don't like that loss of control."

He made a sympathetic noise. "Was your last experience as dismaying as this one?"

"Unfortunately. Except last time I was trying on purpose to remember. This time getting rid of that stuff—"

"Spontaneously triggered the memory?"

"Yeah, what you said."

He *ah-hummed* like a doctor and motioned for me to shut the door, then worked the gears and pointed the car in the general direction of my hotel.

"What's on your mind?" I asked.

"Just an idea . . . I thought a reenactment of your final moments on the boat—"

"I get it, but it's kind of hard to reenact something if you don't know how it was enacted in the first place."

"We know you were beaten and shot."

"You want to beat me up and shoot me?" I said cautiously.

"It is only a suggestion, mind you."

"Let's keep it that way until I can think it over."

"As you wish. After all, I could lose my license by assaulting a client, even if it is in his best interest."

I watched the streets glide past, waiting for the tingling in my left hand to subside. "You still want me along tomorrow?"

He was surprised. "Why would you think otherwise?"

I made a fist and opened it, stretching the fingers. "Because of this. I might conk out on you."

"I'm willing to risk it."

"And because I've met some private inves—agents before, and usually the last thing they want is their clients breathing down their necks while they work."

"That is usually true, but then you don't breathe."

"Funny."

"Besides you are essential to our success. Surely you're aware of the extreme usefulness of your abilities?"

"For sneaking around unseen? Uh-huh, except I'm not too sure what I should be looking for."

"In this case, you might know it when you see it, like a half dozen crates marked as spare parts. You'll have much more freedom of movement than I. You need only to avoid getting caught."

"I figured that much, but how do I get there? I'm not up and around at six."

"You can use my car. I'll leave it at your hotel after I've finished my inquiries for the day. There will be a marked map on the seat showing you how to get to his place."

At a quarter to eight the next night I was out and following his neatly written and meticulous directions. In addition to the map was a sketch of the house and neighboring grounds, and an X marked a shrub-sheltered spot off the road where I could safely park. Paco took his privacy seriously. There were warnings about armed guards, high fences, and even watch dogs, all of which I intended to avoid.

The place was just far enough from town to give the illusion it was in the country. The land around was brilliantly lit by star and moonlight. There was no darkness for my eyes to rest in; even the deepest shadows under the trees had been reduced to soft gray patches devoid of mystery and fear. Darkness had been ended forever for me. Perhaps tonight I would see the man who was responsible.

Twenty careful minutes later I was crouched under the window Escott had designated, mentally keyed up but devoid of the usual physical signs of excitement. My lungs drew no quick gulps of air, my heart wasn't hammering in anticipation of action, I wasn't even sweating. My hands were paper dry. The only evidence of inner turbulence was the iron-hard stiffness that seized my spine. It did help me to keep very still while I waited;

that alone was enough to make me invisible to the occasional patrolling guard. I was just another shadow in the bushes.

Escott softly called my name from the window. The coast was clear, inside and out. My body vanished, reappearing just behind him and still in a crouching position. I came out of it slowly, orienting. We were in a bathroom.

He'd been peering out the small window and then whirled with a stifled jump. "My God, but that's unnerving," he whispered, and I tried very hard not to smile at his reaction. "Are you all right?"

"I'm fine." I stared in fascination at his makeup job—it was perfect. "How can you see through those glasses?"

He pulled out a sheet of paper with a rough sketch on it. "Here's the kitchen, where I'll be. . . . They've set me to washing dishes for now and I've got the window over the sink open if we need to talk. This is the dining room, the guests are still there, about thirty of them, give or take the odd gunman. The caterers are only allowed into these areas, the rest is your territory. Paco's office shouldn't be difficult to identify, but in particular you might seek out the basement. There is a locked door to it in the kitchen, but I'm willing to guess there's another entrance as well."

"You think the locked door is to protect more than just his liquor?"

"I certainly hope so. I want to know where he put all the money he borrowed from Slick Morelli."

"Anything in particular I should look for?"

"Whatever looks out of place in a normal house—or even this one for that matter. Perhaps even your list, if they're careless enough to leave it lying around. In the last week they could have acquired it from Benny Galligar."

"O'Hara."

"Whatever."

I nodded in agreement because he looked nervous. "Okay, don't worry about me. How long will you be here?"

"My group is supposed to leave around twelve. I'll have them drop me off near the car, and wait for you there. You should have as long as discretion allows."

It seemed like plenty of time and I said so. "You better get back to your dishes. If I turn up anything, I'll let you know."

"I've learned to be a patient man, Mr. Fleming. Good luck."

He slipped out the door and I was on my own, without even my reflection for company. I gave him time to get away, then floated out of the bathroom. Considering its proximity to the dining room and kitchen, it would have a regular parade of intruding patrons. Feeling my invisible way down the hall kept me safe, but I'd have to solidify soon to get some bearings. Two men walked past, their voices flat and muffled in my ears. I followed in their wake until they faded away. Pressing what would be my back against a wall, I tried a partial re-forming.

The confusing buzz of background noise became the familiar tones of clear conversation coming from a large room on my right, with double doors leading in to dinner. There was a T intersection down the hall on the left. I picked the left branch of the T and began opening doors.

There were plenty of closets, some small bedrooms apparently belonging to the permanent staff, and another bathroom. It was a water haul so I tried my luck with the other branch of the T and found more of the same, except for one encouragingly locked door. I ghosted through it and felt the floor drop away in a series of descending right angles. It was the other basement entrance. At the bottom landing was another locked door, which also proved useless for the owner.

Inside, I partially materialized and discovered the jackpot. It was a brightly lit laboratory crammed with the kind of stuff I'd last seen at college, when I'd slept through the required chemistry courses. It was nearly as big as my old classroom, but neater and newer looking. The one thing it didn't have in common with higher learning was the lantern-jawed mug sitting at his ease about five feet away from me. Only my lack of sudden movement and his complete absorption in a magazine kept him from spotting my intrusion. I vanished, got behind him, and re-formed.

His face was unfamiliar, but his flashy clothes and callused knuckles were enough to identify his probable line of work. On a table next to him was a half glass of milk with crumbs floating on top and a plate of cookies that he occasionally dipped into. His magazine caught my eye—he was also interested in the Shadow's adventures and halfway through *Terror Island*. Someday I'd have to write Walter and tell him about his mobster fan.

Without disturbing him, I very quietly checked out the rest of the joint. At the far end a door with a glass panel set in it led to a dark service area for the furnace, and eventually went on to the kitchen stairs. There was also a locked wine cellar, a laundry, old furniture, and a lot of dust. Going back by way of the lab, I went back upstairs to the T, down its base, and explored another hall. This area was not very promising, with only some socializing rooms; nothing like an office until I got to the last door. It was locked, but no problem.

Paco liked to show off. The inside of his sanctum looked like a decorator's idea for a president's office. It was full of velvet and leather upholstery, black stained wood, and gold-framed oil paintings of conservative landscapes. The only portrait was of a bullish-looking man with heavy features and pop-eyes. He looked enough like Sanderson to have been a close relative. It was hard to judge how tall he was, for the painting was done on a larger-than-life scale. No memories stirred for me and I wondered how good a likeness it really was.

My training as a detective was limited to what I'd learned watching movies, so I started looking for a safe behind the paintings, but with no luck. The desk drawers were locked, and since Escott didn't want any obvious signs of intrusion I left them alone and sorted through the papers left on top. Nothing important was on them, just some notes about the party and a few doodles.

I tried upstairs and found only more bedrooms and baths, gave up, and snuck back to the kitchen. I could make little sense of the noise and muddle of voices there, and drifted outside to look through the windows. The curtains were open and the sashes had been raised to let in some breeze. The kitchen was steamy and filled with people busy with mountains of food. Peering through one window, I was face-to-face with Escott, who was bent over a pile of dishes and up to his elbows in soap suds. I softly tapped for his attention and told him to go to the cellar door. He nodded dully, as if to himself, staying in character so well I had some doubts whether he'd really heard and understood. But a few minutes later, when I unlocked the door from the inside, he was turning the knob one second and standing next to me on the small landing the next.

I explained the problem with the laboratory: I could get in anywhere, but lacked his knowledge.

He pocketed the fake glasses and rubbed his eyes. "I can

absent myself from the dishes long enough to have a good look. Lead the way.''

We went straight to the glass-paneled door and from the safety of the dark on our side, looked in. His eyes lit up at the sight of all that equipment. He stared at everything for nearly a minute, then grabbed my arm and backed us away.

"What's it about?" I whispered.

He shook his head with a small, impatient movement. "I've got to get in there. Can you get rid of the guard?"

"How permanently?"

"Nothing fatal, if you don't mind—wait, he's moving."

We shrank deeper into the shadows, watching through the glass. The man left the magazine open on the table, massaged his back, stood, and stretched. He checked his watch, yawned, and unlocked the stairway door, then secured it again from the other side.

I darted forward, sieved through our door, and let Escott in. "You've only got a few minutes."

"How do you know?"

I pointed to the now-empty glass of milk. "He's headed for the can to get rid of that, so he won't take long."

"Excellent deduction," he approved, and went to work, prowling the length of the room, inspecting the variety of glass tubes and flasks, and poking nosily into cabinets. In one of them he found a handwritten notebook of some kind and in another was a small safe. He suppressed a bark of triumph, dropped on his haunches, and tried the handle. We were both surprised when it turned and the door swung open.

"What's inside?"

"Something odd," he said more to himself than to me. He opened the book, scanning page after page, visibly puzzled.

"Anything wrong?"

Too occupied to pay attention, he reexamined some sealed glass containers that seemed to be filled with liquid chrome. He tapped one and the convex surface vibrated like a molten mirror. Leaving them, he searched for and located a supply of chemicals in a walk-in closet. He read the labels but opened a container anyway to make sure of the contents. A smell like rotten eggs drifted into the air, and he looked like a kid who'd just gotten everything he ever wanted for Christmas.

"Come on, what is it?"

"No real heat source except those Bunsen burners," he muttered thoughtfully, "but that could be talked around. Well, well! We can leave now."

"Glad to hear it."

He returned everything to its place except the book, and we got out about ten seconds before the guard returned. He got comfortable with his magazine again and began reading.

"Why isn't he at the party?" I whispered.

"Probably shy. Come on."

Back at the kitchen stairs, he sat on the second lowest step, pulled out a small flashlight, and studied the book. Five minutes later he was shaking so hard with silent laughter he had to close it up to get his breath back.

He held it out to me. "If nothing else, this would be proof enough of Frank Paco's criminal tendencies, for is it not well-known that you can't cheat an honest man?"

"What is it?"

He rolled the Latin out slowly and with evident pleasure. *"Magnum opus."*

"What great work?"

"Open the first page, read what is printed at the top."

" 'What is above is as that which is below, and what is below is as that which is above.' What's it about, burying people?"

"A kind of philosophy, a seeking for enlightenment which has since become corrupted and obscured by ignoble charlatans. You saw the mercury and sulfur. All that was lacking was a purifying furnace. This, my dear fellow, is alchemy."

"Alchemy," I repeated blankly. "Paco is trying to make gold?"

"Pah! The man hasn't the education."

"He's got a tame chemist, then."

"More likely a chemist *cum* physics." He shook his head. "Not a genuine one, but a fraud in every sense of the word."

"A con man?"

"Precisely."

"Somebody's convinced Paco he can turn lead into gold?"

"Not lead, but mercury. It's next up from gold on the periodic table. The notes in that book indicate they plan to use radium—"

"Radium?"

"—in some exotic process that will knock an atomic number

or two from the mercury so they end up with either gold or platinum.''

''That's impossible.''

''In theory it seems quite possible, but that is just in theory.''

''It *is* impossible?''

''Given the present state of science, yes, but the idea can be so beautifully profitable if presented in the right way to greedy and receptive ears. This is a confidence trickster of rare genius and no small audacity. It would be an honor to meet the fellow.''

''But where can he get radium?''

''He doesn't have to get any—that's what I found in the safe.''

''An unlocked safe? But radium is more expensive than gold.''

''Astronomically more expensive and far more dangerous to have lying so casually around. Only four years ago there was a case of a Pittsburgh man who died horribly from ingesting a quack medicine containing radioactive salts. The radium they have tucked away in that unlocked safe is nothing more than a convincing substitute. No doubt it was purchased by the mark for a large sum of cash from the con artist's partner.''

''So the phony radium and all this lab equipment are just so much window dressing?''

''A new twist to a very old game, don't you think?''

''Yeah, I also think that maybe Paco is wise to it and pulling the strings of the con man. He's got a lot of money swilling his booze upstairs and might take some of the greedier ones on a little tour down here.''

''A good point,'' he admitted. ''Again, I seem to have underestimated the opposition. All right, we discard the outside con man for the moment and put Paco in his place instead. He chooses a few gullible prospects from his guests, leads them to think he can make an unlimited quantity of gold by using radium as a modern-day Philosophers' Stone and offers them the opportunity to invest—''

''Or help buy the radium—''

''Then the experiments end in failure and Paco pockets the unspent cash.''

''You think he borrowed the cash from Morelli to start with, just to build this lab?''

''It makes quite a convincing backdrop, does it not? I talked with Shoe again today and he was able to confirm that Paco had borrowed a quantity of cash from Morelli about a month ago, before you came to town.''

''You don't think this is connected with me?''

''I really don't know. For the moment the most I'll say is that it seems unlikely.''

''It's a beautiful situation, though.''

''In what way?''

''Paco's left himself wide open—I mean if anything should happen to that lab . . .''

''Are you suggesting we do something precipitant?''

''Any objections?''

''After what Paco nearly had done to me, I don't give a bloody damn what happens to him so long as it's something terribly unpleasant.''

''You got any ideas?''

''Yes, but I want Shoe's people well clear of this before we do anything. Is the car in place?''

''Just like you marked on the map.''

''Good. I must ask you to go there and wait for me. The catering staff leaves at midnight.''

''Sure, but what are you planning to do?''

We'd been too loud, or our voices had carried in some freak way, for the glass-windowed door to the lab opened and the basement lights flared on. Escott's back was to them, and his body shielded mine with shadow. He slipped his thick glasses back on and whispered a one-word order for me to hide. The last I saw of him was his startled expression as I vanished.

''Hey! Who are you?'' Heavy aggressive footsteps approached and braked. ''Hey! I'm talking to you! What are you doing here?''

''I wash up,'' Escott mumbled in the same voice he'd used to such good effect last night. I moved up behind the man; if there was going to be trouble, I wanted to be in a position to take care of it.

''Yeah? Well, what's to wash down here? You dunno, huh? Get back up to the kitchen. Gowan—move. It's more than your ass is worth if you come down here again.''

They both trooped up the stairs. He pushed Escott out, locked the door, and clomped down again. He moved around the basement, checking to see if he missed anyone, but eventually returned to the lab with a weary sigh and shut off the lights. He sounded bored, which wasn't good. A bored man is on the look-out for distraction. Whatever Escott had in mind, we'd have to be careful.

I floated upstairs and outside, appearing at the window as before. Escott was busy scrubbing, trying to catch up on lost time.

"I'll be at the car," I whispered.

He nodded as though in time to some unheard inner music, and splashed another of pile of dishes into the soapy gray water.

The guards patrolling the estate were visible a mile off. I had no trouble avoiding them, but the dogs were another matter. They'd been on the other side of the grounds when I'd first arrived and were now making an importune circuit of my escape route. One of the men had a big mongrel on a short lead that caught my scent. Its ears went flat and he came charging, dragging his master. I like dogs, but this time my vanishing trick was never more welcome.

I was near a pine tree and used it to orient myself, hanging close to the trunk to keep from drifting in the slight wind. The man and dog approached and he let the animal sniff around. However, it did not like blundering into the space I was occupying, and at first contact the dog gave an unhappy yelp and decided to seek something else to threaten that was a little more within his experience. He broke away and ran off, his master in hot and annoyed pursuit.

It was way past time to quietly beat it out of there. The commotion was drawing the kind of attention that was only welcome in a three-ring circus. I formed up solid again and, moving fast, got away from the clown-and-dog act and found the fence I'd climbed coming in. It was a long five minutes of tearing through brush, brambles, and long grass to reach the car and something of an anticlimax once there, since I had nothing to do until Escott came. For the next couple of hours I plucked greenery from my clothes, kicked at stones, and ducked every time a set of headlights appeared on the nearby road.

Shortly after twelve a large truck rumbled up from Paco's and stopped for a few seconds. A single tall figure hopped from the back, waved to someone inside, and was left in the exhaust as the truck drove off. There was a spring in Escott's step, as though he were on vacation and hadn't spent the evening washing dishes for a man who'd tried to have him killed.

"Sorry about that interruption. I'm certainly glad the fellow missed seeing you."

"You didn't get into trouble?"

"Not at all. I think the man was reluctant to inform anyone that a person of my apparent intellectual capacity managed to get down there in the first place, as it would make him look bad."

"Good, I didn't want to have to do anything he'd regret. You going to get rid of that face?"

"Yes, I'm beginning to sweat it off, anyway." He opened the Nash's trunk and turned on a small flashlight with a piece of red glass over the bulb instead of the usual clear covering. He noticed that I noticed. "You may have excellent night vision, but I must preserve my own as best I can."

He fixed the light so he could work, and hauled up a large metal box; the layered, unfolding kind used by fishermen to hold their lures and other equipment. Instead of spare hooks and lines, it contained a wide assortment of greasepaints, powders, brushes, sponges, and a dozen other things I couldn't identify in all the clutter. It was the only thing of his that was not starkly clean and neat.

Working quickly in what for him was very dim light, he removed the glasses, false forehead, some protruding teeth from his lower jaw, a ragged gray wig, and odd tufts of hair. He smeared cold cream on and wiped the rest of the makeup off on a thin towel that had seen better days, then closed the kit up. He shrugged out of the white dishwasher's coat and buttoned a dark shirt on in its place.

"Now we can get to work."

"My question still stands: what have you got planned?"

He reached into the trunk again and pulled out my answer.

"You're kidding. You *carry* that stuff around with you?"

"I try to be prepared and I am not kidding. You can put this where it will do the most good."

"Where? Up Frank Paco's—"

"Don't be crude. He has unwisely indebted himself to Slick Morelli to construct facilities to 'produce' his dream gold. You have suggested that if those facilities were destroyed—"

"Well, not in so many words . . ."

"This could be a setback he can't afford."

"Couldn't he just start over?"

"I think not, since his credibility in the criminal community would be destroyed as well once the story got out, and I can make sure it does. It's cost him a lot to set things up, and he might not be able to clear the debt with his creditor."

"He might get rubbed out."

"That is a possibility. If you have second thoughts let me know now, for this is a felony."

"My murder was a felony. Paco owes us both one, so let's go collect."

6

SILENTLY ENTERING THE house by way of the kitchen, I started to re-form, but became aware just in time to dodge two men making a late raid on the icebox.

"Did you see that?" a distorted voice asked.

"See what?"

"I thought something moved over there."

"Check it out, then."

I held still, even when something alien intruded into my amorphous body.

"Jesus, it's cold as hell in here. Shut that box up."

"You see anything?"

"Nah."

"Boss'll think you're drinking, you talk like that."

"I could use one."

I left them to their food and moved on to the basement. The lab was as I'd left it, complete with the "milk and cookies" guard. Try as I might, I couldn't work up any dislike for the guy, and it took a real effort to tap him a good one behind the ear so I could do my work undisturbed. To make up for the assault, I eased him gently to the floor and thoughtfully folded his magazine into his coat pocket. Then I went through the lab like a dose of salts, opening cabinets and leaving them open, dumping drawers and looking for papers that might be useful. Escott had been thorough, though, and anything really important would be upstairs with Paco.

Now I hauled out Escott's present, a single stick of dynamite with a five-minute fuse attached. It would do the job, but I wanted to be certain of the lab's utter destruction, and for that spent the next few minutes sloshing several gallons of alcohol all over the room. The walk-in storage closet was full of usable items, and anything marked flammable was added to the general mess. I made sure the air vents were wide open. There were no windows to the outside or I'd have opened them as well. After that I gave the gas taps for the Bunsen burners a good twist and listened to it hiss invisibly into the room.

Propping the dynamite on the one clean table in the middle, I lit the fuse with some nervousness. In the five minutes it would take to burn down I planned to be in the car with Escott and tearing down the road back to Chicago.

I hoisted the guard with the sweet tooth over my shoulders, my new strength making him seem remarkably light, then unlocked the lab door that led to the T-intersection and set it to lock again once it was closed. Trudging upstairs with my burden, I opened the second door into the hall and put the man down to one side. My back was to the hall while I was busy with the door. Too late, I heard the sharp clunk of a machine gun bolt being drawn back. My guess that the hallway would have less traffic than the kitchen was wrong.

"Freeze right there, buddy," a voice told me.

I had to obey and wondered how I could stall them. If I left now they might check the basement and, depending on their luck, foil the explosion or be blown up. There were two men behind me. One of them approached, and I raised my hands slowly.

"Stay outta my line of fire, Harry."

Harry grunted in acknowledgment. He searched me with quick, professional slaps. "He's clean," he announced, and stepped back.

"What's going on?" demanded another, more authoritative voice.

"We caught ourselves a burglar, Mr. Paco."

"Check out the lab, Harry."

I made a move to stop him, but was told again to stay put. Harry slipped downstairs. "The door's still locked, Mr. Paco," he called up.

"Then how'd he get Newton out, dummy? Get up here and check 'em. He's gotta have keys or something."

My muscles had gone all tight. Frank Paco's voice had touched a dormant nerve in my brain. I needed time to think, to remember. . . .

"You! Turn around."

I turned slowly, enjoying first the puzzlement, recognition, and then shock on Paco's face.

"Fleming," he breathed softly. Only I could hear him. I felt an awful smile crawling across my features.

The portrait in his office had been too flattering—the artist must have wanted his commission very badly. He'd caught the wide face and pop eyes, but had omitted the ingrained hardness and suspicious set to his mouth. He was shorter than Sanderson, but built much the same; stocky with muscle, rather than flab, and not afraid to use it, but now, because of my face, he fell back a step in fear.

"Mr. Paco?" the man with the machine gun said uncertainly.

The need to assert his authority overrode his confusion. He straightened and glared at me, rejecting his first instincts. And why not? As far as he knew, Jack Fleming had died over a week ago.

"Who are you?"

"My name is Gerald Fleming. I believe you know my older brother, Jack."

Paco seized the explanation as I knew he would. Once more on firm ground, he was able to deal with the situation. "Yeah," he agreed reasonably. "I know your brother."

"You met him the other week, didn't you?"

"Yeah, we had some things to talk over. But you answer the questions here, punk. What are you doing in my house?"

"I thought we could talk."

"We'll talk and you better answer straight. What are you after?"

I said nothing and my bloodshot stare made him uncomfortable.

"This guy's some kind of freak. Take him out and get rid of him."

Harry and the machine gunner each grabbed an arm and marched me past Paco and down the stem of the T. "Get rid of me and you'll never find that list," I shot back. My escort hesitated.

"What makes you think I want it?"

"My brother told me you were after it. He gave it to me. I know you got him. I'll trade you the list for him."

Paco was chuckling. I'd given him a lot to laugh at.

"What if I got it already?"

"Then you wouldn't bother talking to me now." Maybe the bluff would stall things longer. I had no idea if there was enough truth in it to give him doubts, but I was certain I hadn't talked aboard the *Elvira*. He might still want his list. "I came here to look for my brother. You caught me square, but I'm willing to deal."

"I'll just bet you are." Paco came closer, his eyes absorbing my face. I hoped my reclaimed youth would pass the hard study. "I'll deal with you the same as I did with him." His hand came up and he tried to knock my jaw off its hinges. I faked the impact, snapping my head hard over and letting my knees buckle. The two men on either side kept me standing.

Not that I paid them much attention, my guts had gone cold. (They were going to kill me . . . they were going to beat me to death. . . .)

"You hear me, punk?" Paco's voice jolted me back to the hallway. "You start talking. You tell me how you got in here. You tell—"

"Frank?"

"What?" His head jerked around in irritation. Another man strolled up. He was in evening clothes, holding a glass, and his face had the broken-veined, dissipated look of a confirmed alcoholic.

"Ask him what he was doing in the lab. Is the lab safe?"

"He musta got in somehow to get Newton out, Doc," said Harry. "The door's locked now and I don't have no key to check."

"Oh, of course, hold my drink." The man fumbled in his pockets. "I have mine right here . . . um . . . somewhere."

"I told you, I was only looking for my brother," I insisted, needing to sidetrack them.

"Then why were you dragging Newton around?"

"I thought I could use him as a hostage."

Paco didn't believe that one at all, not that I blamed him. He threw a hard punch to my stomach. I doubled over, remembering to force air from my lungs. I sagged between my supports, gagging a little, and hoped my performance was convincing.

"How'd you get in here?" Paco repeated.

"Snuck past men—open window—"

"Frank, do you have your key, I must have left mine—"

"Not *now*, Doc!"

"You'll think not now if he's damaged anything down there."

Paco growled and slapped through his pockets. I straightened, worked saliva into my mouth, and spit right in Paco's face.

It was a more than sufficient distraction. Paco gaped at me, frozen in sheer disbelief. His big hand came up slowly to wipe it away. I found a perverse enjoyment in the situation and let it show.

"Leave it there," I suggested. "On you it looks good."

He went beet red, then hit me hard enough to knock me from the grip of my two supports. Stiff-legged, he bulled after me with his fists ready, and I made a big show of cowering and backing away. Paco struck again and again. I was only distantly aware of the blows, feeling impact rather than pain. He'd wear his hands out before he could do me any real harm now. I put on a good act, though, crying out, throwing my arms up, trying to protect my face and groin and each second moving farther and farther away from the basement door.

I heard it a split second before anyone else and, down already, I just covered my head and lay prone.

The blast roared up the stairs, knocking the bottom door to splinters and shattering every window in the house. The whole structure shook; plaster and framed pictures alike jumped from the walls to the bucking floor. The men in the hall were bounced away by the concussion, and the machine gun went off and tore holes in the ceiling.

Paco, Doc, and Harry were knocked flat, Paco actually somersaulting over me. People were yelling alarms in other parts of the house and beneath it all, like the purr of a tiger, I heard the fire. It was time to go.

I got my feet under me and stood in time to greet the reinforcements rushing in from the dining room. Spotted as the outsider, two of them grabbed me while a third aided Paco. He threw off the helping hands and came straight for me. He halted inches away, glaring.

"Take this bastard to my office. Somebody call the fire department."

They dragged me to the office on the other side of the house. Behind us Paco was talking to Doc.

"Get up, you goddamned lush. We got work to do."

I faked weakness, hoping they might get careless and take their eyes off me for a moment so I could disappear, but there was no such luck, not with the boss right behind them. They kept their eyes and guns locked on my head until Paco came in, dragging Doc with him.

Doc was the worse for wear and dropped onto a couch, holding his head. Paco went to the massive desk, unlocked it, and began cramming papers into a briefcase.

"What's Slick going to say about this?" Doc wondered out loud.

"I already know," said Paco. "And if you got any brains in that skull that ain't been pickled yet, you'll figure it out, too."

"What will we do?"

"A quick trip outta town with a few of my best boys until this blows over."

"An apt phrase."

"And this mug's coming, too. Slick and me screwed up with his brother, but I won't be taking any chances with this one. If I come up with his list and hand it over, Slick will cancel all my IOUs."

"Assuming you get him to talk."

"He'll talk. He don't have his brother's guts."

Oh, yeah?

"What about me?"

"Don't worry, I'll find a safe spot for you until we can set things up again." He snapped the case shut. "Come on."

They opened the door to a smoke-filled hallway. Paco's men were losing out to the fire. He slammed the door, coughing. "We'll take the back way," he said, and started for another door across the room.

Just as he touched the knob, the lights went out. Not knowing how long it would last, I took advantage of the situation. In seconds I knocked Doc and the other two men out cold. The sounds alerted Paco. He swung around, a gun in his hand.

"What's going on?" he demanded. "Doc? Sam? Answer me!"

I grabbed his wrist, pushing the gun away and squeezing. He

grunted in pain, dropping the gun from suddenly nerveless fingers. He was trying not to scream. I eased off, but only a little.

"Fleming, it's you, ain't it? We can still talk. I can still give you your brother—" Now he did scream, my grip on his wrist tightened involuntarily and the bones snapped. He dropped the briefcase and sank to the floor when I released him.

"No deals, Paco," I whispered from the dark.

"What d'ya want? Just tell me. . . ."

What I wanted he didn't want to know. The hate inside me was growing like a separate living thing, and I wanted to turn it loose on this man and let it tear him to bloody ribbons. I picked him up by the clothes and shoved him against the wall. He made a small movement with his left hand. I should have paid attention, but was too crazy to notice. He drew a slightly deeper breath and briefly held it, which was a warning, but then it was too late. The hard snout of a nickel-plated derringer was pressed up under my rib cage and he triggered both shots.

Two red-hot comets tore through me, leaving behind the harsh, ringing aftershock of pain. My body spasmed once for each bullet. I must have cried aloud in reflex, because it hurt like hell. Paco let his breath out in relief and waited for me to fall away.

Instead I slapped the gun from his fingers and laughed. It sounded ugly to me, and I could only imagine what it was doing to him. My lungs ran out of air and I was still laughing, shaking with it, drunk from the look of fear on his face. He fought to get away, but I hoisted him right off his feet and pinned him to the wall. There was just enough thin light coming from the windows for him to see my face. His pop eyes bulged even more, his head shook, and he looked ready to scream, but it was reduced to a whimper that seeped out of his mouth like dribble.

"What's on the list?" I said, giving him a shake to punctuate the question. His heels knocked loosely against the wall.

"N-n-numbers."

"What numbers?"

"C-code—don't know—"

"What do you want it for?"

He was struggling again. "You're dead, I shot you—"

"You're damn right I'm dead, you son of a bitch. You tell me why."

". . . dead, shot you—"

"What is the list for? Why do you want it?"

"Slick!" The name was screamed out. It could have been an answer or a call for help.

"What does Slick have to do with it?"

"He wants . . . Him—you get him. Lemme go, oh God, lemme go!"

"Who killed Fleming?"

"I dunno."

"Did you?"

"No!" The denial was too fast and forceful. "It was Slick! He said to do it. Him!"

"Why?"

"Shut him up. Please, lemme—"

"Where?"

"Yacht."

"The *Elvira*?"

"Yes."

"Who else was there?"

"Fred, he tried to tell me. Oh God, tried—"

"What? Tell you what?"

"You're dead. Go away, go away." Tears streamed down the man's cheeks from his wide-open eyes.

The hot, living hate was banging around inside me, fighting to get free, clouding my brain like the smoke that was just starting to ooze into the room. Our eyes were locked. He couldn't turn away, and then it was too late. He stiffened under my hands like a corpse. His mouth dropped wide and a gagging noise came out. The noise shaped itself, rose in volume, and lengthened into a full-fledged shriek that had no humanity in it. I let go and stepped away. Something else inside me released him as well, and the screaming died away. Paco dropped facedown on the floor and didn't move.

I stared, afraid and wondering what I'd done to him. I was cold all over and shaking, feeling drained and weak. Out in the hall someone ran up, shouting for Paco. The door opened, and smoke billowed into the room along with two blinded, coughing men.

Paco was still alive, but he didn't respond when I turned him over and there was a heart-sinking blankness in his eyes. As surely as I'd broken his wrist, I had shattered his mind. Considering what he had done to me and who knows how many other poor slobs who couldn't hit back, I felt no pity for him. I picked up his briefcase and retreated a few steps through the door we were to use before the lights went out. By then, the newcomers were tripping over unconscious bodies.

"What the hell? They're all out. . . . Mr. Paco? Mr. Paco?"

But Paco was still oblivious.

"We gotta get 'em outta here."

"The back way?"

"Too slow—open the window."

I quietly left while the men were busy lowering bodies into the flower beds outside. No one really noticed as I crossed the open grounds this time. All eyes were on the house. Some of them had been late-staying guests still in evening dress, others were servants, the rest looked like the thugs they were, and all huddled in little groups and stared at the smoke rising from the windows to the sky. Shouts from the other end of the house brought help to the men who were getting Paco out, saving me the trouble. I may have hated his guts, but I wouldn't have let him burn to death.

Turning away, I walked unchallenged out the front gates and down the road. In the distance I could hear the first fire trucks approaching.

Escott was standing on the fender of the Nash, craning to get a better view of things.

"You were successful?" he asked when he could see me.

"Yeah, it was a real riot."

"Anything wrong?"

"No." I got in the car and tried to pull myself together. I felt the same as when I'd hit Sanderson and turned his face inside out, only this time it had been Paco's mind. I wasn't sorry about it, but I was frightened that I had such an ability and of what it might do to someone who didn't deserve it.

Escott started the car and got us well on our way back to the city. He was looking at me, wanting to ask what was the matter, but forcing himself to be patient. I shrugged and shook myself as though I'd solved a problem. It wasn't solved by a long shot, but I could at least push it aside for the moment.

He took my movements as an opening to conversation. "What is in your case?"

I'd forgotten it. "Some of Paco's papers. He seemed to think they were important enough to carry from a burning house, so I took them away instead.''

"Dear me, yes, they should prove to be most interesting, indeed. But did he not see you?"

"Yeah, he saw me, but I passed myself off as my younger brother Gerald, who I invented just then, and he swallowed it.''

"Then will he not be in pursuit of Gerald?"

"The explosion and fire were some big shock to him. I don't think he'll be looking for me at all. He was talking about finding a deep hole and pulling it in after him. If his boys are smart they'll be doing the same thing.''

"If they're smart. What else happened?"

"I think I met the alchemist; they called him Doc. He was drunk, but still had more brains than the others, he nearly spoiled the boom. I last saw him being hauled out a window, guess he got too much smoke. He was worried about what Slick would say once the news was out, which was why Paco was leaving town. Morelli holds all his markers.''

"He may have a difficult time collecting now."

"I . . . I started to remember things, Paco's voice—I nearly had another seizure, but snapped out of it. I found out for certain I was killed aboard the *Elvira* for some kind of coded list. Paco and Morelli were both after it, so it wasn't just the loan and money tying them together.''

"At one point it was you and what you knew."

"When I didn't talk . . . I know they beat the hell out of me before Paco . . .''

(He raised the gun to my chest and fired. The flash filled my eyes, I fell . . .)

My head bumped hard against the dashboard. My shoes were stained with grass and damp. Escott said my name in a worried tone and brought the car to a stop. He pushed me upright against the seat, and I shook my head like a dazed prizefighter, my eyes blinking as I tried to regain the present.

"Fleming?"

"I'm all right." I was a little surprised; the guy was really concerned about me.

"You don't look it," he said.

My ears were ringing from the memory of the shot and I felt weak; my vision was fuzzy around the edges. The shock of memories coming back I couldn't help, but I could handle the cause of these new symptoms.

"I just—just drop me at the Stockyards. I'll walk home from there, if you don't mind."

He didn't.

Maybe I'd talk with him later, for right now things in my stirred-up brain could wait. We were both tired. For something to do I opened the briefcase and rummaged through the papers. There was a lot of junk I didn't feel like wading through just then. No doubt Escott would enjoy every bit of it later. Then I found an interesting item at the bottom of the case which I could immediately understand. If the printing on the homemade wrappers could be believed, I was holding five neat bundles of one hundred twenties—ten thousand dollars all in one lump sum sitting in the palm of my hand. After spending so many years living close to the edge, all that cash felt pretty damn good.

"Who says there's no justice?" I mumbled.

"What?"

"You want some?"

Escott spared a glance at the money and managed not to run us off the road. "Well, well."

"You think it's marked?"

"Knowing Paco, I think not, but it won't hurt to make a thorough check."

"You mean we keep it?"

"Why not? You once asked me if I were rich. I said sometimes. This is one of those times. A little extra cash is always handy."

"I thought you might be above this sort of thing."

He looked pained. "A Free Agent is entitled to whatever rewards his conscience will permit. If this is Paco's money, my conscience can become quite elastic. It is? Then I think we should consider this to be sufficient recompense for our work tonight. I shall put my share to good use, such as interior improvements to my home."

If he meant his two-room office, he could use a lot of help there. I looked down at the shredded cloth on my stomach. "I think I'll get some new clothes."

Escott looked at the holes. "I thought I smelled cordite. What happened?"

"I annoyed Paco."

He wisely decided to leave it at that.

After feeding and a good day's rest I felt a lot better, and the next night I made an effort to find a men's store that closed early, so I sifted through the ads in the papers, squinted at my map, and located a place nearby that might fill my needs. Then I went downstairs, got a handful of change at the desk, and folded myself into a phone booth. The operator put me through to Cincinnati.

"Hi, Mom. What's going on?"

After last night I needed a dose of reality, and happily used up my change talking to her and Dad about mundane things. We argued about money a little.

"Don't think we don't appreciate this, Jack," said Mom, "but you can't afford to be sending us twenty-five dollars all the time. You have to save a little for yourself."

I thought about the five thousand dollars Escott would be bringing by tonight. My current expenses were running about fifteen dollars a week, including rent and tips. My food, of course, was free. At that rate I could easily spare my folks twenty-five bucks a week for the next two years or more. Maybe by that time Roosevelt would have the economy back on keel.

"I'm saving a little. . . . How are my siblings?"

"What?"

"How's the family? Any new nephews or nieces?"

"Yes, Sarah Jane wrote just the other day. . . ." And she went down the line chattering about my three brothers and three sisters and the growing brood of grandchildren, then had to hand the phone over to Dad.

"Where are you staying so we can write you?"

"I'm just at a small hotel for now, and I may be moving on if I find a better place," I hedged. I didn't want them knowing I was staying under an assumed name. I asked him about the store and about his drinking buddies and what he thought about Hitler, safely distracting him away from questioning me. I'm a lousy liar at the best of times and my parents were always able to tell when I was trying to give them the business. The best thing was to keep my distance until I could figure out what was safe for me to tell them about my condition, or if I could tell them anything at all.

"What happened to all that reporting?" he demanded.

"What's all this about an ad agency? I thought all those places were in New York."

"They have a few out here, and they pay good money to bright boys like me."

"Like—what—oh, your mom asks when you coming back for a visit?"

"When I get a vacation."

"When's that?"

"I don't know, I just started. Give me some time to get settled into things."

"You know you got work here if you need it."

"I know, and thanks."

"Well, this is costing you a fortune. Write next time."

"I will, don't worry."

He gave the phone over to Mom, who said pretty much the same stuff, then repeated it all over again to make sure I understood.

"And remember what I said about saving some for yourself."

"Yes, Mom."

"And be careful about what you eat. No drugstore hot dogs."

"No, Mom, I promise."

She said good-bye, gave the phone over to Dad again, and he told me to stay out of trouble, and we said good-bye.

I stayed in the booth for a while, my head down and a cold hard ache inside. I hadn't been really homesick since I first left for the Army as a kid. At least back then I knew I could return again, that home and things would be the same as ever, but that was a kid's thinking. Their lives had changed and I had changed and grown up. I didn't necessarily like the situation, but there wasn't a whole hell of a lot anybody could do about it.

I backed quickly out of the confining space of the booth and went outside, trying to put distance between myself and the loneliness. The depression followed, but its hold lessened with the distractions the long streets offered. Thirty minutes of round-about walking put me in front of a men's shop that had been advertised in the papers.

It was closed and no one would be in the back working late, which was exactly why I picked the place. I didn't need any hovering clerks asking awkward questions about my aversion to mirrors.

I slipped inside and got oriented. The front window shades

had been pulled, but the low level of illumination was more than adequate. Turning the lights on would have just annoyed a passing cop. After poking around, I located a pencil, receipt book, and a pair of gloves, not necessarily in that order, and proceeded to wait on myself.

Careful to print, I recorded the purchase of several shirts, ties, a couple of suits, some other odds and ends, and the real corker: a tuxedo, complete right down to the white fringed scarf to drape around my neck. I figured the scarf would make me look more like Fred Astaire than Bela Lugosi.

The clothes were high quality and with a price to match, but aside from rent and a few tips, I wasn't spending my money on very much else. I overpaid the purchases by three bucks since I was out of small bills, but thought it would be sufficient compensation to the shop owner for my inconvenient nocturnal intrusion. I could have just walked out with the stuff, but I'm basically an honest guy. Besides, if the incident were reported to the cops, they would probably do nothing. The stuff was paid for and then some. They'd have bigger fish to catch than some customer who took self-service very seriously.

After packaging everything up into a stack of long, flat boxes, I tried leaving by the back door in order to avoid witnesses to my impromtu Houdini act. There were alarms on all the doors, set to go off if they were opened, so I was forced to dematerialize to get out. Not all the boxes went through, the ones that didn't tumbled to the shop floor. I made several trips in and out after that, holding the larger ones close. Since I had to enter the back door of my hotel by the same method, I got a lot of practice in that night. The boxes all bore the name of the store I'd "burgled" and I didn't want to be seen entering the lobby at a late hour with an armful of incriminating evidence. Should the story of the honest thief make the morning papers, the last thing I needed was to have some night clerk putting things together. Maybe I was being overly cautious, but sometimes paranoia pays off.

Before midnight had rolled around, my new duds were hung up, their labels removed and flushed. Taking another short walk out the back way, I disposed of the boxes and wrappings in some isolated trash can.

Escott was sitting in my armchair smoking his pipe when I returned.

"You certainly waste no time." He nodded at my open closet and its new contents, and his eyes went to the top hat on the bureau. "Planning an evening out?"

"Maybe. From what I hear about the Nightcrawler Club, I figure a plain old suit and tie wouldn't get me past the hat check girls."

He murmured agreement. If he had questions about how and where I came by the stuff, he kept them to himself.

"Is this a social visit?"

"More or less. I was wondering if you had seen the papers."

I knew what he was talking about. "Yeah, but you know how these things can get distorted. Editors like to punch things up; it sells papers."

"True, but even taking that into consideration, there was quite a lot of copy devoted to Frank Paco's mental condition."

"He must have been running close to the edge. The fire may have pushed him right over—either that or he's faking to keep Morelli from collecting."

"Has your memory come back on anything since last night?"

"Haven't thought about it," I lied. "I've been busy."

"And I as well." He pulled five thousand dollars from his inside pocket and gave them to me.

"Clean?"

"Very clean."

"I'll try not to spend it all in one place. Don't I owe you something, though?"

"For what?"

"For this case, or are you working for free these days?"

He made a noise that was something like a laugh. "Mr. Fleming, I have already received a very exceptional fee for this case and it is safely lodged in my home, all five thousand of it. You have been more than generous, believe me. As it was, I had not planned to bill you anything at all, especially not after you prevented Sanderson from dumping my careless carcass into the river."

"All right, we'll call it even, then."

"You don't keep banker's hours. You have a safe place to keep your share?"

"Don't worry, it's locked away."

"Very well." He changed the subject again, but kept the conversational tone in his voice. "Did you know that several of Paco's key men have been arrested on suspicion of arson?"

"Fancy that," I chuckled.

"I've also been going through the papers you brought out."

"Is it good stuff?"

"It is excellent stuff. I made copies for future reference, and then anonymously turned them over to the right people. If Paco were in his right mind, he would certainly be in jail by now, rather than in hospital."

"Better that he's in the hospital; he can't make bail and leave the country."

"He does have a police guard on him."

"Couldn't happen to a more deserving guy."

"What did you do to him?" he asked in the same quiet tone.

I wasn't ready to talk about it. He could see that, but just sat there and waited.

"Was it something to do with your condition?" he said after a long time.

After all the activity last night I had needed to go straight to the Stockyards, so he knew I hadn't touched Paco's throat. Such an assault might have driven the man around the bend, though at the time it hadn't even occurred to me to try. Escott was fishing around for something more subtle.

I avoided his eyes. "You've seen him?"

"I talked with a nurse who had."

"How is he?"

"The same as he was last night."

He wanted to know very badly.

"Was that a result of one of your powers?"

I caught myself avoiding his eyes again and stopped. "You make it sound like I'm Chandu the Magician."

"More like Lamont Cranston."

He was referring to the introduction of "The Shadow" radio show. Every time it came on, the audience was reminded of his power to cloud men's minds. "Yeah, I guess it was something like that."

"What kind of control do you have?"

"I don't know, that was the problem."

"Are you going to learn how?"

"No!"

He gave me a few minutes to cool down. I paced the little

room and looked out the window for a while. The street was still down there. I thought about Maureen and all the things she hadn't told me.

"Mr. Fleming . . ."

His formality was annoying. "Why don't you call me Jack?"

"I was going to wait until your case was cleared away. I prefer to keep things on a business level with my clients until they cease to be my clients."

I looked at him now. My mind was concentrated and I prayed controlled. His gray eyes had ceased their normal movements and were locked onto mine. It was so damned easy.

"Call me Jack."

His pipe dropped to the floor with a clack, and the tobacco inside scattered from the impact. The movement distracted me just enough. His eyes blinked and his face resumed the expression he had a few seconds ago.

"Where's your pipe?" I asked.

He found it and apologized for the mess.

"But how did it get there?"

"I must have dr—" He let his breath out slowly. "You did it just now?"

"Yes, I told you to do something. The pipe falling was just a side issue. Now do you see why I want to leave this alone?"

"Induced hypnotism . . ."

"No—"

"Jack, this is not something you should avoid, this demands responsib—"

"Am I still your client?"

It was an oddball question and he wondered why I'd asked it. I told him.

"You see how it is? You weren't even aware of what I did. You think it's your own idea. If I told you to jump out the window singing 'Swanee' you'd do it."

"If it were hypnosis, I would not."

"Yeah, I know all that. You can't get a person to do anything against his will—but that's for the normal kind, and this isn't."

"How do you know that?"

"Because I saw what it did to Paco."

"Did you do it on purpose?"

"No—I don't know—it was an emotional thing as well. I don't know how it works, it just happened. It got away from me and

I'm not going to try anything like that again. I have no right to."

"And how do you plan to control it if you choose to ignore it?"

"I don't know. . . . I'll work things out. I could avoid all this arguing by just telling you to forget all this."

"Then do so."

"No. I'm not going to go banging around in your brain with a monkey wrench and have you ending up like Paco."

Escott nodded thoughtfully and refilled and lit his pipe. "I almost wish other people were as morally minded as that, but then I should be out of a job."

It took me a minute to figure out what he meant by that beyond the obvious, but at times I could be pretty damn slow. His needling had been more of a test than curiosity. Apparently my reaction was satisfactory and I almost resented his game. Almost, because if our positions were reversed I might have done the same thing to him.

I tried to laugh, but it came out sour. "Yeah, I'm a goddamned Jack Armstrong."

He stood up. "If you've nothing else planned, would you care to go for a drive? I find it to be quite relaxing and I've something you might like to see."

I didn't, so we did. He took the Nash as far north as the streets led without actually being in the lake, then took an east-west road. He went dead slow past a two-story brick building that took up the whole block. The place was dark except for a couple of upstairs windows.

"The Nightcrawler Club," he said, in case I'd missed the dark neon sign on the front. "I thought you'd like a look at it. They're closed on Sundays."

He drove down a block and pulled over. We got out and walked past the place, then around to the back. I noticed someone standing in the rear alley and told Escott to keep going. We turned away from the club, going north again until we were stopped by a railing that overlooked the lake. We stood only ten feet above the black water, but I hated any kind of height, and kept away from the rail. Escott leaned on it and stared at the garbage swelling against the concrete boundary of the land.

"Who was in the alley?"

"An off-duty waiter, maybe, but he was dressed fancy."

"We can try again later."

He pushed away from the rail and headed east along the water. There wasn't much to see: a few boats tied up, others were at anchor farther out; they all looked asleep at this late hour.

"Do you see anything out there?" He pointed to something large out on the lake. The last time I'd seen it was in profile. Its stern was toward us now, but I had no trouble reading the name.

"The *Elvira*."

"I couldn't be sure of her in the dark, but she is in the same spot she was in this afternoon. Morelli's on board now with his lady friend. He spends his free time there when he can."

"Must be nice."

"What does it bring to mind?"

I shook my head. "Sorry. Right now it's just another boat."

We walked on and made a big circle before coming back to the club. The alley was clear this time, but there wasn't anything worth seeing. It was wide enough for the delivery trucks, and had no more than its share of trash at the edges and the usual loading platform and steps that go with back doors. When I took an incidental breath, the place stank with a wet and used smell—nothing extraordinary—it could be found in any alley with bad drainage the world over.

I shook my head again to his unasked question. As a memory jog, the place was useless. We walked back to the car, or at least tried. The fancily dressed man must have taken a turn around the block himself. It was hard to tell who was more surprised. Automatically his hand went to his belt, where he kept his gun.

"What're you doing here? Get out!"

We were more than ready to oblige and moved away from him, but like a yapping dog, he trotted up behind to make sure we left. Things were peaceful enough until someone else stepped out the back door.

"What is it, Ed?"

"Couple of guys and they're leaving."

"Who are you with?" he said to us.

"Just ourselves, takin' a walk home," said Escott. He had an American accent now and sounded slightly drunk.

"And where's home?"

"Nonayur business. You want us out, we're out." Swaying, he grabbed my arm and started away.

"Ed."

Ed needed no further instructions. He came around in front of us and pulled the gun. I hoped it was too dark for him to see our faces clearly.

"What's the big idea?" protested Escott. "We're goin'."

"In a minute," said Ed. "Turn around and keep your hands out."

He marched us up to the loading dock, the second man joining us at street level. He also had a gun. With his other hand he was pulling out a lighter. While he fumbled to get it working, I felt Escott's muscles tighten. It wouldn't do us any good if those bozos got a clear look at us. While they were watching the sparking lighter, Escott released my arm and twisted backward, grabbing Ed's gun hand and forcing it down. I jumped the other guy and tried to do the same. He had the gun up and fired once, but I knocked it to the outside before it could do any damage. I didn't waste time pulling it away from him, but just hit the side of his head and stunned him. He went down hard and ceased to be a worry.

I checked Escott. Ed had lost his gun and they were both scrambling and rolling on the concrete to get it. I kicked it out of the way and when there was an opening in the punching and flailing, leaned in and knocked him cold. I dragged Escott to his feet, and we ran out of the alley for the car before the one wild shot could bring reinforcements. Escott had the keys out and ready. He opened the passenger door, dived in, and slid over. The Nash was started and in gear almost as fast.

He was breathless with a thin sweat on his face, but his eyes were gleaming happily. The man was crazy, he'd been enjoying himself back there.

"That was good exercise," he puffed. "At least we know they take their security as seriously as Paco."

"That could be a problem."

"But not for you, my dear chap. Thanks for the helping hand, that fellow was awfully fast."

"Anytime. Are you done for the night or do you want to take on any wandering longshoremen just to cap things off?"

"Another time. Believe me, I did not think they'd react so suspiciously. The one on the steps must have seen through my drunk act. A pity, it went over well enough on stage. I shall have to show you my press clippings sometime. Oh, dear."

He pulled the car over fast, the right front wheel bumping the curb as we jerked to a halt. He was still breathing hard and his damp skin was gray.

"Oh, damn. Oh, bloody damn." He pressed a hand against his left side. Blood was seeping freely between his fingers. "The bastard had a knife." He slipped sideways against me and fainted.

7

DR. CLARSON WAS a small man with large brown hands that at first glance didn't look dexterous enough for the work they were doing. His tightly curling hair was cut close to the scalp. He was about fifty, but the gray at the sides made him seem older. His movements were economical, and if he had any opinions about patching up a white man in his tiny examining room at two o'clock on a Monday morning, he kept them professionally to himself.

Escott was out cold again on the exam table. The room was too small for anyone else but him and the doctor, so Shoe Cold-field and I had to be content to cool our heels in the waiting room outside. There were six old wooden chairs, each as scarred as the matching floor, a small table that must have served the receptionist as a desk, and some ancient file cabinets, also of wood. The place was very clean, though, and smelled sharply of antiseptic. Shoe looked worried, but not overly anxious. However shabby the place was, he had trust in Clarson's medical skills.

I was restless and wanted to pace, but held it in check, trying to follow Shoe's example of patience. He sat quite still on one of the chairs, his eyes straying to the doctor and Escott, alert in case he was needed. All I could do was fidget around on my perch on the table and try not to look at the smears of blood we left decorating the floor when we brought Escott in. Bloody damn had been right, my hands and clothes were covered with the stuff. From literature I'd read in the past on the subject of blood and vampires, I should have been feeling something other than sick horror.

The blood on my hands got sticky, and I asked if there was a washroom nearby. Shoe glanced up and led the way out to one down the hall. We cleaned up as best we could, but our clothes would be the laundry's problem.

Things hadn't changed at the office. We sat down again. I chewed on a nail, a habit I hadn't fallen into since I was a kid. It tasted lousy, so I forced my hand down with the other and kept still. I looked at Coldfield and wondered why he hadn't asked for explanations, as he was certainly entitled to do, but then I hadn't volunteered any. I looked at Clarson's back and wondered what was taking so long and if we should call an ambulance.

I had eased Escott down on the seat, pulled out a handkerchief, and pressed it against his side. It soaked through in what seemed like an instant, but I could see now that my reckoning of time had been distorted by fear. With his head level with his heart, he came to after a moment and said something unintelligible, then clearly said my name.

"I'm right here. I'll get you to a hospital if I can find one."

"No. Find Shoe . . . closer."

I had no better ideas and at least I knew where to go. Somehow I got over to the driver's side and drove like hell to the Shoe Box.

Half a dozen dark men jumped when we screeched up outside the place, and I could hardly blame them. A couple came up to the car, and I recognized one man from our previous visit. He stuck his head in the window, his eyes going wide and curious at Escott's huddled form.

"Is Shoe around? His friend Escott's been hurt."

He wasted no time on the tableau, but straightened and shouted to someone by the nightclub door, who disappeared inside.

"How bad is he?"

"Don't know—it's a knife wound; he didn't feel it at first."

"Yeah, that's how they are." He spoke from experience, but didn't elaborate.

Escott's eyes were open, but he didn't seem aware of very much. His lips were blue and a sheen of sweat covered his cold face. I knew shock when I saw it and wished to God Coldfield would hurry. After a couple of years of pressing the sodden handkerchief, I looked up and saw his face in the passenger window.

"Shit, what happened?"

"Knife fight. He wanted to come here."

"It's his lucky night," he said, and looked back at the club entrance and told someone to hurry. That someone was introduced as Dr. Clarson, who peered at Escott and got into the backseat, telling me where to drive. Shoe got in the other side and we took off. Three blocks later I stopped in front of a dusty stairway leading into a dark building. The street-level sign declared the doctor's office was in room 201 and gave the hours.

Shoe took over pressure duty while Clarson went up to unlock things and turn on the lights. Between the two of us, Shoe and I got Escott up to the office, hopefully without inflicting more damage. Escott must have been in some pain by then; his gray eyes rolled up at the harsh white light and kept on going to the top of his head.

As the waiting telescoped, I became very conscious of Escott's soft breathing. Every few seconds I had to stifle the urge to get up and check things. Leg muscles would tighten, then forcibly relax as I willed myself to stay put so as not to break the doctor's concentration. Another twitch would bring up another excuse. For something to do I pretended to breathe. In that small and very quiet waiting room, Coldfield might possibly just notice its absence as Escott had.

Escott . . .

When there was a long, descending sigh in the next room, Coldfield went bolt upright in his chair and looked at me.

The doctor stood up straight and nodded over his work. His had been the sigh we had heard. We crowded into the doorway to see. Escott's clothes had been peeled away, leaving his trunk pale and vulnerable except for the bandages just under the line of his rib cage. Clarson washed up at a tiny sink in the corner and dried his hands carefully.

"How do I handle it, Shoe?" he asked without turning.

Shoe looked at me. "You want to tell me now?"

I told him how it had happened and that it had something to do with Escott's investigation of my case. Clarson shook his head, giving his silent opinion of grown men trying to act like Saturday-afternoon serial heroes.

"He won't be kicking off just yet," he told us. "So I guess there's no harm keeping this between us."

"What do we do now?" asked Shoe.

"Leave him here tonight, let him rest. He lost a lot of blood and got some muscle cut up, but no internal stuff or he wouldn't be here." He didn't specify if he meant the office versus an emergency room or among the living.

"What about tomorrow?"

"We'll see in the morning. I don't want him moved for now. I'm keeping him quiet for a few hours, so you two can go on. I'll call you at the club if there's any trouble."

"Do you anticipate any?" I asked.

"Not really, infection at the most. I cleaned him up good, but knives can be dirty."

Coldfield and I thanked him and went downstairs to the car. There was some blood on the upholstery, but it was dry now. We were just getting inside when a long, bony body lurched at us from behind. It was Cal, the skinny kid who shined shoes, but now he was minus his box and easy smile.

Coldfield was surprised, which for him was the same as being annoyed. "What you doing out of bed, boy?"

"Jimmy told me about Mist' Escott."

"He's all right now—"

"Can I see him?"

"He's not even awake and the doctor says he needs rest. He's not hurt too bad, so come on and get in the car."

Cal looked wistfully up the stairs, then reluctantly got in between us. I drove back to the Shoe Box and Coldfield had me park around the back. Without being told, Cal got out and trotted ahead of us to the back door.

"He lives here?" I asked.

"Yeah, him and a few other boys his age. They earn their keep and it's respectable work."

"What about their families?"

"Some don't have any to speak of. Cal's dad was killed in an accident and his mama works in a bar so she can be close to the booze. When she climbs out of the bottle, Cal will move back with her, but until then he's got a home here."

"In a nightclub?"

The question should have annoyed him, but didn't. "My sister looks after them. This place is a castle compared to where they've been. I make 'em work and when they aren't working, they go to school. I don't force anything they don't want; they can leave when they like, and some do, but the smart ones don't.''

The headline, ''Bronze Belt Boys' Town'' jumped into my head. It would make a good story, but now was hardly the time for an interview.

''Want to come in for a drink?''

''Thanks, but next time. I need to get home and clean up.''

''You got a way home?''

''I can walk.''

''Not in this neighborhood, you can't. Come on, my turn to drive you.'' We went to his newer Nash and got in. He asked where I lived and I told him. ''That's a pretty long walk.''

''I like to walk.''

''In some parts of this town, you're better off running.''

''So I've noticed.'' I handed over the keys to Escott's car. ''Here, I won't be by till late tomorrow, you take care of them.''

''Sure. You still going to mess with Morelli?''

''I have to, now.''

''Take some advice and don't.'' He didn't mention the consequences. He didn't have to since we were both thinking about Escott.

Back in my room I packed my dirty laundry up for the staff to work on. To save trouble explaining the bloodstains I just threw the shirt away. I spent the rest of the night flat on my back and staring at the ceiling from the bed. It was depressing having to sit through the long early-morning hours alone and not be able to watch the dawn and the change of mood a new day can bring. The only good thing was the oblivion it brought as soon as the lid of my trunk came down, and then an instant later it seemed, there was another fresh night ahead of me, as though the day had never happened.

I phoned the Shoe Box first thing and talked to Coldfield.

''You been out all day? I tried to call.''

''Yeah. Call me for what? Is he all right?''

''He's weak, but insisted on going home. I thought you'd want to know, is all.'' He gave me a different address from the little office and I wrote it down. ''You ain't going to tire him?''

''No, just apologize for putting him through all this.''

"It's no one's fault but the s.o.b. with the knife."
I agreed and hung up.

The taxi dropped me at a row of two- and three-story buildings that looked old enough to have escaped the Fire, or had been built immediately afterward. Kids played in the quiet street, and parents sat on the steps and fanned themselves in the twilight. It was a respectable middle-class neighborhood. It hardly seemed suitable for Escott, but then again I couldn't think what else would have been right.

I rang the bell of a brown brick building of three floors and Cal opened the door.

"Hi, Mist' Fleming. Shoe said you was coming."

From somewhere close inside, Escott said, "*Were* coming, Cal."

Cal grinned and said it again correctly, standing back for me. It was a small entryway, with a rack on the wall to hang hats and coats. Directly ahead were stairs leading up into shadows. On their left was a hall going through to the back of the house. An open set of double doors were parallel to the stairs, and beyond them was a cramped sitting room, where Escott was lying on an old chintz-covered sofa. He was in a deep purple bathrobe; the color made him look more pale than he was. There were tired circles under his eyes, but he seemed glad to see me.

"Come and sit down. Will you have some tea?"

The question was for Cal's benefit; I politely declined. "You look better than last night. How do you feel?"

"Tired, but I'll live through it. Shoe invited me to stay at his place, but I wanted to come home. We finally compromised, and he let me go, but only on condition that Cal stays over and keeps an eye on me."

"Good, I was afraid you'd be alone."

At second look, the place only seemed cramped. The high ceilings made the floor area appear smaller in proportion. The floor was highly polished, reflecting the lamplight and a few comfortable old pieces of furniture. Several pictures hung by long wires from the upper moldings. They were all large mediocre prints of naked women reclining on clouds with naked babies and doves, and were hardly consistent with Escott's character.

"Did this place come furnished?"

He noticed where I was looking, his eyes crinkling. "Do you like them?"

"They're . . . interesting."

He didn't miss my expression. "You have excellent taste. They shall no doubt prove profitable to the junk dealer as soon as I can get around to it."

"They came with the house?"

"Yes, certainly. It has an interesting history. I have it on good account from my neighbors that the place was once a bordello."

"The previous tenants *are* gone?"

"Yes, the owner died some time ago, the place went for sale, and I was able to buy it quite cheaply, as no one wanted to live here. You know, I still occasionally have to turn away an old customer who hasn't heard the news yet. My life is not dull—sometimes odd, but never dull." He sipped his tea. "Shoe thinks I should talk you out of pursuing your own case and to turn it over to the police."

"You know I can't go to them the way I am."

"I know, but Shoe doesn't. He obviously has decided that I have no further interest in it because of this little incident."

"I'm not too surprised; he mentioned it last night. I am sorry about this. If I'd been faster—"

He shook his head. "No one else could have been faster, I've seen it and you did save me, after all, and I am grateful. Forget about it, I'll be up and doing soon enough."

Cal came in with a glass of water and a small bottle of pills. "It's time."

Grimacing and accepting two, he washed them down quickly to get it over with, then Cal took the glass away to the kitchen. As soon as he was gone, Escott spit the pills fastidiously into a handkerchief and tucked it into the robe's pocket. He drank more tea to wash away their taste.

"What gives?" I asked.

"They're morphine. I've seen what it can do to people, and I'd really rather endure the pain. At least I know it will go away. Clarson is an excellent fellow and discreet, but he really should know better. I had an armful of the stuff this morning and could hardly do anything for myself."

I wondered what he could possibly feel up to doing in his condition. "Do you need anything now?"

"Only more patience."

"You aren't talking me out of this mess?"

"We're enough alike that I know better than to try."

"I'm going there soon."

"Tonight?"

"Tomorrow. I want to give them time to cool down from last night's fracas. They wanted to know who we were with. You think they thought we were Paco's men?"

"Possibly, or any of a dozen smaller gangs out for trouble. I'm inclined to think they were just naturally suspicious. What do you plan to do?"

"I was a journalist two weeks ago. . . . I'll just check things out like it was any other story and see what happens." Vague at best as an idea, but it had worked for me on other occasions and had turned into acceptable copy. I was hoping to turn this into my missing memory.

Escott was visibly tired, so I wished him well and left, walking around the city for a couple of hours. Coldfield was right about some places being dangerous, but I was a big boy now and could take care of myself. I was looking things over, getting acquainted with the streets and the personality of each block, slowly working toward the Stockyards and my inevitable stop there.

By now I had ceased to be too squeamish about the blood drinking. That oddball reaction had hit me on my second visit there. My first feeding had been done in a kind of panic; "you must do this or die." It had been quick, dreamlike, and with no time to think. My second visit had been more leisurely, and when it came down to brass tacks, I almost balked. The thought of opening an animal's vein with my teeth and sucking blood from the wound was nauseating, but out of necessity I had to push the thought from my mind and get on with the business. Intellectually, I still had trouble handling the process, but by now I was at least getting used to it. It helped to think of it in terms of a habit, like brushing one's teeth; boring, but it had to be done.

The blood completely satisfied my hunger and gave me strength, but its ingestion was a far cry from sitting comfortably around a table with friends and socializing into the small hours over real food and drink.

Leaving the yards, I wandered a long time until I found an all-night theatre and went in. Leslie Howard pined after Merle

Oberon in *The Scarlet Pimpernel*, and I watched it three times in a row, until I was rooting for Raymond Massey to win. He never did, so I went home and read the papers until dawn.

The personals still carried my question to Maureen, but had no reply. I told myself again I was a fool to hope after all these months and should just give it up. As always, I gave a mental shrug. It wouldn't hurt for just one more week, it really wouldn't.

But it really did. The trick was to ignore the hurt and keep hoping.

The tuxedo fit well enough. I was one of those lucky ones who could buy things right off the rack, even pants. The new patent leather shoes were a bit snug, but they'd be well broken in tonight. A mirror would have been useful, for I was interested in how young I appeared. I'd fed heavily last night to obtain good color as well, as I planned to pass myself off as Gerald Fleming again.

I transferred some cash into a new wallet and worked the stiffness from it. The rest of my money was locked in the trunk with my other personal papers. The wallet had a little pasteboard card with lines for printing one's name and address. I filled it in with the name of Gerald Fleming, a phony out-of-town address, and the name of Jack Fleming as someone to contact in case of an emergency. As a legal ID it was totally useless, but better than nothing at all. I draped the white silk scarf so it hung in front, and finished things off with the top hat.

I left by the back door, partially from paranoia, partially from the idea that if anyone in the lobby glommed me in this memorable getup they'd raise my rent. A few blocks away I caught a cab and had it take me to the lion's den.

Tonight the windows of the Nightcrawler were bright, and fancy people were streaming in and out even at this early hour. I paid the driver and trotted up the wide steps in order to slip inside with a knot of revelers, but found my way suddenly blocked by an agile mountain disguised as a man in a tuxedo. He had short blond hair, small eyes, and a chronically grim set to his mouth.

"Good evening," he said civilly. I mumbled a reply of some kind, noting he was giving me careful study. His eyes flicked to some grillwork set like an oversized vent in one branch of the U-shaped entrance. The darkness of the small room beyond wasn't quite adequate to hide the man with the gun who sat there. He nodded and the mountain stood aside and let me by. I pretended not to notice this exchange, as they decided I wasn't a dangerous character. It was favorable to be underestimated. I looked young and hopefully innocent—all that was needed was a touch of stupidity. Considering some of my antics from the past, that would probably be very easy.

The doorman did his duty, but I paused at the threshold with a brief attack of doubt and insecurity. Though it would have been too dangerous for him, I wished Escott was along. I missed his confidence. Despite the advantages I had now, I could still get scared. For just one second I nearly turned back, but a silly-looking woman with frizzed black hair and too much makeup caught a look at me and whooped hello. Her party had preceded me coming in and were already more than a little drunk.

"Whatcha waitin' for, a streetcar? Come on in, cutey," she shrilled.

I couldn't stand this kind of drunk, but went in before I started thinking again. She latched on to my arm.

"Isn't he cute? Hey, Ricky, isn't he cute, isn't he?"

Ricky said, "Yeah," and swayed a little. How had they qualified getting in if the watchdogs had been so careful with me?

"That's how I like 'em, tall 'n cute," she told Ricky reproachfully. I hadn't been cute since I traded my short pants in for an older brother's hand-me-downs, but let them drag me inside. Stepping away from the door, I heard the men behind us chuckling. Good. If they found my situation something to laugh at, they might also think me harmless.

As politely as possible under the circumstances, I detached myself from the lady's grip and checked my hat and scarf in with the first of the many stunning blonds that worked there. Platinum was the dominant color, apparently a requirement for employment. They wore short black dresses decorated with silver sequins in the pattern of a spider's web. Over their hearts were black, red and silver pins of stylized spiders, all of which were a nice gimmick to tie in with the name of the club.

With difficulty, I turned my attention from the girls to the rest of the place. It was very noisy. The barrage of conversation trying to be heard over the brassy orchestra was like a riot in a large dog kennel. With that image in mind it was easy to categorize the patrons. There were a few high-class ones with pedigrees, but the overwhelming breed represented were the mutts; well-dressed, but mutts all the same.

Another blond came up and led me to a table the size of a dinner plate and told me the waiter would be by shortly. The place was surprisingly busy for a weeknight, but well organized. In less than a minute a young man appeared and took my order for Irish coffee, which also appeared in less than a minute. I pretended to sip, though bringing it to my lips was an act of will, and I had to stifle a gag. For distraction I looked around and caught several unescorted young ladies giving me a hopeful eye. I wasn't that handsome—they were working girls. I had no inclinations for that at the moment, so my gaze slid past to the swaying couples on the floor below. The band wound up the music, the dancers dispersed, and the lights went down. A single spot picked out another platinum blond leaning against the grand piano. She was in something long, white, and silvery, a nice contrast to the brief black skirts of the other girls and a perfect complement to her long shimmering hair.

She sang something sad and shallow in a voice that was surprisingly good, filling the room and hushing even the worst drunks. As with any woman I noticed, I was comparing her to Maureen, looking for something wrong, but for once the lady was holding her own. She finished her song, and the lights faded and came up, but by then she was gone, leaving her audience wanting more. The band cut to another number and couples began to venture onto the floor again. I looked up and saw a pretty girl smiling at me, holding a tray full of tobacco products.

"Bobbi always knocks 'em dead," she observed with a nod toward the stage. I made a business of picking out some cigarettes and got her to talk a little. In two minutes I found out where she lived, when she got off work, the time of Bobbi's next number, the location of the gambling rooms, and the requirements to get inside, which were specifically a lot of cash and the willingness to lose it fast. Her interest cooled and she moved on, apparently having had experience with gamblers. I'd seen the type as well; men who would rather gamble than make love, more fool they.

And here I was trying to imitate them. I abandoned my table and drifted over to a guarded door marked PRIVATE. The large man there asked my name. I gave the one I was using that night

and was slightly disappointed to get no reaction. He consulted
a telephone, a buzzer sounded, and he opened the door wide.

It was another big room, but much quieter, lit by crystal chan-
deliers and dimmed by cigarette smoke. I'd been in places like
this before, but never when they were in one piece. Usually I
was hot in the wake of a police raid making a written account
of the destruction and noting down who had been arrested for
what. Prior to tonight I had never been able to afford this sort
of decadence. It felt great.

At the money cage I bought two hundred dollars in chips,
blanching inwardly at the small pile they made in my pocket.
For something to do, I lit a cigarette and studied faces. Not one
of them was familiar, which was all for the best, since I didn't
want to be noticed right away. I wandered around, looking for
Slick Morelli. He was either not there or my memory was not
cooperating the way it had at Frank Paco's. Maybe I was expecting too much from my traumatized brain.

Giving it a rest, I found an isolated corner and got into a
blackjack game, winning ten dollars and losing fifty before re-
alizing I could cheat without getting caught.

The dealer's face had about as much expression as a dead fish,
but he had no control over his heart rate. When the immediate
noise level occasionally subsided, I could just hear it. Every time
he dealt the house a good hand it beat just a little louder and
faster, and after some concentrated practice at sorting out the
internal signals my rate of winning rose marginally. I didn't win
every time, that was impossible with the other players and the
natural fall of the cards, but I had enough of an edge to win
more than lose. In an hour I left the table a thousand dollars
ahead, excited at the prospect of a new vocation in life.

Circling the room again, I looked at the new faces, checking
out the suckers at the roulette tables and slot machines. One of
the machine patrons was the singer, Bobbi. She looked just as
good, if not better, close up as she did fifty feet away on stage.
Now she was wearing a black sequin-trimmed wrap over her
bare shoulders. It must have been to provide some modesty to
her stage gown, but since the black material was practically
transparent it had just the opposite effect.

She pushed a coin into the slot and hauled the lever down
with just enough precise force, indicating long practice. She got
a cherry and two lemons. Her face revealed no disappointment.

Her moves were automatic: push in a coin, yank the lever, and wait, push in a coin . . . I was getting hypnotized. She won a small pot, added the money to the stack she kept ready, and started over again. I wondered if she'd rather gamble than make love.

She noticed me out of the corner of her eye. Just my luck, the first emotion I inspired in her was annoyance. "The floor show's in the next room, ace."

"Sorry, didn't know I was intruding."

"You shouldn't look over other people's shoulders."

I moved around to her front field of view and angled so I could look out across the room. Tapping out a cigarette, I offered her one.

"They kill the voice and stain the teeth," she told me, pulling the lever down with decidedly more force. I put my props away unlit and offered to buy her a drink.

"No, thanks, and before you ask me why I'm here, I'm supporting my crippled mother down on the farm."

At least she was talking to me. She didn't say anything I wanted to hear, but she was talking. I watched her play the machine. There was more strength than grace in her automated movements, but the view was very absorbing.

"You know Slick Morelli?" I asked.

She kept up the rhythm, but her eyelids flickered. "Doesn't everybody?"

"Where is he?"

"Somewhere around."

"Can you point him out?"

"You think I'm the party hostess or something? Go talk to one of the boys over there." She jerked her head in the direction of the door. The movement dislodged a wisp of hair. She paused long enough to brush it with her fingertips, using the gesture to glance at me before going back to the machine. I tried to keep my smile neutral and non-threatening.

"I heard that yacht of his is for sale," I tried. "The *Elvira*."

She laughed. Another coin, down came the lever. I didn't see the result. She put in another coin.

"Why not? He needs the money."

This time the lever stayed up. Her eyes slid over to mine. I expected blue, but they were hazel. She studied my face, trying to fit me into a category and finally deciding; it was anything but complimentary. "What do you want?" she said wearily.

"An introduction to Slick?"

She almost asked why, but thought better of it. "Go talk to one of the boys."

"They're not as pretty. My name's Gerald Fleming . . . I think Slick will want to talk to me about my brother Jack."

The names meant nothing to her, which was a relief.

"Jack met him two weeks ago, they were aboard the *Elvira*."

Her heartbeat went up suddenly, but she kept her face straight.

"He's built just like me and much the same in the face, but he's in his mid-thirties."

Nothing new, she was still reacting to the mention of the yacht.

"Frank Paco and a guy named Sanderson were there, too. Fred's dead now and Paco is headed for a nuthouse. . . ."

She went white at those names, but still tried to cover it with a kind of defiance. "So what?" She wore a soft flower scent, but underneath the roses I could smell fear. I asked her why she was afraid. She didn't deny it. "Death and taxes, what else?"

Slick Morelli or me?

She kept her eyes on the machine. "I think you'd better go now."

"I'd rather stay."

"Suit yourself, it's no skin off my nose."

"A guy could get discouraged."

"Good."

"I know Slick killed my brother."

She had a lot of control, but now the fear smell was drowning the perfume. She went on playing, pretending she hadn't heard.

"If you see him tonight, pass that on. I'll be around."

"You're not kidding, are you?"

"No."

"Why do you think he—"

"Because I was at Frank Paco's last dinner party, the one with the hot finish that made all the papers. I overheard things. Slick's name came up in the course of the conversation."

"Aren't you being kind of stupid to march in here like this?"

"Maybe, but Slick won't hurt me because I've got something he wants."

"What?"

"The same thing he wanted from brother Jack, but didn't get."

"Okay, be cagey."

"The less you know the better it is. I don't think you want to be in the middle of things."

"So everyone tells me. Why should you care?"

"You remind me of someone."

"Thanks a heap."

"She was afraid sometimes, too."

She watched me, troubled and wary. I shut up and moved away, there was no more to say to her and I couldn't trust my voice. Maureen was still too strong within me and I was feeling guilty for being attracted to Bobbi. She was as beautiful as Maureen, but in a different way; she was also vulnerable and worked hard to hide it. She gave me a lot to think about and I drifted blindly for a while. I lit more cigarettes, but didn't inhale. My body allowed me air to speak with, but rejected all foreign substances but one, and I had tanked up on that last night. I puffed superficially and added to the haze.

In one of the alcoves a little away from the noise, a serious poker game was in progress. There were five players, but most of the chips were on one side of the table in front of a totally bald fat man with a tangled brown beard bunching along the edge of his jowls like a baby's bib. Just as I strolled up one of the players threw down his hand and folded for the night. He left with a sweat-slick face, his body giving off the kind of reek that only comes from a habitual gambler, the kind that loses. I was the only observer of the game, the fat man probably won far too often for it to be of any interest to onlookers.

The cards went down and he raked in another pot, neatly stacking his chips according to color with his short, flat fingers. There must have been nine thousand dollars in front of him.

"Care to join?" he said, not looking up.

"No, thanks, I'll watch." I didn't like poker, tending to agree with Ambrose Bierce, who defined it as a game played with cards for some purpose unknown. I'd been listening to heartbeats and knew my little trick would be totally useless at this table with these veterans of the bluff. To test it, I mentally played a hand against the fat man, looking over the shoulder of another player. I lost repeatedly, as he registered about as much emotional reaction as the felt-covered table. All hands were alike to

him. Bored, I finally left, sliding quietly out of the alcove. The
fat man's glassy soulless eyes followed me before they snapped
back to his cards.

After patrolling the room once for Morelli, I went back to the
blackjack table and settled in for some serious gambling of my
own. As a game to play, it was much faster, and I enjoyed the
mental workout it gave. Before I knew it, two hours were gone
and I was the only player left. It increased my odds of winning,
I had the dealer's reactions down well enough by now to practically read his mind.

I flipped up my last card—it was a straight blackjack, I got
them occasionally. It was time to quit. Hardly believing it, I
gathered up fifty-eight hundred dollars in chips. At this rate I
could buy Dad a whole new chain of stores. My conscience
wasn't chafing a whole lot. It was Slick Morelli's money and he
owed me.

Shuffling the chips away, I looked up, my eyes locking on to
Bobbi's face. She moved without hurry across the room, not
smiling, not frowning, carefully blank. She sat on the stool next
to me and gave the dealer a quiet signal. He closed the table and
left.

"You gave up on me pretty fast. Why?" she asked.

"I thought that's what you wanted."

"I don't know what I want right now."

Dance music filtered in sporadically from the club room as
the door opened and closed. I caught her scent again—roses and
fear. It was strangely exciting. Her skin was very light and in
the shadow beneath her jaw I could see the veins throbbing with
life. I could smell that, too.

Keeping very still, I waited for her to look up at me. She was
so very beautiful and the first woman I'd wanted in a long, long
time. When she finally looked, I suggested we leave the room.
She stood and let me follow her through an unmarked door at
the back. We were in a dim hall, silent for her; for me it was
filled with the uneven rhythm of her lungs and the booming of
her heart. She let the wrap slide back from her shoulders as her
arms went up around my neck. The length of her body pressed
warmly against mine, just as I had wanted it. I caressed her
hair, tilting her chin up and kissing her red lips.

But the passion was all one-sided. Her face was empty of all
thought or feeling, her mind was in some neutral state, waiting

for my next suggestion. I backed off in doubt, then, suddenly knowing it was wrong, I turned away.

As a living man I'd never forced myself on a woman, and I wasn't going to start now. My changed nature had provided me with an all-too-easy route to seduction. Maureen completely avoided the use of this ability. She had wanted a willing lover, not a slave.

Bobbi's arms hung loose at her sides, and gradually awareness returned to her eyes. If she had some idea of what I'd been doing, she made no sign. Perhaps she thought her own desire had brought us here. I put a hand on the doorknob, hers stopped me.

"I think I should go."

"No." Her voice was hardly above a whisper. "I had to tell Slick what you said."

"I know, it's all right. That's why he sent you after me."

"Was it that obvious?"

"Just unexpected."

"I can get you out from here. I'll tell them you got wise and ran."

"Too risky for you, though."

"I'll be all right." Her breathing was back to normal and she still held my hand. Her face was tilted up again and she was free from any form of suggestion now. I lowered my head and kissed her and felt elation when she responded. I wanted to stay there, but reluctantly had to draw away. There was a pleasant kind of pressure building in my upper jaw. It was different from hunger pangs, but just as intense, pushing out my canines. While things were still manageable, I pushed them back into place with my tongue. Now was not the time or place for that sort of thing.

"This isn't Slick's planning," she said.

"I know."

"Look, maybe I can meet you tomorrow—"

"Tomorrow night. I have to talk with Slick first."

"Why?"

If I tried to answer that one we'd be there all night, which under any other circumstances would have been most desirable. I shook my head and smiled a little. "I'll take you back before you're missed."

She crumpled. "I hate it when he makes me do this. He said it was a joke, but I know better. He wanted me to get you outside, for you to meet me out front so you're seen leaving the club.''

"I'll oblige him, but we'll leave you out of it."

"But you're a fish on a hook now. Don't you see?"

"Like my brother?"

She was trying not to shiver. "I don't know about him, I really don't. Two weeks ago Slick spent several days on the yacht. He came back exhausted and in a bad temper, maybe your brother had something to do with it, but I just don't—"

She looked like she needed a pair of arms around her, and I did the best I could. "Don't worry about it, it's my choice. I'm leaving now, by the front door."

"He'll kill you," she said with certainty.

"No, he won't." It was too late for that, but a person doesn't have to have a bullet drilled through his heart to be emotionally dead. I smiled again, got hers in return, and felt alive for the first time in years.

8

I TRADED MY chips for cash at a grilled window under the hard gaze of two gunmen and folded the money away. The cashier made a big point of inviting me back again tomorrow night. He must have figured my beginner's luck would have worn out by then.

The band was playing a last slow number and I emerged from behind the door marked PRIVATE. Bobbi had gone around by another door and was on the dance floor, floating in the arms of a man who was holding his face close to her gleaming hair. Some guys had all the luck. It might have been Morelli, but I was only guessing.

The tables had lost most of their patrons. One whole section had been roped off and the mop-and-bucket boys were busy cleaning it. I collected my top hat and scarf, giving the girl at the counter enough of a tip to wake her up, and left by the front entrance.

I wondered how much line they were going to give me before hauling me in.

The cool night breeze off the lake felt clean and moist. The place was probably an Arctic hell in winter, but now things were just right. There were still a few hours before dawn. If they planned to try anything, I hoped the night would be long enough to accommodate them. I turned left along the front of the club, walking slowly. Behind, two sets of shoes were keeping pace with mine. I stifled a smile.

Between streetlights I paused and glanced back. One of them was the walking mountain, the other was the guard from the casino door. I tried to not be overly optimistic that they were after me. They could be underpaid enough to just want my newly acquired money. I continued on and turned the corner. There were two more men standing in the way. One of them plucked a toothpick from his mouth and flicked it away. He must have seen that one at the movies.

The guys behind caught up with us and completed the quintet. To make it look right I tried to duck past them for the open street. They were fast and professional and didn't even muss my clothes, but then I was not using my full strength to fight them. With arms held pinned to my sides and the white scarf over my eyes, I was marched quickly back to the club.

From the length of the walk and the smell at the end of it, we were going in by the alley entrance. I made some stock verbal protests until one of them shoved my own handkerchief into my mouth. This was done only to shake me up. If I'd really started to yell for help, they'd have been a lot rougher. In silence I was dragged up some steps and over a linoleum floor. From the left-over smell of grease, I guessed it was a kitchen. We trod on wooden floor for twenty-eight paces, then I was stumbling up a flight of stairs. Knuckles rapped on wood and I was shoved forward.

The door shut. I stood on carpeting in a room with two sets of lungs; one right behind me, probably the Mountain and the other about eight feet in front. A light switch clicked, and I felt a gentle warmth on my face.

The scarf was yanked down. The warmth came from a flexible desk lamp whose bulb had been angled to shine right in my eyes. The rest of the room was dark, but it didn't matter; the man trying to hide behind the glare was quite visible to me.

He was medium sized and dark haired, with a pale olive complexion slightly marred by old acne scars on his cheeks. In his young thirties, he had a set of sweet dark eyes that should have been on a woman. He would have been handsome, but his nose was too pinched and he had what looked like a razor cut for a mouth. His stare was intense and I shifted uneasily.

He smiled approval at my reaction.

I checked the room over so as not to look at him. It was a plain working office, but with a nice rug, a couple of paintings of ships, and an expensive desk-and-chair set. On the desk was a phone and blotter, in the corner behind me stood a file cabinet.

There was no other place to sit, though some dimples showed in the rug where chairs had been. He was smart enough to know how well such minor intimidations can undermine a person's confidence. He sat relaxed behind his desk, gave me a good once-over, then raised one finger as a signal to the man behind me. Hands probed, and my wallet, half a pack of cigarettes, and a book of matches were dropped on the desk. He opened the wallet, ignoring the money, and his eyes rested a moment on the little pasteboard card.

"I think you can consider this an emergency," he began. "Would you like us to put you in contact with your brother?"

Figuratively speaking, I could breathe a little easier. I'd worried he wouldn't have accepted me as Gerald. I didn't answer, but squinted at the light as though trying to see past it.

"I heard about you being at Paco's. They said you wanted to trade the list for your brother. I know where he is and I'm willing to deal with you."

It was simply stated and the truth, but I didn't think he was dumb enough to think I was that gullible. He was only feeling me out.

"Are you willing to deal with me?"

"Only if you're Slick Morelli."

He didn't answer except to move his hand slightly. The Mountain came up on one side and buried his knuckles in my stomach. That hurt a little—very little—and I faked the rest, going down on my knees as I had done at Paco's; no imagination, these guys.

"You can call me Mr. Morelli, Junior," he told me. "Now say thank you."

I was pulled to my feet and punched two more times before I got bored with the business and said what he wanted. There was a purpose to it all; get me to give in and obey him once and it would be that much easier for me to give in later about other things. He knew his business. I'd seen it done in other situations. The faces changed, but the technique remained constant. I let the Mountain hold me up and concentrated on breathing. Under the circumstances, they were both bound to notice if I stopped.

"Now, where is the list?"

Again, I said nothing; my memory had it in a place I could not reach. They'd killed me over it before, and they'd certainly try again—a difficult job in my present state, but not impossible. I had some control this time, though, and would stall to try and learn more, hoping my contact with them would trigger a memory.

Morelli opened a drawer in the desk, drew out a long black cigar, and fitted it into a silver holder. The skin on my head began crawling in different directions, my left hand twitched, and I fell back a step into the Mountain. He held me firm as Morelli looked up and saw my fear. The reaction had come boiling up without warning, and it was all I could do to stifle the urge to tear away and bolt out the door. He finished lighting the cigar and blew smoke at the ceiling.

"Start talking, Fleming."

A film was over my eyes. I blinked uncontrollably. My hands jerked up to rub them clear.

("Start talking, Fleming.")

The Mountain's grip kept me on my feet or I'd be on my knees again.

(The cigar stink filled the little room. Its burning end pivoted from my eyes and pointed down to my left hand. The pain shot up the arm, into the brain, and came clawing out through my clenched teeth. I tried to tear away from it and the binding ropes. . . .)

The Mountain shook me out of it. My jellied legs found the floor and I stood under my own power, staring at Morelli with hot rage. I wanted badly to let it out, knowing what it would do to his mind; good revenge for my past pain, but it would accomplish nothing. My eyes tracked another cloud of smoke. His leisurely manner reminded me that he had all the time in the world, I only had until sunrise.

"What did you do to Jack Fleming?" I asked. "How did you get him?"

"I ask the questions, Junior." This was punctuated by another punch.

"Did you have Paco shoot him?"

I was on the floor now and felt the distant blow of a shoe in the back of one leg. I made an appropriate noise in response. The Mountain bent down to pick me up. For the first time he spoke, whispering in my ear.

"Tell him what he wants, kid. He won't let me let up."

So he was supposed to be my friend, he had some pity for me. Maybe if I cooperated he'd pull his punches. Bullshit.

"Where is the list?" Morelli pretended he hadn't heard his boy speak.

I was made to stand. Favoring my kicked leg, or appearing to, I shook my head. The Mountain hit again and that's when I overdid my act. It was by accident, or by sheer clumsiness, that my body pitched too far and too fast off balance and my head connected hard with the edge of the desk.

The thing was made out of very solid mahogany.

Lights flashed behind my eyes, there were waves of dizziness, and if I went under they'd think I was dead. They'd sink me in the lake again and this time I might not come up. My eyes fluttered, I felt myself falling, but it was just the Mountain turning me over.

Breathe, keep breathing.

He was watching me closely. I looked back, concentrating on pumping my chest up and down and fighting the pain in my head.

Breathe, breathe until the worst of the shock passes.

"I thought he was gone for a second, but he seems okay, now," said the Mountain.

"Then wake him up." Morelli sounded infinitely put out. "And, Gordy, you be more careful with him this time."

He poured a glass of water I didn't want in my face and I spit it from my nose and mouth like poison. The door opened and a chair was dragged in. They put it under me. Perhaps Gordy the Mountain was getting tired of holding me up.

"Tell him what he wants, kid," he urged.

My head was bowed, I gently checked the sore spot. There was no blood, but it *hurt*. It hurt far more than Paco's gunshots. I remembered the time and let the sleeve ride up my wrist for a glimpse at my watch. Not good, but better than I expected.

Morelli was still behind his desk, puffing on the cigar. The office was hot despite the air-cooling system, filled with smoke and the stink of sweat. Now I was glad they'd thrown the water; it would give the illusion that I, too, was sweating.

"I'll clue you, Fleming. You talk now, or you are dead meat. We will work you over and you will die. Talk and you will live."

For how long? I wondered.

"Where is the list?"

Same old song. I stalled and let Gordy earn his keep. He was not too creative, but he had a lot of endurance and muscle. He needed it since I kept falling from the chair as part of my act. It was a long and brutal quarter hour before I finally broke. I'd seen it done before in movies, in real life. I gave them the full treatment: sobbing, pleading, anything I could think of, and it was exactly what Morelli wanted to see. He was feeling good now; he'd ground a man down, opened his guts, and not even left his chair.

I slid to the floor and made friends with the carpet, curling up to nurse bruises I didn't feel. It kept my face hidden and my voice muffled. Both were always dead giveaways whenever I tried lying. Between moans and groans I spun them a line of how Jack had passed the list on to his baby brother, but kept the details to the bare minimum; too many and they wouldn't believe it.

"Very good," said Morelli. "But where is it now?"

"I took a room at Jack's hotel and waited for him. I figured you'd already been there and wouldn't come back again, and there was a chance Jack would for his stuff."

"Smart, Junior. Keep talking."

"It's at the hotel, hidden in the basement. I'll have to show you where. You'll never find it otherwise."

They had a lot of trouble swallowing that one, and it took a large chunk of the time I had left to convince them they had to take me along.

My eyes were covered again, but this time they spared me the handkerchief. We went downstairs and waited in the kitchen. A car rolled up and stopped, its engine idling quietly. They opened the door, guided me down the concrete steps, and I was shoved into the backseat. I slumped low as if in bad shape—actually I was worried about the ever-present rearview mirror.

Gordy was on my right and another man was on my left. They each had a hand tightly gripping my wrists, taking no chances on my making a sudden move. Morelli sat in the front with the driver, occasionally giving a direction.

We crossed water once, twice, there were several turns, and we waited in silence for traffic signals. The car finally slowed and parked, the motor still running. The right-hand door opened and Gordy dragged me out. He pulled the scarf down and the first thing I saw was a gun ready in his hand. Next to him was the casino guard, who had a hand inside his coat like a latter-day Napoleon. His body blocked my view of Morelli in the passenger seat. Dead meat or not, he was careful not to let me see his face. It was fine with me, I was sick of it, anyway.

"Go and get it," he said.

The hotel was a block away on the same side of the street. Maybe the night clerk would remember me, but I wasn't planning to test him. I'd only gotten them back to this neighborhood because it made the story I told more plausible. I wanted them nowhere near my present hotel.

As before, they marched along, gripping my arms. I was in luck, for a change. They'd have to pass the entrance of an alley that ran between the hotel and the next building. There was a risk they might catch on to my unusual strength, perhaps they'd put it down to desperation. It wasn't getting any earlier; pretty soon I would be desperate.

We breasted the alley and I shook free, connecting a mild backhand hit in the gunman's stomach and pushing Gordy into some garbage cans. He recovered fast, and was up and after me before I'd gotten halfway down the alley. His friend was catching up as I came to the wood fence blocking the far end. I went over it with an agility that surprised me, landed like a cat, and pounded away, gaining a good lead.

The fence protected a street lined with residential brownstones, each with steps and railings and deep doorways. There were plenty of places to hide if necessary. I went to the right, wanting to gain more distance before vanishing. That was one trick they didn't need to witness. I was looking for a suitable place to duck when one of them did the unexpected. It must have been the gunman, Morelli had forgotten to tell him I was needed alive.

What felt like a sledgehammer blow caught me between the shoulder blades. The pain made me forget my aching head for the moment. I was in mid-stride when my body was lifted and thrown off balance by the impact. I tried to keep my legs under me, but the shock to the system was too much, and they buckled and failed. I rolled hard onto the sidewalk, carried on by impetus until I hitched up against the wheel of a parked car. The two men trotted up and turned me over.

I'm too much of a joker not to take advantage of such a situation. Besides, it was a way of getting them off my back. I gave it my best, pulling my hands up to cover what should have been the exit wound and hoping it was too dark for them to see the lack of blood. As they approached, I gasped, twitched convulsively, and slowly let my last breath shudder out in a horrible rattle. I stared at them with glassy eyes. They stared back, then Gordy bent down to feel for a pulse in my throat. He straightened and looked at his buddy, shaking his head.

"You're up shit creek," he pronounced.

I was right about it being the gunman and saw why I hadn't heard the shot; a bulky silencer was fixed to his weapon. It was enough to damp the sound down so the local residents continued to sleep.

A half minute later the car rolled up and Morelli erupted out before it stopped. He glanced once at his men, then glared down at me. I was sorry for not drawing my death scene out long enough to give him a cryptic message to worry about. He whirled on his men. Gordy pointed at the other guy, who had gone all white. Morelli went all purple, the neck tendons coming up as though to break through the skin. His body shook with rage and his breath came in short gulps. He'd gotten one last chance to find his precious list, and this guy had stupidly taken it from him. He snatched the gun away and, using it as a club, laid into him. When he finished, there was another body decorating the sidewalk. He gave the bloody gun to Gordy and stalked back to the car. Gordy picked up his buddy and followed a minute later.

"What about him?" he asked. They were out of my line of sight, but I could imagine his gesture in my direction.

"Leave him. He's got no wallet, they'll think he was mugged. Leave him."

The car doors slammed and they drove away.

I lay on the sidewalk and counted my blessings. When I stood up and felt my aching head I was in the mood to consider everything else. I was out of the Nightcrawler more or less in one piece and Morelli thought I was dead. On the down side, my new suit was a disaster area, I was missing fifty-eight hundred bucks and I still didn't know much more than when I'd begun.

The sky was getting lighter and I had to go home. I started around the corner to my old hotel, but thought better of it. There was a remote chance that Morelli might be there, or return the next day and find out about the guy in the ventilated tuxedo wandering in and asking for a cab. No, that was a very bad idea. I kept walking, moving quickly in hopes of finding some other open business, or better yet, an available cab. No such luck occurred and by now the light was hurting my eyes.

I was anxious enough to make an illegal entry into a closed drugstore on a corner and used their phone to call for transportation. There was still change in my pockets, so I left some on the counter for a pair of their darkest sunglasses and went outside to wait, scanning the street in worried hope. I was tied down to the place now, unable to move until the damn cab arrived.

The gentle gray light from the east was blinding, and I could hardly see him when he did come. Tumbling into the back, I promised him a two-dollar tip if he could get me to my hotel in as many minutes. With that for motivation, he poured on the coal.

When we reached the hotel, he had to follow me up to my room for the money, but I had to stumble down to the lobby again to pick up a key. My door was locked and my normal method of entry would have sent the man screaming into the streets. I was on a friendly basis with the night clerk, though, and that saved a little time. I persuaded him to give the driver the money and to put it on my bill. He did it with a smile, God bless him, gave me a key, and I fled upstairs.

The sun was up now. I was moving through syrup and going blind. I found the keyhole more by luck than anything else and shoved the door shut, sinking to the floor. My head felt ready to explode from the weak reflected sunlight filtering through the window. I crawled to my trunk, but it was locked. I tried to seep inside but couldn't; the light was searing my brain, I could hardly think. Where was the damn trunk key?

I groped in the closet, tearing the pockets of my old suit. Wrong guess. The bureau, I left them in a drawer. . . . Crawl over and visit them . . . Middle drawer, under the shirts . . . I groaned with relief as my stiffening fingers brushed them and clutched.

I fumbled forever with the trunk lock and was ready to just break it off when it finally flipped open. I pushed the lid up, forced my legs to straighten, teetered a second, and fell inside. The proximity of my home earth helped, and my arms had just enough flexibility left to pull the lid down again, shutting me safely away from the light.

Then consciousness was whipped away like dust into the wind.

Someone was knocking at my door, but it was too close and loud. It was the trunk lid. Escott was the only one who knew I slept here, so I said come in and it opened a crack. I thought I saw a dim oval floating in a sea of purple sparklers.

"Are you all right, old man?" it asked. "I've been trying to call for an hour."

I shook my head, which made it ache more. I wanted him to go away and let me rest.

"Good Lord, you look like death warmed over. Let me help you out."

I started giggling like a fool and let him pull me up. It seemed that lately all I ever did was let other people haul me to my feet. I felt weak, though, and let him, until I remembered he was still recovering from that knife wound and the strain of lifting me wouldn't be doing the stitches any good. I put a hand on his shoulder for balance, got my legs out of the trunk, and stumbled for the bed, flopping on it. It felt great to stretch out. Something cool and wet was soothed over my forehead, a washcloth. Escott was a mind reader.

"That's an extraordinary goose egg you have there. How in the world did you get it, or are you up to questions yet?"

I tried to open my eyes again, rubbing them clear with the cloth. Purple sparklers still floated around, so I had to locate him from the direction of his voice.

"What's the matter?"

"I got caught by the sunrise, I can't see anything."

Considering the situation, I must have sounded idiotically calm. I felt his fingers propping my lids gently open and heard a match strike. I thought I could see it as it moved from side to side.

"You're tracking light and your pupils are reacting to it."

"Then maybe it's temporary."

"Are you in any pain?"

"Only from the goose egg."

"You have a nasty hole in your shirt," he observed calmly.

"It matches the one in the back."

"You must have had a very interesting evening."

This time I took the opening and told him briefly what happened last night, just leaving out the part about Bobbi and the blackjack game.

"Have things improved?" he asked, meaning my sight.

"A little, I think." But I was only being optimistic and kept involuntarily blinking to clear my eyes.

He waited a moment before cautiously suggesting the Stockyards as a remedy. I'd have to stop being so sensitive about my feeding habits.

"It might help," I agreed. It couldn't hurt.

He was apparently relieved at my reaction. "I'll be happy to guide you, but won't there be a bit of a problem with both of us trying to sneak in?''

''There's so much coming and going, we probably won't be noticed. Are you up to it?''

His voice, at least, sounded stronger. ''I've had a good forty-eight hour rest. The stitches are itching and that means they're healing. I've even sent Cal home.''

''Okay, if you're sure. Can you help me change?''

He did and somehow got me down the backstairs to his car. I thankfully left the rest up to him. He parked us close in and then put something into my hand.

''What's this?''

''Your dark glasses. They were in the bottom of your trunk. Should we run into anyone they will lend credence to any story I give them about your blindness.''

''As long as they don't become a permanent part of the act.''

''See here, if any blood will do, wouldn't it be easier if I just found a friendly dog?''

I was shocked. ''A dog? I *like* dogs, I couldn't—''

''It was just a suggestion,'' he said hastily.

I got out and waited for him. He took my arm and guided me slowly along the sidewalk, down curbs, up curbs, and from the noise and jostling of bodies, past the front gates of the Yards. The cattle stench was very strong now, I could hear them clearly and very close.

''Try to find a place that doesn't look busy,'' I advised.

He said nothing, plainly thinking me crazy since most of the place was busy all the time. There was a long, soggy walk for us before he finally found a spot that met the requirements.

''Fence,'' he said. ''Shoulder height, wooden, there are several cows on the other side.''

He didn't need to tell me, I could sense them. I felt for the fence, then glided right through it.

I guess I should have warned him. He drew a shaky breath. ''You could make a fortune haunting houses. That was quite an entrance.''

I made no comment, my hands were already reaching out to a warm, shaggy body. I calmed the animal with soft words and felt my way toward its head. I knew just where to go in. If nothing else, my fingers could guide me to the right spot, but I paused and looked back to where he was standing.

"Escott?"

"Yes?" he whispered back.

"Would you mind not watching?"

"Er . . . um . . . not at all, old man." His feet scraped as he turned around. Maybe he didn't understand why I was so touchy about this, but at least he respected my feelings. I could trust him to stay turned.

The ache in my head subsided quickly. I stood slowly, feeling much stronger. The stuff spread a wonderful warmth all through my body like a slug of smooth liquor, but without the drunken side effects. I took off the cheaters and tried my eyes out. The purple sparklers were fading, and I could just make out Escott's outline above the fence and went over.

"I think I'm okay now."

"Your eyes—"

"They're clearing already."

"They're . . ."

"What?"

"Nothing, I'm glad . . . may we leave?"

Escott clearly did not care for cattle at all. We got back to the car without incident and scraped our shoes off. Things were improved enough that I was able to drive, but Escott was more tired than he wanted to admit and remained quiet. It was fine with me, since I wanted to think. My first waking hour had been too occupied with trying to recover and all my day time had been spent in total oblivion. I couldn't remember dreaming, perhaps I no longer did.

Physically I was all right, emotionally I was angry. It was still inside me, ready to be directed at Morelli or myself. I could have walked out of the club at any time last night, but stayed and went through the wringer again, hoping to find a memory. Except for the humiliation suffered at allowing another man to hit me when I could have hit back, I wasn't really hurt. Oddly enough, I felt no grudge against Gordy; the man's manner had been so completely neutral through the whole business that I thought of him only as a tool in Morelli's hand. I also remembered the bloody wreck of Sanderson's face. That had held me back, that and not wanting to tip my supernatural hand to them.

There was a kid I knew in the Army whose right hand had been shot clean off. I saw him years later wearing an artificial hand covered with a glove. He'd gotten into the habit of hiding it in his pocket and pretending it wasn't there, and each time you looked at his eyes they stared hard into yours demanding that you pretend as well. There was another kid in the same unit who'd lost a leg from the knee down. I met him again in New York while doing a story for the paper. He was the lead dancer and director of a polka troupe. He, too, was ignoring his injured limb, but in a different way.

My vampirism was just a peculiar condition, like a health problem. If I respected the rules it imposed I'd have less trouble, and that made it more acceptable to my confused brain. There were definite compensations for the rules, though. Otherwise I'd be at the bottom of Lake Michigan, forgotten and unavenged, along with who knows how many others. I'd changed in a greater sense than my grandfather could ever have imagined, but I'd been fighting it. That was why I'd been reluctant to have Escott watch as I fed. Had our positions been reversed I doubt if the thought would have even crossed his mind.

My anger had a direction now.

Morelli thought that kid brother Gerald was dead, and so did all his boys. It was a unique situation, certainly one of which I intended to take full advantage.

"I'm going after Morelli again," I said.

Escott nodded. "I can't think of a more choice subject for you to turn your talents upon. Have you worked out a plan yet?

"Yes. In fact, you inspired it back at the Yards."

"Indeed?"

I explained my idea. With a chuckle he approved and added a few touches of his own. We changed direction to go to his house, picked up some stuff, then went back to my hotel. While I took a bath, he worked on my perforated tuxedo shirt.

"I certainly wish I could be around to see his face," he said, blowing lightly on the wet gore to dry it. Gingerly I put the shirt on, doubling my chin to get a good look at my front. A large part of it was covered with what looked like blood, but was actually some very realistic-looking stage stuff Escott had developed himself.

"The trouble with real blood," he said cleaning his paint brush, "is that it dries out, gets sticky, and goes brown, but this will stay nice and fresh looking. Unfortunately, it doesn't wash out, but in this case that hardly matters."

"Nope, the bloodier, the better," I agreed. It was good to be doing something positive, not to mention sneaky, like a kid out on a college prank.

I had good color again, but Escott opened his makeup case and toned it down, putting circles under my eyes and hollowing out the cheeks.

"At least your face has the right underlying bone structure for this sort of thing. I find nothing more tiresome than trying to thin down a full face."

"That's never been one of my problems." I'd always been on the lean side. "Did you learn all this in the theater?"

"Yes, in Canada. I was apprentice to the makeup artist of a Shakespearean company for three years. I was also props, scenery painter, set builder, and as you know, occasionally played a part. I'm especially fond of character parts. The Soothsayer in *Julius Caesar* was one of my best roles, though hardly an effective one, considering that Caesar chose to ignore me."

"Got any similar warnings for me?"

"My dear fellow, in all fairness, I should call Mr. Morelli and warn him. He is in for a rough night. There, you don't look quite so bad as Banquo's ghost, but you'll do. It's subtlety we are striving for, after all." He gave me the keys to his car.

"But I couldn't—"

"I insist. Tonight, at least, so that you need not be delayed waiting for a taxi. You can drop me back home again and go on to the club from there."

It made sense and I was very grateful for the loan. As he pointed out, I might have a problem getting a cab driver to take me as a customer the way I was got up now.

"Look, I know you must be tired—"

"Nonsense, it is *not* doing anything that tires me out."

"Well, I thought if you felt well enough tomorrow you might ask around for a car for me."

"That should be no trouble. I have a friend in the business. New or used?"

I gave him enough money for a good used one. I had no preference of model as long as it was dark in color and fairly anonymous. I drove him to his door and promised to tell him all the details tomorrow, then I turned the nose of the big Nash north and headed for the Nightcrawler.

Parking a block away and out of sight of the club, I carefully locked things up and went down the dark street, trying to look inconspicuous in the bloodied tux. It was damp and quiet; the hard heels on my dress shoes made a lot of noise against the sidewalk, at least to my ears. Having made a wide circle to avoid the front entrance, I eased into the alley, found it empty, and tiptoed up the concrete steps to listen at the kitchen door. A lot of activity was going on within, but I slipped inside anyway, feeling my invisible way along in the general direction of the twenty-eight-pace-long hall. They'd done me a favor with the blindfold last night, for it was very close to the method of travel I used now. I felt my way to the stairs and ascended, then partially materialized at the top to get my bearings.

The upstairs hall matched the one below, but was longer, running the length of the building. Just to the left and across the hall was a likely-looking door for Morelli's office. The rest of the hall had doors at regular intervals. Some were open with lights inside, and nearby a radio was playing, competing with the orchestra down below in the club.

Things seemed deserted for the moment, so I took the opportunity to check out the area. A partially solid form made it easier and quieter to move and my senses weren't so muffled, though it was almost like swimming in the air. I went to the office first; it was empty and I moved on to other rooms. There were several bedrooms, bathrooms, and a second set of stairs on the far east end. About a dozen of Morelli's boys seemed to be permanent residents, at two to a room. The place was like a hotel. The next door down from the office led to a much larger bedroom, probably Morelli's. I took a good look around, opening drawers and being generally nosy. He had a large tiled bath, a well-filled closet, and a door opening to a slightly smaller bedroom. From the decor and scent I knew it was Bobbi's.

She'd be downstairs, probably in the casino. If she'd been singing, I would have heard her. I wondered if she knew what had happened last night. Morelli might not have told her. It was something to hope for, anyway.

On the ground floor was another hall running roughly through the center of the building at right angles to the first, and it ended in a closed door. The hall served as a buffer zone between the casino and the nightclub. The door gave joint access to the hat-check stand and the casino cashier. I got curious as to where they kept the money they raked in, and went back to Morelli's office. After a short search, one of the boat paintings on the wall swung out on hinges, revealing a combination-lock safe. I was unfamiliar with such things, but had read a lot of lurid literature about them and seen a few in movies. I'd be able to hear the tumblers clicking into place and for the moment had nothing better to do. The office door was locked, so there'd be enough warning to vanish in case of an interruption.

Playing with the dial was harder than it looked, and about a minute after I started, heavy footfalls were coming in my direction. I pushed the painting back, stood behind the door, and disappeared.

They twisted a key and the doorknob at the same time and three bodies burst into the room, hitting the lights. There was silence for a while as they went over the place. I felt the tug of moving air when they whipped the door away from me.

"He must have got past us," said someone.

"He wouldn't have had time." It was Morelli's voice.

"Then maybe the trip is on the fritz."

They tested it out. I got the idea that the second the painting swung open it set off a signal elsewhere in the building. It was working fine, but Morelli left a man to keep an eye on things while they searched the rest of the place. The other two left. I waited a decent interval until he settled into a chair. From the noises he made he seemed disgusted with guard duty. I quietly materialized before him, and his expression when he looked up was worth a million. I had his complete attention, and that made the rest easy.

"Don't move," I told him.

He didn't.

"I'm not here, you can't see me, you won't remember me. Take a nap."

He folded his arms over the desk blotter, lowered his head, and dozed off. I watched and listened, but he was genuinely asleep. I suddenly shivered all over and stifled a nervous laugh. Had it once been like this for Lamont Cranston? Only the Shadow knew. . . .

I went to the painting, swung it open, and waited.

My man woke up when the door crashed open. I could imagine everyone looking at the painting in vain, since it had been thoughtfully pushed back into place.

"Did you touch it?"

"I never went near it, Slick, honest! I been in this chair the whole time."

Morelli growled and they tested it out again with no better results. There was a brief argument and in the end a second man was left to keep the first company. I waited long enough to give Morelli time to get downstairs, or wherever it was where he spent his evenings.

The two men were facing each other, one behind the desk, the other in the chair in front. They were quiet, but from the small sounds produced, a deck of cards was in use. The first man had already been primed, hypnotizing the second was just as easy. They both got sent off to Slumberland, and I repeated my act with the painting.

The next armed invasion was more fun. Morelli cross-examined his two stooges, unfairly accusing them of a lot of things, and then kicked them out, electing to remain there himself to do the job right.

It was exactly what I wanted.

I let him settle down. He made some calls on the house phone and then ordered up some coffee and a sandwich from the kitchen. He swept the cards into a pile and dealt out a hand of solitaire. I was behind him, partially materialized, and watched with interest. The hand didn't come out so he cheated until it did. I went away for a moment when his snack came and left him undisturbed as he ate. With what I had in mind, he'd need all his strength.

When he was quiet again, I moved in, covering him like a blanket. Previous experience informed me that in this form I was on the cold side. He began to shiver almost immediately. I clung around him as he got up and fiddled with something on the wall, probably the air vent. He paced up and down, then got on the phone and made an irritable inquiry on the state of the air-cooling system. We both waited until the return call came that stated everything was working fine. He slammed the phone down and poured another cup of coffee to warm up. I drifted away, coming to rest on the chair I'd occupied last night.

By very slow degrees I became visible, until I was sitting solidly in front of him, staring with blank, wide-open eyes. I thought my initial appearance should be underplayed.

His reaction was quite gratifying.

Perhaps he'd first noticed something just on the edge of his vision as he'd looked down at the cards, something that didn't belong. The eye automatically tracks movement, but I wasn't moving, only gradually becoming *there*.

His eyes snapped up and grew until they were as wide as my own. His heart lurched and his breath stuck in his throat, and he stayed that way for nearly a minute, apparently too terrified to look away or even move. I thought if I said boo (and I was very tempted) he'd go completely to pieces, so I kept still and slowly faded away.

Escott had said that my antics were unnerving. Now I was getting a firsthand look at their effect on the uninitiated.

He was frozen in place for some time, his heart fighting against his rib cage. Cards and cold coffee forgotten, he got up and circled the chair. As soon as he touched it I blanketed him again to give a brief chill and then pulled away. He jerked back as though he'd been burned instead, and he was backpedaling for the door.

I heard his steps retreating down the hall. While he was out I eased the door shut and locked it. Going to the desk, I gathered all the cards up into a neat pile, which I left in the exact center of the blotter, faceup. The top card was the ace of spades. I opened the hinged picture again, shutting it and vanishing just as the door was unlocked.

He wasn't the first inside; he left that to Gordy, whom I recognized by his sheer bulk. Morelli was upset, but too proud to show it in front of his men, or to explain why he'd called them back so urgently. They went over the room inch by inch, testing the safe out again with negative results. I spent the time wrapped around Morelli to stay out of everyone's way and to wear his nerves down some more. He was gritting his teeth to keep them from chattering.

Then he noticed the cards on the desk.

"Which one of you did that?" he demanded.

They were all innocent and said so. He shut up, probably brooding on the significance of the top card. In the end, he pitched all of them out, except Gordy. The chair went out as well and another was brought in. He left the door open and had Gordy stand in the hall to watch the stairs.

He fidgeted awhile, getting up and patrolling the room, then dropping behind the desk in disgust. He had no further use for the cards and just sat there, fully alert and listening. I decided to fulfill his expectations.

I appeared quite suddenly on the floor, recreating the position I'd been in when he saw me dead on the sidewalk last night.

It was a real sensation.

He shot to his feet, sending his chair over with a crash that brought Gordy in just too late to see me.

This time Morelli had him stay in the room.

He ordered up some more coffee and lit a cigar; just the thing for his nerves, as far as I was concerned. I waited patiently.

Gordy's suggestion for a game of pinochle was ignored. Neither man spoke much. Small wonder.

The coffee came and went. Morelli got up and said he'd be back in a minute. After all that liquid and the chills, I knew where he was headed.

He chose to go to the big tiled one in his own room. In his absence, I gently put Gordy to sleep and turned out the room lights. After making sure it was clear, I shut off the hall lights and then waited for Morelli to come out. When he did, he got very cold again. He hesitated in the fan of light from his bedroom, not wanting to venture into the dark hall.

"Gordy?" His voice was not normal, nor very loud. He had to repeat himself several times before Gordy responded. The office light came on.

"Yeah . . . Slick? Why are the lights off?"

"What the hell were you doing sitting in the dark?"

"I dunno, I looked up and they were out."

"Did you put 'em out?"

"No, boss!" He sounded hurt. "Maybe one of the boys is playing a joke."

"Then you go find 'em and tell 'em it ain't funny."

"Sure. Now?"

"Yes, now!"

Gordy trundled off, stopping at the other occupied rooms to talk with the boys. Morelli's teeth were chattering, so I gave him a break and preceded him into the office. He opened a desk drawer and brought something out that clunked heavily when he put it on the desk. It wasn't hard to guess what it was. Well, if it gave him a sense of security, fine. I'd just have to undermine it.

I partially materialized in front of him, my hands reaching out. He blanched, brought the gun up—it was a police .38—and let fly with all six chambers. In this halfway state I felt the bullets tickle through. They made sensation, but no pain. Nevertheless, I rocked back as though hit, and vanished. The room was full of smoke as his men charged in looking for something to shoot at, and they all asked questions, even the quiet Gordy. Morelli declined to answer and just said the gun went off by accident.

"Six times?"

For a gangster he was a lousy liar. "Shut the hell up and get out!"

They got out.

I hung around until four A.M. By then the club and casino were long closed, and the money counted and locked away behind the picture of the boat. Prior to opening the safe, Morelli had pressed a button under his desk, which I understood deactivated the circuit of the burglar alarm. At the time, everyone was out of the office while he twirled the combination lock open. No one was there to see me peering over his shoulder and getting all the numbers.

He was feeling better after shooting at me and I'd been quiet for some time, which restored some of his confidence. All the same, he left two men in the office with the door open and strict instructions to keep their eyes in the same condition. Then he went to bed.

Twenty minutes passed, and things were quiet. I put the men to sleep, found the button, and turned off the alarm. It took another quarter hour of twisting the damned dial around before getting the combination right. I'd been off on the last number and had to experiment. It was frustrating work and bad on my nerves because I had to keep half an ear cocked on the hallway, ready to vanish if I heard someone coming. In retrospect, I'm sure the time spent was pretty good for a complete novice. It certainly was profitable.

I was an honest thief, taking only my fifty-eight hundred bucks in smaller, used bills, though there was considerably more inside. I shut things up again and put the alarm back on. They'd have a fine time trying to figure out how the money got lifted.

I wanted to make a final grand call on Slick before leaving and more than that, look in on Bobbi, but the clock said it was late and I had to allow for car trouble or unexpected delays of some sort on the journey home. Playing it safe, I left, but promised myself and Morelli another performance.

9

THE NEXT NIGHT Escott came by a little after sunset. He'd found
a year-old dark blue Buick and said the dealer guaranteed it for
at least a week. The interior was clean, the engine sounded
good, and the outside only had a few dimples on the metal to
show that it was no virgin.

"I had a devil of a time with the paperwork," he told me.
"The dealer wanted you there to sign things before I could have
the car."

"How did you get it, then?"

"I didn't. It was your cash up front that persuaded him. That,
and the veiled threat of finding another dealer who was less
particular. Just sign here."

I signed here. He gave me the keys and I gave him my thanks.

"It was nothing at all. Have you a driving license?"

"A New York one. I had to sell my old wreck to get me out
here. Why?"

"I was curious if you planned to acquire one for Illinois."

"Good question. I would if I could."

"I could do something about that as well. We resemble each
other a bit in build and features, I could work at forging your
signature and just go in for you."

He seemed wistfully eager to break the law on my behalf and
I said as much to him.

"Well, this is a unique opportunity for a new experience—is
there something amusing in this? I am serious, the law does not
look lightly upon forgery."

"I know, but you don't have to do this."

"I don't mind a bit. To me, this is rather like going to a speak during Prohibition—have fun, but don't get caught. Now, depending on the expiration date of your old one, sooner or later you will need a new driving license, or would you prefer to have the police ticketing you for want of one?"

"I doubt if I'd let things go that far, but I see your point."

"Good. Of course, you know your best cover is to remain anonymous. The less people notice you, the safer you are."

"You talk like I'm some kind of Bolshevik spy or something."

"They're called Communists now, or is it Socialists? But you have the right idea. Prior to your—shall we say—conversion those years ago, what was your attitude toward vampires?"

"I generally thought about Theda Bara if I thought about it at all, but other than that I didn't believe in them except as a myth."

"What better shield could one ask for?"

He had something there. We returned to my room and while I told him about last night's show, he made my face up again.

"Suck your cheeks in. . . . All right . . . raise your brows. . . ."

"Wish I could see this stuff."

"Yes, I can do a very effective job, if I do say so. You're looking a bit more gruesome tonight, I'm allowing for decomposition."

"How thoughtful."

"I knew you'd appreciate it. I could bring a camera next time. It would be interesting to see if your image can be recorded on film."

"I have wondered about that."

"There." He made one last touch-up and I relaxed my stiff neck. "Now, as we say, 'break a leg.' "

"Hopefully Morelli's."

"Have you taken into consideration he's probably checked up on you by now? He might be wondering why the papers carried no account of a body being found on that street the morning you were 'killed.' "

"Well, this is Chicago and that kind of thing does happen."

"Not that often, but all too true at times. He's bound to have friends in the police and other departments who are in a position to find things out for him.''

''I'll be careful, but as far as he's concerned, I'm a ghost and he's not about to tell anyone he's being haunted.''

He chuckled. ''Then have your fun—''

''But don't get caught.''

I parked my car in a new location, locked it, and walked a quick two blocks to the club. The place was busier, if that was possible, and there were more men out front. They loitered around, the lines of their monkey suits spoiled by the bulge from various pieces of lethal hardware, and checked the face of each new arrival. Morelli must have really been impressed last night, but I couldn't figure how he thought posting extra guards could protect him from supernatural forces. I gave them all a miss and vanished while still across the street in the cover of a doorway. There was always some disorientation, but I was improving, especially when it came to moving in straight lines. The street was a nice wide-open space, that could easily be crossed, and when I came to the outside wall of the club, I went up like an elevator. Feeling around for the window, I seeped in and materialized in Morelli's bathroom.

Its door was open. I edged an eye around the jamb and saw Morelli fixing his tie in front of a big mirror, getting ready for the evening ahead. It would be a memorable one for him.

I started things off by turning the taps on in the tub and flushing the toilet. He came quickly to investigate, probably without thinking, and stopped short when he saw the empty room. With slow cautious movements he shut off the water and looked around. It didn't take long, but by then I was in the bedroom, easing open all the drawers of his bureau.

From under the bed I followed his progress by watching his feet tour the room. He angrily slammed one of the drawers shut, charged the hall door, gave it a jerk, and glared outside. No one was there to receive it, so he closed the door and began checking the closet, Bobbi's room, her closet, and under the beds, drawing a blank each time. He then made a circuit of the walls, tapping on them with something hard. This was puzzling until I realized he was looking for secret panels. While he was busy inside the closet, I floated back to the bath and flushed the toilet again.

He was there in a shot, standing on the threshold, trying to keep one eye on the bath and the other on the bedroom. He rattled the flush lever uncertainly, took the top off and peered at the mysteries within. Out in the bedroom I flicked the lights off.

He noticed immediately. The switch was by the hall door. He'd have to cross a large dark space to get to it. If he waited long enough, his eyes would get used to the dark and he could cross with ease. He didn't. With more steadiness than I would have had, he left the comfort of the bright bathroom and crossed over. His heart was pounding, but he forced himself to walk at a normal pace. After all, there was nothing there in the dark that wasn't there in the light. Personally, I'd always found small comfort in that bit of logic. His sedate pace gave me plenty of time to materialize at his feet and trip him.

He went down hard, stifling a cry and throwing appearances to the wind. Scrambling to his feet, he was clawing frantically for the light switch while still a good ten feet away from it.

I wanted to use Escott's makeup job while it was still fresh, so when the lights came on I was practically nose to nose with Morelli.

At that point I think anyone coming into the room would have scared the hell out of him, but the fact that I was only inches away and not looking too healthy to boot could explain his reaction. He couldn't bolt out the door, I was in the way, but by now he was beyond coherent thought. He fell back from me with a scream and fainted away like some fragile heroine from a silent movie.

I couldn't pause to laugh, that kind of yell would bring his bully boys. I moved fast, pulling drawers onto the floor, ripping the bedclothes out of place, and then ducking into the closet. I used the last few seconds to relieve the hanging rod of a fine collection of suits and coats before disappearing.

Gordy yanked open the closet door; I knew it was him from his size and the quick way he moved. He surveyed the wreckage, made sure no one was hiding under the mess, then backed out. In the room there was quite a commotion as attempts were made to revive Morelli. His body was searched for any extraneous bullet or knife holes, and the other rooms were combed for intruders. None were found, and when Morelli did wake up he had no good explanation for his blackout or the tumbled condition of the room.

His patience ran out quickly, as well as his temper, and having been found in such an embarrassing state didn't improve things. He kicked all of them out except Gordy, who didn't talk much.

"Find out if anyone new came in tonight," Morelli told him. "Use this phone."

It took only a minute. "Six of them, boss," he reported. "They came in with a bunch of regulars and have been in the bar all evening."

Morelli growled and kicked one of the drawers. "Some jerk is playing jokes on us." I noticed the plural. He wanted to include everyone in his haunting to keep from being too isolated by the ghost. Otherwise it might mean the ghost had a legitimate grievance against him; which I did.

"I'll check up on all the boys." Gordy was keeping his tone carefully neutral. Perhaps the thought that Morelli was going nuts had crossed his mind.

"I want you to check up on Fleming."

"Sure, boss, which one?"

"Both, but especially the kid brother. Find out what you can, when he got into town, who claimed the body and where they are. Wake up people if you have to, I want to know tonight."

"Sure, boss."

They left the room together, stopping off at the kitchen to send someone upstairs to clean the mess I'd made. There was no point in troubling the hired help and I stuck with Morelli, literally. He was feeling cold again. Gordy went off to get his information, leaving Morelli to restlessly pace the club and casino while I hung around him like a pilot fish. He stood this for half an hour, then headed for the back exit. His car was ordered up and he left a message that he'd return at closing time. I enjoyed a short ride, albeit a blind one, and had no idea where he was going. He parked and got out, and I remained behind and materialized for a look around. We were at the waterfront, the car resting on a concrete pier that jutted out like a breakwater. It must have been a solid piece of construction going down to the bottom from the land, or I'd have felt the pressure I always experienced being over water.

Morelli was just disappearing over the edge of the pier, where steps went down to the water. I left the car and quietly followed. He was easing into a small boat. I pulled back before he could see me. Out on the lake, serenely anchored in deeper water was the *Elvira*. All by itself, my left hand twitched and clenched.

Morelli rowed clear of the pier. I was standing under a light, so he couldn't help but spot me. He broke off rowing and gaped, the current slowly taking his boat off course. I kept still, a scarecrow figure in stained and tattered clothes, watching him. Gradually I faded to nothing. Limited though my acting experience was, I knew how to make a good exit.

I moved back beyond the light and reformed. Morelli was rowing quickly toward the *Elvira* where three crew members were standing by to help him aboard. Chances were they'd been watching him and hadn't noticed me, which was fine, I planned to be his exclusive ghost for the time being.

It took ten minutes to walk back to the Nightcrawler. I strolled slowly to give things time to settle, and went in by way of the bath again. The cleaning crew was efficient; the place was back to normal after my rampage. Next door, someone was talking in Morelli's office, Gordy from the sound of it. I lounged against the wall and eavesdropped; it was better than radio because I was the star.

Gordy was on the phone, vainly trying to get information on my nonexistent kid brother. He seemed an expert at delegating tasks, for he was calling people up, giving them the name of Gerald Fleming, and telling them to get a line on him. Almost as an afterthought, he threw in my real name. Some of the calls were to New York, and I wondered if I should start sweating. No mutually familiar names were mentioned and his tone indicated he was long used to dealing with the people on the other end. Somewhere out there was a very large network of eyes, ears, and busy little pencils. He hung up and we both waited.

In ten minutes the first incoming calls started. Locally, the police department never got a report of a body fitting Gerald Fleming's description, dead or otherwise. No area hospital had me with a gun wound lurking in any of their beds. When the hotels began reporting in I was glad for registering under another name. He received a single call from New York that stated I was an out-of-work journalist who'd left to look for greener pastures in Chicago. It was depressing to hear it put that way, but for once it was good to have a thoroughly undistinguished career.

The office door opened and someone else puffed into the

room. The voice was naggingly familiar, but I just couldn't place it.

"Anything?"

"No, Mr. Lebredo." Gordy sounded respectful rather than neutral this time

Mr. Lebredo lowered himself into a chair with a sigh. "What did Miss Smythe have to say about him?"

"She said he couldn't sleep and that he kept the lights on all night."

"And you?"

"He's been acting pretty strange."

"So we've all noticed," he said dryly.

The phone rang. "Yeah? Go on . . . all right." He hung up. I'm beginning to think that the kid just dropped outta the sky. No one's heard of him."

"If his name really was Gerald Fleming."

"Slick said he was a younger version of the other guy. There's no doubt it was the brother and he was a green as a stick, he even had his name in his wallet. He was just a stupid kid."

"As you say." There was silence for a while. "Fifty-eight hundred was missing from the safe; fifty-eight hundred was what Morelli took from him. No one else has access to the safe that we know of, therefore Morelli might be trying to pull something. If it was for no other purpose than to buy a bauble to keep Miss Smythe happy, I shall let it go, but you keep your eyes on him as usual."

"Yes, sir."

"And don't forget the errand I want done. You've still got the address?"

"Yes, sir."

The man got up and left. I was curious about his looks and waited until he was down the hall, cracking the bedroom door a little. I was stumped for a moment because he was away from the original surroundings I'd first seen him in, but I did finally remember the fat poker player who'd invited me to join the game. He looked about my height, but had Gordy's weight, none of it muscular and most of it in his ass. Lucky Lebredo, half owner of the club, was apparently playing a game other than poker behind Morelli's back.

He waddled downstairs and I quietly shut the door. Hours stretched before me, unbroken and uneventful. I could go back to the hotel and wait there until Morelli returned, but decided to hang around. I wanted to see Bobbi again and was hoping she might come upstairs sometime during the evening. It was a slim hope and a foolish one, but something to think about.

Hardly being in a fit state to greet her, I went to the bath, stripped off my coat and shirt, and scrubbed at the makeup. It was stubborn junk, but I left a lot on the towel as I rubbed my skin raw. Escott had used cold cream to clean his face, maybe Bobbi had some lying around. I decided to look and at the same time borrow one of Morelli's shirts.

I shut off the taps and went alert. Someone was moving around in the next room. I peered past the door; Morelli's mirror reflected most of the room, including Bobbi, who was just about to leave.

"Wait!" The word was out before I could think.

She whirled in surprise. "Who's there?" She backed against the door, ready to escape.

"It's me, Ja—Fleming. I'm in the bathroom," I added unnecessarily.

She visibly relaxed, then tensed again. "What are you doing here?" she hissed. "Slick'll kill you."

"You told me that once before, but he didn't." It was a relief to know Morelli hadn't told her of my apparent demise the other night.

"You've got to get out of here."

"It's all right, believe me."

"Why don't you come out?"

"I'm getting dressed and I'm bashful." It was true. I was very shy of that big mirror out there.

She made a noise, it might have been a laugh.

"Why don't you come over here?" I suggested.

"Where's Slick?"

"I left him aboard the *Elvira*. He said he'd be back around closing."

"I didn't know he was gone, I thought you were him in there. Why are you here? The way he looked the other night—"

"We came to an understanding."

"And what about your brother?"

"We're working things out." I wanted to change the subject. "Would you turn the light off?"

Her hand moved to the switch and paused. She looked like

she wanted to question why, then thought better of it. We were both grown-ups. The light went out. I threw the towel in the hamper, picked up my shirt and coat, and shut off the light.

She was halfway across the room and had to stop, uncertain in the dark. Her arms were crossed, hands gripping the elbows hard as she looked in my general direction. If she was afraid, I could easily change her mind, but that would have been a cheat, and I hate cheats, so I held back and let her decide what to do. I already knew what I wanted to do. Dressed in something white with simple clinging lines and silver combs in her hair, she was unsettling and inspiring.

"You're very beautiful tonight." Not the most brilliant or original thing to say; she must have heard it often enough, but it was the stunning truth.

"Why are you here?"

A reasonable question. I didn't answer.

"Did Slick send you?"

"No. I thought you didn't like being too curious."

"I think I have a right to be this time."

"If you're worried about him, he won't be back for hours, so relax. I'd rather talk about other things." I cautiously moved closer, but didn't quite touch her.

"Like how you survived the other night? I saw how he was. How'd you get out of it? He'll kill us both if he finds us."

"I said we were working things out."

"Is a night with me part of the deal?" She had no illusions of her effect on men. She took it for granted in the same way other people breathe. Her question also left me fairly shocked.

"Good God, does he make you—"

Her jaw lifted and set, taking the wind out of me.

"I'm sorry—I—Slick knows nothing about me being here. I think maybe I should go now."

"You really would leave, wouldn't you?"

"Very reluctantly. I'm here because I wanted to see you again. I was going to wait in the downstairs hall after I—"

"And get spotted by half the staff? That makes a lot of sense."

"So who ever said I had brains?"

"But how did you get here? He *must* know."

I shook my head, forgetting she couldn't see me.

"You're doing this just to see me?"

"Do you want me to stay?"

She considered the question carefully. That was something else I liked about her, the way she listened and weighed facts, an ability no doubt sharpened by living close to people like Morelli. "Only if we lock the door."

"Consider it done," I said, and moved to do it.

"Fat lot of good it'll do. Slick isn't the only one with a key."

"I'll bet he's the only one who has any business using it, though, but he's not here, so let's forget him. What else would you like?"

"Does it matter to you what I like?"

For the men in her past and very likely the present, that might not have been a very important consideration. "Yes . . . it matters to me very much."

"You confuse me."

"I do? How?"

"I shouldn't feel this way, I—it's just bodies, after all."

"Not for me, it isn't."

"You're different?"

I thought of a loaded answer and dismissed it. "Yes."

Her arms reached tentatively forward, her hands brushing lightly down my bare chest. Standing so close and scented with roses, fear, and now desire, she was like a white candle and I was just beginning to feel its gentle heat. Her heartbeat drummed so loud in my brain I could hear nothing else. If she'd told me to leave then I doubt I'd have had the ability or understanding. Something primitive and as old as time overwhelmed all conscious thought and all caution, she was in my arms and nature was taking its course.

A hot minute later she pulled away. "Not here, not in his room—this way." We went to her room, and she locked the door and turned her back, lifting her hair out of the way. I undid a few strategic buttons and the white silk fell in a heap around her ankles. It was a happy surprise to learn that like Jean Harlow, she disdained the wearing of underclothes. In another second we fell into the bed.

My basic method of lovemaking was the same as when I'd been alive, and I'd never received any complaints, but knew this time from the signals my body was sending out that its ultimate expression had changed considerably. I was in the delightful situation of being able to lose my virginity twice in one lifetime.

There had once been the incredible sensual joy of being on the receiving end of Maureen's special kisses. Now I understood why she'd been unable to describe what it had been like for her.

My lungs were pumping regularly, not to breathe, but to smell. The dark scent of red blood rushing swiftly beneath her skin was maddening. I was going too fast and had to pause, my lips were already seeking out her warm, taut throat. Shifting slightly, I took in the other pleasures her body offered, exploring her soft mouth and testing the firm muscle underlying her smooth skin. She was no stranger to the act and did all she could to please me, but as I learned long ago, my greatest satisfaction came from pleasuring my partner. I did my best, with the steady roar of her heartbeat stimulating rather than distracting me. She let me know she was ready, but I held off as long as I could, held off. . . .

The kiss was painless to her, but not without its own unique intensity, and her body shook from it for as long as I held her and drew into my own starved body the hot, salty essence of her life.

After many long, long moments I gradually pulled away. Her hands slid around my head to keep me in place, wanting me to continue, but I was afraid of going too far and taking too much. I was aware of my inexperience and didn't want her to suffer from it. She sighed acceptance finally and arched her back, pushing her head deep into the pillows. Through half-closed eyes she smiled, her lids drooped shut, and she dozed lightly, her heartbeat returning to normal. With an ear pressed against one soft breast I listened to the rhythm as declining waves of warmth surged and ebbed through me.

Earlier in the evening I'd ignored the first faint tickle of hunger, planning to visit the Yards later, but that would have been mere feeding. This taking of blood was lovemaking, and for a vampire, there was a chasm of difference between the two.

I eased my weight from her and lay on my side, stroking her hair with my free hand. It had been too long since I'd really touched anyone. So long that I'd almost forgotten how good it was to hold and be held. Distantly through the walls I heard the band playing something slow and sentimental, then the phone in her room began ringing.

"Damn," she said. "I have to answer that." I didn't ask why, but moved so she could get out. A minute later she returned and snuggled in again.

"That was the stage manager. I had a number to do and missed it."

"And you told him you were sick. Are you?"

"I think you know better. I never felt anything like that before that lasted so long."

"But you're not hurt or dizzy, are you?"

"I'm fine, I'm terrific."

I tilted her chin to one side with a finger, looking closely at her neck. The marks were surprisingly small and there was no apparent bruising. Her hand slid onto mine, which she drew up and kissed.

"I guess you are different. What did you do to me?"

"If it felt good, does it really matter?"

"I just don't want it to have been a fluke of my imagination."

"It was real. I take it you didn't mind that we didn't follow a more traditional method?"

"No, this was so much like it, but more . . ." She shrugged. "I can't describe it, I only know I want to feel it again."

"That might not be good for you now. I'll come tomorrow night."

Her face clouded. "What about Slick?"

"I can get rid of him."

"What do you mean? Kill him?"

"Why do you think that?"

"It's something you get to expect after a while. I have no illusions about what he is or what I am to him. We've used each other to get what we want. It's an old story."

"It sounds very empty."

She didn't want sympathy, and a hard edge crept into her voice. "I know it is."

"Do you have to use him? What is it you want?"

"I have it now. I'm the top singer in a top nightclub and I'm on a local radio broadcast once a week. Slick makes sure I meet the right people and I keep him happy. When he gets tired of me I'll use those contacts to move up in the business."

"But are you happy?"

"Yes, I think so."

"Is that why you were working that slot machine so grimly the other night?"

"That was just boredom. Even this place gets boring. I don't like all the people here and I get tired of being stared at, but Slick likes me to mingle. He likes to show me off."

"But he doesn't like you to get too friendly."

"At least with the wrong people. But sometimes it's good, it's really good, when I'm on stage and the spotlight hits me and the music comes up—that's what I really want. That makes me feel so alive and I don't care what I have to do as long as I can stay there and sing."

"He's in a dangerous business. What would you do if something did happen to Slick?"

"There are always others like him, and he's not so bad. My first boyfriend used to hit. Slick likes to roughhouse, but at least he doesn't hit me. Then there's the other owner of the club"— she went very still—"but I'd never go to him for anything."

"Who's he?"

"Slick didn't tell you? He's the fat poker player, Lucky Lebredo."

"Colorful."

"Just don't get in his way. Slick can be mean, but Lucky is worse, and he's a lot smarter. He's like some big spider, always watching things."

"He watches you?"

"What do you think? He hasn't laid a hand on me yet, and I don't plan on ever giving him the chance. I think he and Slick have some sort of understanding about me."

"Nice guys."

"You said it."

"Do they have an understanding about Gordy as well—about who he really works for?"

"Slick doesn't know about that and neither should I, but sometimes you overhear things."

"Like what?"

"I just caught the end of it, but Gordy and Lebredo were having an argument, or something pretty close to it. Lebredo asked him if he were planning to be awkward in the same way Mr. Huberman had been awkward, and then Gordy backed down, and I've never known him to do that with anyone before. Even Slick knows where to draw the line with Gordy."

I remembered the Huberman scandal; it had been the nine-day wonder tabloid editors dream about. Someone had thoughtfully provided them with some especially lurid evidence of Huberman's romance with a knockout of a blond who was not his wife. Tame enough stuff, it happened often enough, but not always to senior state senators. The real lid came off when the general public was made aware of the true sex of the blond. Huberman was found on the floor of his office with the muzzle of the gun still in his mouth and the back of his skull blown off.

"Does Gordy like girls?"

"Sure, he does. I see what you're getting at, but that's not it. Lebredo's got something else on him."

"Maybe it's time you left this place."

"Not now, but soon. I'll leave when I'm ready."

"But—"

Her eyes snapped. "Don't go all protective on me, I can take care of myself."

"Okay, I can see that." She was right, it was none of my business.

"Mrs. Smythe didn't raise no dummy."

"I'm not arguing."

She took me at my word and calmed down. "You going to tell me your life story now?"

"Not tonight."

Her hand went to her throat. "But I want to know about what you did. Is it because you're really different, or that you know something new that I never heard of till now?"

"Yes," I chuckled.

"To both? Don't be a kidder."

"I'm not."

"Then what's this about?"

"You ever hear the one about the one-legged jockey?"

"Yeah . . ."

"Well, I kinda have the same thing. It's a sort of condition—"

The sharp cough of the gun was the only warning we got.

Preoccupied with each other, we hadn't heard his approach in the other room or noticed the light under the door. Perhaps he'd come to check on Bobbi after she'd missed her cue, and then heard us talking. The second after the bullet blew off the lock, he kicked the door open and lurched into the room like a boulder coming down the hill, or maybe I should say mountain. It was Gordy, playing the watchdog for his boss.

He didn't know me in the dim light spilling from Morelli's room, but I was a man in a place where I shouldn't be and that was enough of an excuse for him to break things up. His gun was already up and aimed. I had barely gotten to my feet. I half expected the impact of a bullet, but he thankfully restrained himself and didn't fire again. Bobbi's breath caught in her throat, but she held back the scream. The room was dead quiet except for the squeaking hinges as the door swung a little in the aftershock of its sudden opening.

I raised my hands slowly, uncurling the fingers, tore my eyes from the silencer-encased gun barrel, and stared hard at his face. All his attention was on me. Good, I wanted him to ignore Bobbi altogether. A few seconds had passed, and I listened for the arrival of reinforcements, but none came. There was a chance for jumping him then. It was possible despite the distance between us, but there was also a big, bad chance of Bobbi picking up a stray bullet, so that was out.

He finally spoke. "Walk over here, pretty boy."

Better, he wanted me out of the room. I held his eyes with my own and moved slowly, hoping Bobbi would know enough to stay where she was. I didn't speak or look at her; the situation was tenuous enough, and I wanted Gordy to concentrate on me alone. For each step I took forward he backed up into the light of Morelli's bedroom. Bad. I wanted it dark. Pretending to squint, I kept my hands in front of my face. This made it harder to watch his movements, but by now I'd cleared the door and Bobbi was safely out of the line of fire.

He sensed I was planning something. The angle of the gun shifted downward. "Move and I'll blow your balls off."

Vampire or not, that kind of threat will stop any man in his tracks.

"Hands away from the face."

There wasn't any choice, I'd have to play it out and see what would happen. I straightened, lowered my hands, and looked him in the eye.

He still didn't know me right away, but then the last time he could consciously recall seeing me I'd been belly-up on a sidewalk, fully clothed and apparently dead. Now I was shirtless, disheveled, standing, and apparently alive. Small wonder the dawn came slowly.

The lids peeled back from his eyes. I kept very still, staring at him, hoping he was as unnerved as I had been. He took a backward step toward the door and kept on going until he was on the threshold.

"*Run,*" I whispered.

The idea must have already been in his mind. He flinched, turned, and retreated heavily down the hall.

Bobbi heard it; she was out of bed and peering past me, a few dozen questions on her face. I quickly grabbed up my discarded clothes.

"What did—"

"I can't explain now." I kissed her good-bye and darted out after Gordy. He was thumping down the backstairs. I pulled on the shirt without buttoning it and shrugged into the coat, not an easy thing to do while running, but I was able to keep up with him. He reached the bottom, looking indecisive, and turned for a backward glance. I ducked, dematerialized, and followed down after him.

Uncertain of his route, I hung close to his coattails and was able to stick right along with him. He went through a door into an assault of noise, and I guessed we were in the casino. Here he stopped and caught his breath. Maybe he only wanted people around him. At a more sedate pace he moved through the room and passed into a smaller and much quieter area, probably the cloak room.

"Hi, big boy, what's up?" a girl asked him.

He didn't answer, but pushed past her to an even smaller room where the coats were hung. I heard a click and sensed he was working at something with his hands. A little unsteadily, he began repeating a call sign. He was using some kind of short-wave radio and trying to contact the *Elvira.* I moved in close to hear both sides of the conversation. Unfortunately he began shivering, but it couldn't be helped.

They had a poor connection, and I hardly made out Morelli's voice.

"Yeah, Gordy, did you find out—"

"Boss, he was here, I saw him, I saw the kid."

"You *saw* him?"

"In your room—he was real, he was alive—"

"Shut up and get out here, I'll have the boat waiting."

"He's still up there with Bobbi—"

"*What?*"

"I caught them together, but I had to get out. Jesus, you shoulda seen his eyes."

"You left her?"

"I couldn't help it, I had to."

"Then get your ass back up there and get her out, you hear me? You get her out and bring her to me. . . ."

At this point I left, groping through the back door of the cloakroom and solidifying. The long, dim hall dividing the casino from the club stretched ahead. It gave backstage access to the bandstand and led to the farther of the stairwells. I raced to the far end and had to dissolve again because of two men sitting and smoking on the steps. I re-formed in the upstairs hall, hurtled into Morelli's room, and locked the door. Bobbi had just finished pulling on some clothes.

"Gordy just called Slick about us; he's supposed to take you to the yacht."

"So?"

"So I don't think he's going to throw you a party."

"Don't worry, I know how to handle it. I was more afraid that Gordy was going to shoot you just now."

"Never mind that, I've got to get you out of here."

"This place is packed with his boys. Tell me how you plan to get past them."

"I want you out of here."

"I know, but I'm staying put. I can handle Slick and I won't split on you."

"Bobbi—"

"If Gordy's coming up you have to leave. Slick won't hurt me, but he'll kill you for sure. I don't care what sort of deal you have going."

Before I could lose my patience, Gordy was banging on the door. He wasn't alone this time.

"Slick's closet—get inside!" She shoved me in the right direction. I felt like I'd wandered onto the stage of a French farce.

"Bobbi, I'm opening the door now," Gordy called.

"Keep your shirt on!" She opened it first.

For form's sake I got in the closet just long enough to vanish and was out again, keeping close to Gordy.

"Yeah? What is it now?" she demanded. She didn't sound at all like a woman who'd been caught doing something she shouldn't.

"Slick wants to see you. You're going for a boat ride."

She didn't ask why. While she threw on a light jacket, they searched the rooms, then hauled her downstairs to a waiting car. Invisibly, I went with them. She might have known how to handle Slick, but I didn't have her confidence in him. All too well I remembered the guy he'd beaten to a bloody pulp with his own gun.

When we got to the docks I had a real check to face, the free running water of the lake. Any and all instincts I had or had recently acquired were sending out emergency alarms, and it took a lot of effort to ignore them. I clung to Gordy like a lamprey as we got into the rowboat. I didn't care how cold it made him.

There were two men to handle the oars, but my presence aboard made it hard work for them, and they were panting from the effort by the time we drew alongside the *Elvira*. Bobbi was handed aboard, then Gordy followed struggling up the ladder as I hung on. I thought he was going to fall in, but he was very strong and someone lent him an obliging hand and pulled hard. We both lurched onto the deck. The craft was big enough to give me some stability, but my back hairs—if I had any in this form—were still up. The whole yacht, big as it was, had given a shudder as I came aboard.

"Wind must be kicking up," someone remarked.

"I felt that, but there's no wind, that was current."

"Are they here yet?" I heard Morelli's irritated call from a short distance. Gordy moved toward the source, herding Bobbi ahead of him. We went below.

From the size of it, we were in the main cabin. I found an unoccupied corner and settled in to listen. Things were quiet at first, I could imagine Morelli giving Bobbi a good looking over, trying to read her mind.

"Who was he?"

"You know already, Slick, so why play games?"

"You tell me his name."

"It was Fleming, the guy you sent me after the other night." There was a long silence.

"Well, what's the matter? Didn't you want me to do it? He said you sent him."

"Shut up!" There was another long pause, his voice calmer and colder when he spoke again. "Did you screw him?"

"No." She sounded disappointed and disgusted. "Gordy interrupted things."

"Then get out of here. Go to my cabin." There was movement and the door opened and shut.

Morelli sounded tired. "Gordy, tell me what you saw."

Gordy was less excited than when he made his call. "She missed a show so I went to check on things. I heard them through the door and shot it open. He was in bed with her and got out fast. For what it's worth, his pants were still buttoned. I didn't know who he was at first, but then he came out and I saw it was the Fleming kid."

"Go on."

"I *know* he was dead on that sidewalk. You saw him. So how does he show up alive now? Is he twins or something?"

"Did you see how he got in?"

"No, and I don't know how he *could* have got in. Secret passages, maybe?"

Morelli's brief and obscene reply shut him up. He must have forgotten about looking for such passages only a little while ago himself. "He could have bribed someone, it happens. What did he look like? Was he normal? What was he wearing?"

"Pants and shoes, I didn't see no shirt or hat, but I wasn't there long."

"What was his face like?"

Gordy didn't understand what he was after. "It was a face, just like we left him, but God, his eyes—"

"What about them?"

"I swear, they were red . . . there was no white showing at all."

"Red? Solid red?"

"I saw him like I see you now. The light was good, better than this. I get the creeps thinking on the way he looked."

"Well, don't," he snapped. They were quiet, then Morelli started again. "Look, I know there's something weird about all this and Fleming, but there's no sense in going chicken about it. We'll stay on the boat for the night after we close the club, then tomorrow we'll really look into everything."

"Sure, boss."

"I'll be in my cabin."

I followed him out. The passage was short. He found another

door and went through. I found another corner near to, but not quite touching, Bobbi, who was sitting on the bed.

"Well?" he said.

"Well what?"

"Gordy saw you two together."

"Being together doesn't mean we slept together."

"Maybe you didn't have time to sleep."

"What are you bellyaching about? It was your idea for the sleeping arrangements, not mine, and you've had a dozen other girls up there since I moved in, and I've never said a word, not even when I was in the next room."

"You'd be in the same room if I wanted two at once. You like your job too much."

"Two at once, that's a laugh. You can hardly keep it up for five minutes."

"You were caught, you bitch, so start shedding and I'll show you what kind of damage I can do in five minutes."

"No."

"If you can put out for a dead man—"

"What do you mean, did you kill him?"

"Yeah, I killed him. He was shot dead in the street two days ago, or didn't he tell you that?"

"You're crazy."

"You can ask Gordy, he was there. You like to screw corpses?" There was a tearing of cloth and the struggling sounds of two bodies against each other. She slapped him and cursed, but he forced her back and down. His mistress or not, I felt compelled to interfere and closed around him like newspaper over a mackeral.

Seconds later he gave his first shiver. "What are you doing?" he asked. Vague as the question was, it was no surprise that she couldn't answer. He moved off her, falling back against a cabin wall his heart going fast. "You're here, aren't you? Why don't you come out? Come on, Fleming! I know you're here!"

Bobbi sat still, probably deducing she was locked in with a dangerous lunatic. I didn't want to push him too much, so I eased off to let him get over his chattering teeth. Neither of them moved; Morelli was listening and Bobbi was watching him.

"Are you all right?" she asked.

"He was here, I knew he was here. He didn't want me touching you."

"There's no one here, Slick. No one."

"Didn't you feel the cold? He was here, he's probably still here, watching."

"You're crazy. I'm going to my room."

"No! You'll stay here."

"What for, more roughhouse?"

"If I want it, yes."

"It's always what you want, isn't it?"

The argument started to build again and that's when I saw my mistake. All the guff between them had been some sort of ritual. They were quickly working up to another knock-down-drag-out. Bobbi had been with someone else and Morelli was reasserting his claim and using his body to do it. Bobbi had said she knew how to handle him, and as for Morelli, I suppose it was none of my business how he expressed his masculinity, as long as he wasn't really hurting her.

They were yelling now. She goaded him one step too far and then he was on her again and they got down to serious sex. I was not happy about the situation, but left them to it, exiting the cabin. No one had shown up to investigate the noise yet— apparently the crew were used to the histrionics.

Gordy was still in the main cabin, helping himself to the liquor cabinet before he dropped on a window seat to rest. He seemed to be facing out into the room, making an unobserved materialization difficult. I found my corner again, hoped it was out of his immediate line of sight, and tried to solidify.

I tried. It was like pushing a train uphill, caboose and all. I got scared, wondering if my remaining in a prolonged state of disembodiment had become a permanent thing. I tried again, harder. The train moved a little, but it was exhausting. The next time I really concentrated, visualizing each part of my body, willing it to come into being. There was weight. Arms felt like this, legs supported, eyes . . .

Like pouring cold molasses, I re-formed, the effort leaving me weak. Gordy spotted me right away, but he was surprised and it was little work to tell him to stay quiet and take a nap. He slumped over without a peep, leaving me to an undisturbed recovery.

Solid again, with my heightened senses running at full, I was immediately and urgently aware of the vast amount of water all around. Now that I had back hairs again, they were at attention from the lower spine to the top of my head. There was little I could do about the situation except to try and ignore it if possible.

The cabin was smaller than I thought, and I knew I'd been here before. My left hand, keeper of the memory, was twitching of its own accord. I tried to hold it still with the other. Outside I heard the occasional conversation of the crew, though I couldn't tell how many were aboard. Farther away were some distinct and unmistakable thrashing noises, and from the other sounds they made, they seemed to be enjoying themselves.

A glance around the cabin revealed the bar, table, and chairs and a safe squatting against one wall. Thinking it might have a similar alarm system, I checked the small desk next to it. Almost in the same spot was the on/off switch. It was off now and though there might not be anything valuable aboard, it was worth a try while I had the chance.

It was unlikely it had the same combination as the one at the club, but for the moment I could think of nothing better to do. The tumblers were clicking at the same spots, though, until I got to the last one and had to experiment. My mind wandered between the clicks. I was worried about the difficulty I'd had materializing. The fact that I was over open water was the obvious reason for the trouble, but some illogical twinge of guilt was nagging me about the fact I'd drunk human blood for the first time. Despite my extremely happy experience with Bobbi, I wondered if it made me some sort of monster, after all. As far as the books, the movies, and even the dictionaries were concerned, I was an altogether evil parasite. There was an extraordinary amount of bad press available on vampires and I was understandably worried. All I had to refute it was my own limited experience.

I didn't feel evil. True, I was a predator, but unlike other hunters, I left my prey alive and in one case, feeling pretty good afterward. I knew I felt better. Perhaps it was just the euphoria of lovemaking, but I did feel stronger. Maybe human blood was the perfect nourishment, it was hands down certainly more exciting and pleasurable to acquire.

The last tumbler clicked into place and the door swung open. Inside was a bundle of cash and unlabeled envelopes full of papers. This stuff looked more like Escott's specialty and there might not be a second opportunity at it, so I folded everything up and stuffed my pockets, leaving the cash. I was a crusading reporter, not a thief.

"Don't move," Gordy said behind me. My attention had wandered too far, and I'd forgotten to keep an eye on him. He told me to turn around.

For the second time that night his gun was on me. He was on the window seat, but far from relaxed if I could tell anything about his thudding heartbeat. Still, he was remarkably calm about facing the supernatural. I doubted I would have had anywhere near the same moxie. I thought about putting him to sleep again and turned it down. It was better to wait for Morelli to come; it was time to settle things up.

He called to someone topside and told them to get Morelli. From the straining noises coming from the cabin down the way, such an interruption would not be welcome. I suppose I could have delayed things for another crucial moment, but why should one of my murderers have any fun? I listened, trying to keep a straight face as the errand runner knocked on the door. Morelli breathlessly told him to go away. The runner delivered his brief message. Morelli told him to go to hell. The runner left, his job completed and the damage done. Morelli had to work hard to get worked up and now his concentration was thoroughly broken. After a short while, he gave up and things got quiet. In another minute he came charging in, loaded for bear.

"Goddammit, Gordy! What—"

Gordy just pointed at me with his free hand.

Morelli went all white in the face. I was getting used to seeing him in that color. He was looking rumpled already, with his hair messed up and wearing only a bathrobe. I hadn't improved things.

"Oh, God, it's him," he said out loud, but only to himself.

"He's the one I saw, Slick, except his eyes aren't red now."

No one moved. Perhaps Morelli was afraid I'd vanish again. It was tempting, but if I failed I didn't want to in front of them. The fewer weaknesses shown, the better.

"Look at his clothes, there's the holes and the blood's still there." Gordy stood to be in a more functional position to shoot.

Morelli was indeed looking at me. He noticed the clothes; I still hadn't buttoned my shirt and its tails hung sloppily out front. He also noticed that Escott's makeup job was gone.

"He looks real enough," he said, trying to generate some

courage. His eyes dropped to my chest. "It can't be the kid, this guy's never been shot."

I beg to differ.

"Or there was a mistake on the street," said Gordy. "Joe never hit him, after all, the kid faked it."

"Then what about the other stuff?"

"Some kind of trick, like you said. He could have drugged the boys and robbed the safe. See, I got him red-handed just now."

Morelli looked past me. "Where are the papers?"

"In his pockets."

"Empty 'em," he told me. It was the first time I'd been addressed directly. I didn't move. If he wanted his papers he could damn well get them himself. He ordered me again, lost his patience, and came for them. As exasperated as he was, he approached me like a ticking bomb, giving Gordy plenty of target area in case I tried something. He threw all the stuff on the table and checked for other things. My wallet came out, my old one. I should have left it at home, but one can't think of everything. He looked at the papers inside.

The shock was almost physical. The wallet he held was supposed to be on a weighted body at the bottom of the lake, not in his own shaking hands. He dropped it and if possible, his eyes were bulging more than than when he'd first walked in the room.

Gordy sensed the change. "What's the matter? Slick?"

Morelli's thoughts flashed over his face. He was trying to understand, trying to put reality right again and failing.

I smiled.

He broke. "Shoot him, Gordy! Shoot him now!"

The gun was already level with my chest. Instinct made me throw myself to one side. The bullet caused a brief bright flash as it crashed through my skull, leaving behind white-hot pain. The force of the shot and momentum of my dive carried me forward, out of control, and my head connected with a solid crack on the sharp corner of the wood table, with all my weight adding to the force. By comparison, the bullet had been a pinprick. I lay stunned and still by the sheer agony that enveloped me.

My body was turned over. My eyes stared at the light, unable to shut out the glare.

"Must have just glanced him," said Gordy. "There's a wound, but no hole. I coulda swore I hit him square, though."

"Is he dead?"

A heavy hand on my chest, then he shut my eyes. I couldn't have moved if I wanted to. "He's dead, see for yourself."

Before he could, there were quick steps and the door was thrown open. "Slick?" It was Bobbi's voice, frightened. "Oh, my God."

"Get the hell out of here! No, wait—look at him, is he the one? Is he?"

"Yes," Her throat was congested with tears. Grief for me or shock, I couldn't tell.

"Shut up and get out!"

Yes, Bobbi, get out so you don't have to see—

"I said get out!" The door slammed. She retreated down the passage, trying to stifle the sobs.

I'd been in such pain before and in this same cabin, lying helpless in the heat with voices and questions, the air thick with sweat and smoke, the stink of my own body burning my lungs.

I slipped into the nightmare, embracing the horror of memory like a lover.

Lover—Bobbi—

No, Maureen.

Maureen . . .

10

WE WERE LAUGHING at some private joke. It was good to hear her laugh, she did it so seldom, but when I turned to look at her, she was gone and the smile within me died.

I woke from the cessation of motion as the train stopped. It was a familiar dream, I used to hate it, but not anymore because I needed the shadow memory of Maureen to know that I'd once loved her and felt alive. She might have been saying good-bye to me this time, though. New York was behind me now, good memories and bad, and I wanted to start fresh again. That was what I told myself while threading through the crowded train station with my two bags. It wasn't much of a lie since I wasn't much of a liar, but the best for the moment, it would have to do.

Chicago was not windy today, it was late summer and the humidity was up to lethal levels. The walk from the station was unpleasant, the bags dragged hard on my arms, and the sidewalk threw the heat up in my face as though it were my fault. I was getting punch drunk from it until a hotel with the right price on the sign invited me into the shade. It was cheap, though not quite a fleabag. Later, if the money got too low, I'd end up in one of those, but not today.

Unescorted, I trudged upstairs to look for the door that fit my key. In these days of the Depression the hotel couldn't afford the luxury of a bellhop. The room was no worse than I expected, small and impersonal, with a sagging bed bolted to the floor, an ugly bureau and a chair to match, but it had a private bath and a phone and came with a fan, which I immediately turned on. I opened the window wide to let in the late-afternoon street exhaust and stripped out of my damp suit. I ran cold water in the tub and dropped in. Later on I'd hunt up a hamburger and read the papers to decide which one deserved to employ me.

The water was just rising past my chest when the phone rang.

I moaned and cursed, being one of those people who have to answer no matter what they're doing. It had to be a wrong number, the only person I knew in Chicago was the clerk downstairs. Lurching out and leaving a wet trail, I picked up the earpiece and said hello.

"Jack Fleming?" It wasn't a familiar voice.

"You got him, what is it?"

"Jack, this is Benny O'Hara from New York. You maybe remember at Rosie's bar about a year ago—"

Benny O'Hara, a little guy with big ears who gave me a tip on an arson story in exchange for five bucks and a drink. I'd let the cops in on it, they caught the guys, and I got an exclusive for the paper with a by-line.

"Yeah, Fourth of July, make it look like fireworks did it, collect the insurance. I remember."

"Listen, I saw you leave the train station and followed you. I thought you could help me—"

The same old story. He needed a soft touch, but I couldn't afford it this time. "I'm sorry, Benny, but I was just on my way out—"

"No, wait, please, this is important!" He sounded desperate, I hung on out of curiosity. "You gotta listen. I've got something big for you, a hell of a story, believe me."

"I'm listening."

"Can you come down and meet me in the street? I can't tell it all on the phone. Please, Jack?"

"What'll it cost me?"

"You mean what'll it give you? This one is red hot."

"Arson again?" I joked.

"Please, Jack!" He was in no mood for humor.

"All right, I'll be out in a minute."

"Just walk outside, turn right, and keep walking. I'll catch up with you."

It seemed overly dramatic, maybe he did have something important. If I came to an editor with a hotshot story ready to roll, so much the better my chances of getting a job, and with better pay. It was worth a try. I told Benny to hold tight and hung up, trying not to sound too eager.

Dried and dressed, I left the hotel, following his directions, scanning the faces around me for his. About a block later he appeared at my elbow.

"Don't look at me, for Chrissake!" he said in a low voice.

The glimpse I'd gotten was not reassuring. He always looked to be just this side of starvation, that was normal, but now he was haggard and twitching at the edges. I wondered when he'd last slept.

"Just keep walking and I'll tell you everything."

"For how much?"

"I'll tell you. When I'm finished you can take it or leave it."

Now, that was out of character. If I hadn't been on guard before, I was now. "Who's following you?"

"Nobody yet, I think, but we can't take chances. Just keep walking."

I kept walking.

"Ever hear of Lucky Lebredo?"

"No."

"He's a local gambler, owns part of the Nightcrawler."

"He owns a worm?" I said blankly.

"It's a nightclub," he said, pained. "Used to be a big speak, then it went in heavy on the gambling when he got part of it."

"Illegal, of course."

"Is LaGuardia Italian? Anyway, he's a name here to some people, but keeps a low profile and stays out of the way of the gangs, so not many people know him or his piece of the club."

"So what's this about, Benny?"

"Did Rosie tell you what I do for a living?"

"She said you were a locksmith," I replied with a straight face.

"Rosie's a swell gal."

"Benny—"

"Okay! I'm getting to it. I have to take advantage of an opportunity when it comes up 'cause there ain't that many of them these days for locksmiths. I gotta flop with this friend of mine, and every Wednesday he has room in his place for a big-time poker game. These guys use thousand-dollar bills like other people use matchsticks. Sometimes the game goes on for days. It's usually out-of-town guys lookin' for some fun, and there's different ones every week, but Lucky never misses a game. He's a real crazy when it comes to poker and he always wins.''

"I've heard of people like that."

"You gotta see to believe this guy. I swear, one week he went home eighty thousand dollars ahead. You gotta figure he don't declare that on his income tax."

"How is it they let you in on this game?"

"I don't play. My friend tells 'em I'm a bodyguard. He lends me a gat for the duration and I hang around and look tough. Some of these rubes even believe it, they treat me like Capone himself, and they tip good to boot. Anyway, I keep my eyes open and one night I decide to follow Lucky home, just to protect him, you understand."

"I understand."

"Well, he goes on into this house, and for a guy with that much money it ain't much of a house, so I figure he must have piles of it lying around unspent and unprotected. Maybe he might like to hire someone to guard it for him when he's out."

"And you decided to apply for the job?"

"Naturally, but the next night when I went back he was gone, maybe off to the club, but I tried the door, anyway, and imagine my surprise when it just opened right up. I thought maybe something might be wrong inside, so I had a good look around to make sure there wasn't no burglars."

"Go on."

"Thank goodness there wasn't and a good thing, too, because—I swear this is the truth—he walked out the door and left the safe wide open. I mean, how careless can you get?"

"Tsk-tsk. Very careless."

"Now, I thought it would be a shame if all that cash were to disappear into the wrong hands, so maybe I should take care of it for him."

"Very thoughtful of you."

"I thought so, too. There were a lot of large bills there and I don't have nothing to carry them in, so I pull out this big envelope from the safe that looks empty. There's only two sheets of paper inside, they don't take up any room, so I start stuffin' money into it and the whole kit and kaboodle leaves with me. When I get back to my flop I count things out and that's when I get a good look at those sheets of paper."

"What was on them?"

"They look like some kid was playing with a typewriter. Both sheets are covered with a lot of punctuating junk and numbers top to bottom, both sides of the pages. I figure right away it's some kind of code, and I like puzzles, so I try to solve it."

"And?"

"And it wasn't so easy, but I did it, and the stuff on those pages is enough to blow this state wide open."

"What is it, then?"

"A blackmail list. The names are big ones, ones you wouldn't expect to be there. It gives the names, where they live, the location of the stuff that's against them, everything. I checked."

"Oh come on, Benny."

"I swear! I got it with me and now I gotta get rid of it."

"Why? And why me?"

" 'Cause you're not on the list, 'cause you're new in town, and none of these mugs know you."

"What mugs?"

"One of Lucky's boys and others. They're with the Paco gang, they been after me for days, I can't get outta town. They've got the stations covered. I can't buy a car, boat, or bicycle without them finding out."

"And you want to foist this off on me? Turn it in to the cops."

"Don't you see anything? There's cops on the list—judges, lawyers, newspaper people—anybody with something to hide is on it. They'd bury it and me, too, if I went to them. I tried. But you're clean, you can do something with it, you can make a story out of it."

"What do you want from me?"

"Just some help getting out of the city. I can take care of myself from there."

I'd always been an idiot when it came to thinking out the long-term consequences of snap decisions. "What have you got planned?"

"You're a square guy, so I can trust you. I give you a couple of notes and you go buy a car for me, but in your name, then all we gotta do is drive outta town. You drop me in some burg in the next state, then I'm on my own and can lam it from there. For that, you keep the car and the list. Lucky and his boys don't know you from whosis, so you'll be safe, too."

"That sounds okay to me. When?"

"Right now. I gotta get out today before my nerves go. Take a turn into that alley ahead and wait for me. If things are clear, I'll be there in a minute."

I went into the alley, walking half its length before stopping and turning around. It was dim and quiet. I took off my hat and wiped at the sweatband with a handkerchief. My only company was a one-eared cat picking through the garbage. Down the middle of the alley ran a trickle of water, and overhead someone's laundry hung dejectedly in the still air. I hoped Benny would hurry.

Long before I thought of leaving, his scrawny figure appeared at the other entrance. His gait was a peculiar hopping walk, as though he were about to break into a run and always changed his mind at the last second. He hitched up close, puffing with his eyes darting all over in nervous jerks. He was looking down at the heels for all the dough he claimed to be holding and had the calm demeanor of a chain smoker who'd just run out of cigs.

"Now we gotta be careful," he warned me, and gave me a thousand-dollar bill.

"Is this for real?" I'd never seen one before.

"Like Sally Rand's feathers. You might want to change it for smaller bills, but you can get a really good car with it. I can't cash 'em myself on account of I don't look that respectable enough, but for you it'd be easy."

Not that easy, but maybe if I changed into my better suit I could pass muster at any bank. "Okay, now where's the list?"

"Right here and welcome to it." He pulled out two sheets of paper folded double and gave them to me. I opened them up. As described, they were solid with typed symbols and numbers.

"How do I read this stuff?"

"It's easy, just substitution—"

Someone coughed off to the left. It was an oddly regular cough, coming three times very close together. Benny's small body jerked and three large red holes appeared in his head, chest, and stomach. He fell into the dirty little stream on his side and lay oblivious in the water, pop-eyed and forever surprised.

I won't defend my reaction, if it was cowardice or self-preservation, but I hurtled out of that alley and into the street as though my ass were on fire.

Terror is a great stimulant. Three long blocks later I was still pelting down the sidewalk at full steam, leaving a trail of disturbance and sometimes destruction as I negotiated obstacles in my path. I never looked back. The temptation was there, but it would have cost me speed and headway. I just couldn't take the risk. Heat and lack of endurance took their toll, though, and I was forced to slow down; my passage through the afternoon rush was too noticeable, anyway. I ducked into a big department store and tried to collect myself while still moving.

The list and the thousand-dollar bill were still in my hands. I tucked both away into my wallet and thought about calling for a cop. That might be a bad idea, though, since as a witness I was no good. I had, God help me, seen Benny die, but hadn't even glimpsed his killer. There could be more than one, from his talk. What story could I give, anyway? That I had accepted money from a thief to help him out? The truth wouldn't do at all, and from experience I knew I was a lousy liar. I kept moving, hoping to come up with some plan before somebody aced me.

I was just starting to feel safe and looked around. Even as a stranger to the city I had no trouble recognizing them. I'd seen the type in lineups in New York. They could look like anyone physically, but there was a hard-to-define attitude that set them apart from ordinary people. A predator's hardness, perhaps, but I had no time to analyze the quality because they were coming after me.

I located the back exits, tore through the stockrooms, upsetting employees, and burst outside onto a narrow street where freight trucks made their deliveries. The street ran into a larger one, with more people and hopefully safety. I heard feet pounding behind me and dived into the crowds.

We played this game for nearly an hour. There were five of them, three on foot and two in a dark green Ford that followed me after I jumped into a taxi. They were smart and certainly professionals. I was a stranger in their territory and really didn't stand much chance of getting away, but had to keep trying to avoid Benny's fate.

I thought of dropping the stuff in plain sight. Perhaps that was all they were after, and I was too unimportant to bother about. It seemed right, but there was absolutely no indication they would be so cooperative. I kept going.

I was getting very tired. The taxi dropped me on Michigan Avenue, though it had given me a small respite, I'd have to go to ground soon. I needed time to rest and think and a safe place to do it in. That's when I looked up and saw the massive limestone structure of the Chicago Public Library. Libraries had often been quiet sanctuaries for me, so I went in.

The first floor was useless, too open, full of newpapers and people reading them. I took to the stairs. The second floor was a haven for civil War relics, but not for me. I puffed up to the third landing and was greeted with the welcome sight of rows and rows of bookshelves. Like a fish returning to water, I slipped between their ranks and found a vantage point where I could watch the avenue and the stairs.

I owed the taxi driver a medal for losing the Ford long enough for me to get to cover. Far below, its green roof cruised up and down the avenue for half an hour before they gave up and moved on. No dangerous-looking types came inside and I relaxed and retreated deep into the shelves.

First I'd get rid of the list, then I'd get out of town until things cooled off; maybe even go home for a while and rest. I could write up a detailed account and send copies to the local D.A., the Feds, the papers, anybody I could think of who might be wondering who bumped off Benny O'Hara. It might not do any good, but it was as much as I was willing to risk at the moment. Seeing a man getting shot to pieces under your nose will take the starch out of anyone's backbone, and I never thought of myself as particularly brave. The last few hours had been so frightening I was ready to quit the papers altogether and go back to helping Dad at the store.

At the moment, though, I was getting hungry and felt that the promised hamburger was long overdue. The mind deals with the shocks, but the body goes on prosaically dealing with the basics of living.

Standing on my toes, I placed the two sheets of paper on the top of one of the shelves in the back. The aisle was clear, no one had seen me. I made a note of which section I was in, and left, knowing they were safe as they'd ever be.

I found a back stairway and used it to make my cautious way into the street again.

The coast looked clear, no green Fords, no hard men, but I kept pace with the thickest parts of the crowds for many long blocks before relaxing enough to find a cafe. A small, busy place called the Blue Diamond smelled good so I went in and managed to get a table at the back. I ordered steak with everything instead of a burger, and while I ate I made notes on a napkin about what happened in my personal shorthand. I stalled over the meal, drinking coffee and having an extra dessert so as not to put off the waitress. When it was dark I left her a good tip and ventured into the streets.

Taxis cost, but walking back to the hotel was too much for my feet. Besides, I had no idea where it was, just the name of the street it was on. I gave it to the driver and hoped he'd take a straight route. It didn't take long, he knew his business and dropped me at the right corner as far as I could tell, although it seemed different in the dark. I was still nerved up and tired, a bad combination.

I kept my eyes open, but wasn't too worried. The men who chased me couldn't know where I was staying since Benny had been so careful. Poor Benny.

And then it was poor me.

Two of them appeared out of nowhere. They must have been watching the whole street knowing I might come back. I was practically lifted from my feet and trotted forward. The green car came up, a door was pulled open, and I was hustled inside. The whole operation didn't take more than five or six seconds and I was being driven off to parts unknown.

The three of us staged an impromptu wrestling match in the backseat as I did my best to get out and they did their best to prevent it. Once I managed to get my hand on the door lever, but a fist hit the side of my head and another one gouged my kidneys.

"Hey, settle down back there!" the driver growled.

A few more hits and I was in no condition to continue the argument. They shoved me on the floor and kept me there face-down, their heavy feet resting with some force on my back and legs. I was dizzy from the punches and scared, and the swaying motion of the car in those claustrophobic conditions wasn't helping.

"I'm going to be sick," I said to the floor.

"What'd he say?"

A little louder, I repeated myself.

There was some laughter from the front seat, but the guys in back didn't think it was so funny. The one nearest my head took off my hat, turned it upside down, and shoved it under my nose.

"You get any puke on me and I'll pop your eyes out," he warned.

I gulped back my gorge and tried to get air in my lungs. It was a long, tough ride, but I managed to keep my dinner down. We pulled over once and the driver got out for a few minutes, leaving the engine running. The car rocked as he squeezed back behind the wheel.

"Frank says we bring him to the boat, then you guys take a hike until he wants you again. Georgie, you take the car back to the house for me."

"When do we get paid?"

"Tonight at the boat, the usual."

"Come on, Fred, we been after this guy all day."

"Then argue with Frank, I don't pay the bills."

Someone tied a rag over my eyes and I was hauled from the backseat with my arms fixed behind me. Two men had to hold me up since I couldn't balance. I smelled and heard the water lapping all around and had immediate visions of Lake Michigan and cement shoes. I tried tearing loose, collected a breath-stealing gut punch, and was dragged down some steps. The next few minutes were confusing as I was tripped into something that felt alive under my feet. I lost balance again and without my arms couldn't stop the fall. My left elbow hit something hard and so did my knees. I tried to twist to get upright, lost it all again, and my head snapped back and the hard thing caught me behind the ear. Despite the blindfold, lights flashed in my eyes before the dark closed everything down.

It felt like I'd been asleep for weeks and was only now coming out of it. Some men were talking and I was annoyed that they were holding their discussion in my private bedroom. I wanted to tell them to get the hell out, but my mouth wasn't cooperating yet.

"On ice and intact," a man said. I remembered his name was Fred.

"You call that intact?" was the ungrateful reply.

"He put up a fight, what can I say?"

"You boys been paid yet?"

"No, Mr. Paco."

"Okay, here, and keep your traps shut. Get lost and forget

today ever happened. Fred, you stay with me. Georgie, take the car back home.''

"Right."

Men shuffled away. It didn't sound like a very large room and I still had a slight feeling of movement all around, which I attributed to my half-conscious state. My head hurt and I was sick in the stomach, and the more awake I got, the more hurts made themselves known. I started remembering other things, none of them too pleasant.

"What did they do to him?" said Paco.

"He took a fall when we put him in the boat."

"Wake him up."

Some water was dribbled in my face. That was when I realized they'd been talking about me. I thrashed around and shot fully awake and painfully alert. I couldn't move much, being firmly tied to a chair, but the blindfold was off, not that what I saw was very reassuring.

The large lump holding the water glass was Fred. The shorter, more bullish man behind him was Paco. Neither of them looked friendly.

The room was long with a low ceiling. The walls were oddly curved. I deduced we were on a boat and a big one. That explained the movement and my bad stomach; I was a poor sailor.

"He's awake," said Fred. He and Paco drew back from my field of vision. My chair was in the middle of the bare floor facing a table. Leaning on the table was another man, darker and thinner than his friends. He unhitched his hip from his perch and came over to me. I heard a click and a slender, long-bladed knife appeared in one hand. The edge was so sharp it hurt to look at. I stiffened as he bent down near me.

"Take it easy, buddy," he said, and cut the ropes. I could hardly move as they dropped away but tried flexing my limbs. Not a good idea, they went from numb to pins-and-needles pain as the blood started resuming its job.

"You want a drink?"

I managed a nod. He made a sign and Fred brought me a stiff double whiskey. I would have preferred water, but took what was offered. It was good stuff and made things comfortably warm inside. My benefactor smiled at me, I'd have smiled back if he'd put the knife away. Fred took my empty glass and returned it to the built-in bar. He was looking at Paco as though waiting for a signal. Paco was looking at the third man, whose attention was on me.

"I think you know why you're here," he said. He had thick long lashes on his eyes, a woman's eyes, and I didn't like the expression in them. "Stand up."

There was no reason not to, though I wobbled a bit and had to use the chair for support. Fred came over and pulled everything from my pockets and dumped it on the table. They went through it. I said good-bye to the thousand-dollar note. They looked at me and Fred was smirking.

"I knew the little shrimp passed him something."

"What else did you get off him?" asked Paco.

They found the napkin my notes were scribbled on, but it wasn't what they wanted.

"He's a reporter," said the third man. Fred laughed. They looked with interest at an old press pass he'd taken from my wallet and read my identification. "How long since you seen New York, Jack R. Fleming?"

"Look, I don't know what you want, I just got off the train today—"

"Did little Galligar call you in to help him?"

"Galligar?" Probably Benny's Chicago name. "I don't know what you're talking about. This little guy starts talking to me in the street. He's got some kind of crazy story right out of *Black Mask* that I don't believe and says he'll give me a thousand bucks if I can get him out of town. I figure maybe the bill is a fake and he's trying some kind of new con game, then somebody shoots him so I took off."

"Why don't you tell me the story?" he said, looking at my notes.

"He just said some guys were after him because he lifted some dough from the wrong people."

"Who's L. L. ?"

"Louie Long or Lang, I think, I don't remember offhand." I sank back into the chair, tired. "The initials are only for my memory, I'll make up something later."

"What do you mean by that?"

"I'm a reporter, but I also write fiction. A real-life experience like that is too good to waste. I was thinking to do the whole thing up as a story and sell it to one of the detective magazines, maybe even make a book out of it. If I had to live on a reporter's pay I'd starve to death, so I write stories as well.''

They stared at me. For a few seconds I thought they believed it, then Paco burst into laughter. The other two joined him and my hopes sank.

They next made me strip and I swayed for several minutes wearing nothing but gooseflesh while they went through my clothes. Piece by piece they tossed everything back, even my wallet and papers, except for the large bill, which remained on the table.

"I know he had it, Mr. Morelli," said Fred, using the man's name for the first time. He didn't seem annoyed at the slip, which disturbed me. I'd heard the name before and something of the man who owned it, but saw no advantage in letting them know that, figuring my best chance with them was to pretend ignorance. "The other boys with me will tell you that, too."

"Was he in your sight the whole time?"

"Well, no, but we were right with him and we got him—"

"Put a lid on it, Fred," said Paco. "You lost him long enough for him to stash it somewhere."

"Hide what?" I tried to sound frustrated and angry. It was easy.

"The list."

"What list?"

"The one Galligar slipped you."

"All he gave me was a cock-and-bull story and that money, and then someone shoots him. I figure they'd shoot me, too, so I ran. Take the money, I don't want it, just let me go."

Morelli interrupted Paco's reply. "All right, Fleming, we will be happy to let you go and you can keep the money. I'll even give you another thousand for all the trouble we put you through. You tell us where you put the list and you can go."

"I don't have any list!"

"I believe you. Just tell us where it is."

"I don't know."

He sighed. "Then we may have a problem."

No problem for him, he just stepped back to give Fred enough room to swing. I tried to fight back and fight dirty, but he was too big, too experienced, and too fast. We broke some things up bashing around the cabin, but no one minded since I was the one falling over the stuff. I moved for the door, but he anticipated it, grabbed me from behind, whirled me around, and laid into my stomach. He stood back to catch his breath and I slid to the floor, unable to move. After a minute he hauled me up and dumped me into the chair.

Morelli bent down to my field of view. "You feel like talking yet?"

I couldn't answer right away, in fact there was only one thing I felt like doing at the moment. He saw it coming, said "Oh, shit!" and backed hastily out of the way. I had just enough strength to lean over the chair arm before giving up the steak dinner and the double whiskey onto his deck.

None of them thought it was particularly funny. I did, but wasn't laughing. I just hung over the chair arm and tried not to look at the stuff. The acid smell filled the room and drove out Morelli and Paco. They made Fred clean it up, having decided he was to blame. He wasn't a happy man and cursed the whole time, most of his more colorful abuse aimed at me.

When Fred finished he dragged me out on the deck. There were lights way in the distance, too far for me to swim in my condition, not that he gave me the chance to go overboard. He shoved me against a rail and bent me double so I was well over the water. With a heavy arm around my neck he pried open my mouth and stuck a finger inside and nearly down my throat. I bucked against this, choking until he pulled it out, and then I retched into the black water. He did this twice more until he was certain I was cleaned out, then let me drop on the deck.

Utterly exhausted and panting like a dog, I hated Fred more than I ever thought possible. If I had a weapon or the strength, I would have cheerfully killed him.

I never had the chance, he took me down below.

Morelli and Paco were there, Morelli with one hip resting on the table much as I'd first seen him. Paco was sipping a beer next to the bar. Fred practically carried me to the chair and dumped me in it. Except for a faint tang in the air, there was no sign of what had happened.

"You don't look so good, Fleming," said Morelli. He still had the knife out. He used it to slice the tip from a cigar and spent a minute lighting it properly. He blew the smoke in my direction. "Now, do you want to talk, or do you want to let Fred hit you some more?"

I didn't want either, so I kept quiet. Fred hit me some more.

He stopped occasionally to catch his breath and Morelli would ask me his question, get no answer, and then Fred started all over again. I harbored some hope that he'd get tired and go away, but when he did Paco took over—and he had brass knuckles.

They came as a bad surprise. Just when I thought it was impossible to hurt more he jabbed them hard into my ribs. The first time it happened I cried out and that encouraged him. He was still fresh, slightly boozed, and enjoying himself. I fell out of the chair and he kicked me until Fred put me back again. They were careful with me. They left my face alone, it'd be hard to talk through a swollen, battered mouth, and they wanted me to talk. I knew if I did and they got the list I'd die. It was a very simple conclusion, even in my present state I could grasp that. I kept quiet and let them hit me. I wanted to live that much. After a while I stopped reacting to the punches and Morelli told him to lay off. Good old Morelli, my friend, I thought before I stopped being awake.

They took a break, had a meal, and started again. The cabin got like an oven and the air was an unbreathable mixture of sweat, cigar smoke, and booze, though the windows were open. With surprise I saw clear blue sky and sunlight lancing through white clouds. It had to be an unreal vision. Men just didn't beat up other men on days like this; then I'd get a whiff of my own stink and know otherwise.

Morelli gave me some water at one point, my tongue felt like it was someone else's property. "You can save yourself a lot of grief, Fleming. Just tell me where you put it."

I must have been feverish. I heard someone laugh a little and say: "Where the sun don't shine."

He threw the rest of the water in my face. It felt good until I passed out again, which felt better.

I woke up. Something sharp in the air was burning my nostrils. I shook my head away but it followed. They'd turned up smelling salts from somewhere and were using them to keep me awake. It was necessary at this point, I kept conking out on them.

"Never mind that," Morelli said when my eyes finally opened. He had more water and gave it to me. It tasted odd, but I drank without thinking.

They left me alone and I started to drift away from the pain, but never quite made it, whatever was in the water wouldn't let me. My heart started pounding hard and fresh sweat broke out all over, I felt breathless. The hurts numbed by a few hours' rest began anew. To my humiliation, tears began flooding down my face. Fred and Paco found it very funny. Morelli just sat and smoked another cigar, letting them do all the work.

By mid-afternoon they took a break.

"I don't think he knows," said Paco, drinking another beer.

"Don't be a sap. He knows, but he won't talk. If he didn't know he'd be making up another story about it or telling us he doesn't know. But this guy don't talk at all. He knows."

Fred yawned. "I gotta sleep," he said to no one in particular. He went out.

"Maybe we should go back and get Gordy," said Paco. "He's good at this stuff."

"Nah, Lucky's got him busy looking for Galligar."

Paco laughed. "He'll need a set of gills to do that. My boys took care of him good."

"They screwed up, you mean. If they thought to shoot both of them we wouldn't be stuck here now."

"I know, but we'll get him to talk. You wouldn't think he'd be this stubborn, would you? Stupid, but he's got some guts."

Their voices faded away. I dreamed about Benny, an uneasy Jewish-Catholic now buried forever without services from either faith, just another guy out of Hell's Kitchen scrambling for a buck.

I dreamed about escaping. If I could get overboard with a life preserver I might be able to make it to shore. Even the prospect of drowning looked preferable to another session with Fred and Paco. All I had to do was get up off the floor. Fat chance that, they'd done their work too well.

I dreamed about Maureen, dark hair and rare laughter, a nervous girl, looking over her shoulder, but needing love and giving it fully in return. Was she safe yet?

I dreamed, but could not rest.

Hours later I opened my eyes. The lids seemed to be the only part of my body that could still move. I felt like a shattered piece of glass held together with weak glue. The wrong touch and everything would fall to pieces. It hurt to breathe and the air was hot in my lungs. The windows were still open, but there was no ventilation.

I wasn't thinking too straight, because even that hurt, but I wanted to get to one of the windows. Once there I'd think of what to do next.

It was only ten feet away. Three steps for a healthy upright man, a few miles for me. Under it was a padded, built-in window seat. If I could get to it I would . . . but I couldn't quite remember.

I squirmed forward six inches and rested. I'd have to go easy and keep the glue intact. Six more inches and rest. Repeat. My shoulders ached from the effort, but then so did everything else, tell them to shut up and cooperate so we can—what? Window seat. It was a little closer. Six inches and rest. Window seats have windows, windows have air, we need air. We need to rest. Oh, God it hurts. . . . Shut up. Six inches and rest. Tears again, waste of energy, but they wouldn't stop. Eyes blurring, from tears or pain? Where was the window? Rest. Don't move, just lay down and die, serve them right. Anger. How dare they reduce me to this? How dare they make me crawl? Twelve inches that time. Anger was good, stay mad and escape. Keep crawling and hate their guts for it. Crawl so you can come back and do this to them. Crawl . . .

But the glue came apart before I was halfway there and for a long time there was nothing.

"Jeeze, you wouldn't think he'd a made it that far." My admirer was Paco. I was looking at his shoes. I wished he'd give me a good solid kick in the head and end it all, but he was no pal to do me favors.

"Put him in the chair," said Morelli.

No, please don't bother.

They put me in the chair.

I fell out of it.

They tied me to the chair. Wrists and ankles. Rough hemp rope. I looked at it, not knowing what it was.

"Fleming."

Oh, go away.

"Fleming." He tilted my head back. I choked on some whiskey. Something had happened the last time I drank, but I couldn't remember.

"Wake up, Fleming."

I was awake, unfortunately.

"Look at me."

No, go jump in the lake. There was a lake all around us, which struck me as insanely funny. It hurt to laugh. Save it for later and laugh then, if there was a later. What was in the whiskey?

"Fleming, look at me or I'll cut your eyelids away."

That got my attention, but I didn't look at him, only the slender knife in his hand. Yes, it was possible they could hurt me more. The look in his eyes, his dark feminine eyes, promised that much. Lightly he drew the blade across the back of my hand, sure as a surgeon. Blood welled up from the cut. Yes, he could hurt me.

"Fleming, you've got to talk to us, you've got to tell us where it is. Believe me, we've been going easy on you. You've only got a bad bruising so far, nothing that won't heal. If you don't talk it will get worse and we'll start breaking things up inside you. You could bleed to death on the inside. Tell us where the list is and I swear on my mother's grave, I swear we will let you go."

I almost believed him. Talk and die or don't talk and die, anyway. I'd be damned before I'd give them the time of day. They won't kill me, not unless I told them and I'd never give them the satisfaction. Stupid, Paco had said. Yes, and stubborn.

"Fleming, did you hear? Do you understand?"

I nodded or at least tried to. My head dropped so all I could see was my lap. He pushed it back and I was looking at the ceiling which kept moving around every time I blinked. Something went down my throat. I gagged and coughed.

In a little while my heart began to race. I was more alert. Fred put his hand in my field of view.

"You see these?" he asked.

Yeah. Brass knuckles. He gave me a good look at them.

"Mr. Morelli says I don't have to pull my punches anymore."

I caught a fresh whiff of stifling cigar smoke. "Talk, Fleming."

No, I'm too stubborn—

"Fleming . . ."

No.

"Fred."

Oh, *God*.

He hit me twice and we both felt the rib give way. I heard someone's sharp whimper and passed out.

It was daylight again when I woke. I was lying down, hot and shivering, with an ache all over as if my bones were too big for the skin and trying to bust out. Fred was looking at me. There was as much compassion in his face as a slab of concrete.

"What?" he asked, and leaned closer. I must have said something. I tried to remember.

"Leak."

"Tell me where the list is and I'll help you."

"I . . . can use the toilet or the floor . . . you want another mess to clean?"

He did not.

In the end he had to find a container to bring to me at the window seat. When he tried to stand me up it was too much to bear. I lay helpless and watched it dribble into a tin can. There wasn't much and it was dark with blood. I was sick again and thankful there was nothing in my stomach.

He went away and told them I was awake. Somehow they kept me that way, hours or days went by. I lost track of time when the fever set in. Morelli gave me some aspirin and had them lay off me awhile. My buddy.

The broken rib reminded me of its presence every time I breathed. Now and then I even thought of escape, but then we all dream when we're sick.

The day, from what little I saw of it, clouded over. There was some concerned talk about a storm, but no one made a move toward shore, except Fred, who, storm or no storm, wanted to go home. I heard something ominous about just one more try.

I was tied up in the chair again. The three of them were looking ragged, but still had the benefit of soap and water. I could only imagine what I was like with a thick growth of beard and no food for the past few days, not that I cared.

Morelli made his little speech, he had to repeat it several times before I understood. All I wanted was for him to douse that damned cigar so I could breathe.

Outside it began to rain. There was little wind with it, just the steady soaking kind of fall that farmers liked. Too bad it was all going to waste out here on the lake. It got dark. They turned on the cabin lights and added to the heat inside.

"Talk, Fleming. Where is the list?" He waved the lit cigar near my eyes. I thought I was past feeling more pain or even more fear until he twisted it down into the palm of my hand. My tongue bulged against my teeth, I tried to tear away, vision blurred.

"Where is it?" Again and again until my wrists were bloody and my hand red with burns. My throat was raw, I wondered if I'd been screaming.

"Talk, Fleming."

He stood back and let Fred have another try. Fred was out of patience and wanted to get to shore. He took it out on me and smashed in another rib. I felt things coming loose inside. He was finally going to finish the job, and I'd be out of my misery.

But I didn't want to die.

We were at the stern of the boat. They'd given up and were heading for shore. Morelli stood in the shelter of the hatch that led below, Paco was holding me up as Fred tied something to my ankles.

"Slick says we're not far from the house," Paco was telling Fred. "One of his boys will row you to the dock. You walk to the house and pick up the car and meet us at the pier by the club."

"Can't he call for his car at the club or get a cab?"

"He says that's out. Lucky's got his car to look for that damned list and we gotta get back before he wises up to what we're doing. Cab drivers, we don't want; they got eyes and ears."

"All this work and nothing to show for it."

"Yeah, well, you gotta know when you cut your losses." He lifted my face to his. "This is your last chance, Fleming. Where is it?"

Where was what? I couldn't remember.

"He's too far gone, Frank."

"Fleming? Ahh, the hell with him. Hold him up, there's one more thing I been wanting to do."

Fred held me up. Paco pulled out his gun, a big one and he aimed it at my heart. It finally dragged a response from me. My last scream drowned out its roar as he fired.

I felt nothing. A tug and a jerk of the body and then blessed release from the pain. My body was pushed backward, somer-saulting into the dark water, and I sank quickly, leaving a stream of bubbles homing toward the surface. The weight of my ankles pulled me steadily down into cold, unbearable pressure. If I'd been breathing I'd have surely suffocated. The pressure grew and grew and I began to fight it. Something inside wanted out. It seized my inert form, encompassed it . . .

I floated, just another bubble compressed into a moving plastic sphere by the water. I was going to float to heaven.

I made it as far as the surface. The thing that saved me now drove me over the water. Some instinct rushed us straight to the nearest shore. My mind didn't question this, it was perfectly normal the way the most outlandish things are normal when you dream.

There was weight again. Solidity. Rain soaking my soaked clothes. Wind against my face, the same wind that drove away the clouds.

I looked up and winced at stars as bright as the sun.

11

THE SILHOUETTE OF a head eclipsed the lights of the cabin. It looked familiar. I moved my hand in a feeble gesture to it, my fingers brushed against heavy satin. Not too far away I heard a woman draw a sharp breath, making a little surprised noise, the kind women make when they open a drawer and find a bug lurking in their frilly things. My fingers closed on the satin, but let go almost immediately because there was no strength in them. The angle of light changed on the silhouette and revealed some bony features.

"Take it easy, old man, there's no hurry."

Escott? What the hell was he doing here? I blinked and made an effort to get my eyes working again. He was a little green in the gills himself, and for some odd reason he was wearing that silly purple bathrobe of his. My hand had clutched at the heavy quilted lapels.

"Isn't that too warm for the weather?" I asked idiotically.

"There was no time to change."

"Why not?"

"My invitation here was rather abrupt."

I thought about that one and blinked fully awake. "What the hell are we talking about?"

"You're concussed. Just take it easy and you'll sort things out soon enough."

He made it sound as though everything were fine, but something was going on that was very wrong, and I couldn't take it easy until I found out what. I got my elbows on the floor and pushed. Escott helped and I was sitting up, resting my back against a table leg. Feeling for damage, I found a bloodied patch on my head. It was sticky and the hair was matted.

Escott moved and I could see the rest of the room. I was the center of attention of four pairs of eyes.

Bobbi caught my attention first. She'd been the one who gasped when I first moved; she couldn't be blamed for that since she thought I'd been killed. She was in a loose black garment, her version of a bathrobe. Her face was drained of color and pinched, her hazel eyes wide with whites showing. She sat rigidly on the window seat, her hands clutching the edge of the cushion with her shoulders up by her ears. I smiled at her and tried to make it reassuring with a slight wink, and she relaxed, but only a little.

Next to her but not too close was Slick Morelli. His eyes were big, too, his whole body radiating tension. Of the two of them, he was the most frightened. For him this was the third time I'd returned from the dead. God knows what was going on in his mind as he stared at me.

To the left, backed against the cabin door, was Gordy, his head crowding close to the low ceiling and his silenced .45 automatic in his big hand. It wasn't aimed at me, but at Escott. Maybe he'd wised up somehow, I couldn't tell with him. He was looking more worried than scared and his eyes would twitch to one side, then back to me.

The fourth pair of eyes were sunk deep in gray hollows, studying me and missing nothing. They were eyes that should have belonged to a victim of starvation, but their owner was anything but underfed, chronically unsatisfied, perhaps, but not underfed. The brown bristle of the beard ringing his lower face camouflaged the spare chins and made his head look like it was growing straight from the shoulders without the convenience of a neck. The skin on his bald dome was dull, and I wondered if he was unhealthy or just shaved too much. He alone looked almost relaxed, but then he apparently knew exactly what he was dealing with, in his hands and cocked with the wood bolt aimed at my heart, was a crossbow.

Escott followed my gaze and looked apologetic. "Sorry, Jack. He turned that one up from my collection."

"How much does he know?"

"Rather a lot, I fear. Allow me to introduce you to Lucky Lebredo, the rightful owner of the list."

"I know he's the owner."

"Then you know I want it back," he said. He spoke as though the least amount of contact with me, even verbal, would somehow soil him.

"How did you find this out?" I gestured at his weapon.

His eyes flicked from me to Escott. "Tell him."

Escott sighed and settled himself against the other table leg. "I'm afraid it got started when you rescued me from Sanderson and Georgie. Mr. Lebredo, through channels he refuses to divulge, got my name from Georgie Reamer. Being interested in Paco's activities, he became curious as to why a relatively unimportant private agent as myself should be so permanently put out of the way, and how I managed to avoid such a fate. Georgie said I had help, and so Mr. Lebredo had a watch put on me and I was followed. He must have been a very good man, too. My trips to your hotel were noted and he became aware of our association, and had you followed as well."

"Even to—"

"Yes, even to there."

Lebredo had a look of supreme disgust on his face. It was fine with me; I didn't like him, either.

"He learned of our visit to Frank Paco and of the little incident in the alley behind the club which cost me a bloodletting. He learned that you had been killed, apparently at least, by Morelli's man during a clumsy attempt to search for it and found you in your trunk and wondered how you got there from the street. The same day he visited your room to search for it and found you in your trunk and wondered how you got there from the street. The earth in your trunk struck him as being very odd. He is not an ignorant man, nor an especially superstitious one, but it did require some effort to piece his bits of information together to a logical, if unlikely conclusion. Your plaguing of Morelli confirmed his guess, and tonight he decided to make his move."

"So he kidnapped you to use as a lever?"

"Yes. As I said, I had little choice in the matter when three of his men came crashing through my door. I couldn't put up much of a fight with these stitches, either. I am most frightfully sorry about the crossbow."

I looked at Lebredo, he made me forget how much my head hurt. There wasn't much to read in his face except for disgust, and that got old pretty fast, so I looked at Bobbi instead to see how she was taking all this. She was holding up fairly well, considering she was learning some things about me the hard way, that is, if it was making any sense to her. Her mouth tightened. I think it was meant to be a smile, at least she wasn't afraid of me and that was something.

"I want the list," said Lebredo in a flat voice. "I want it tonight."

"It talks," I said.

The crossbow moved slightly, I was one finger twitch away from dying permanently. "Gordy," he said.

The .45 went off, the big silencer cutting the roar down to a manageable level. Escott jumped, jerking his hand. The bullet had gone between his spread fingers where they had rested on the floor. One of them had been nicked, he put it to his mouth. The guy had real guts, he wasn't even shaking. His eyes were on Lebredo, bright and cold. If their places had been suddenly reversed, Lebredo would have been dead and not easily.

The fat man ignored him and spoke to me. "I will give you that one warning. The next time Gordy will shoot off his arm."

Things were still, hearts and lungs were working hard. There were too many to tell one set from another, but I didn't need that kind of information to know he wasn't bluffing.

I drew a short breath. "Okay. I'll get it for you."

"Jack—" said Escott.

"It's all right. I've remembered. Between Morelli and this boat, things jogged into place. I know where I left it." I looked at Morelli. "I also know what you and Paco and Sanderson did to me."

"But it wasn't—" protested Morelli.

"Be quiet, Slick," said Lebredo.

"But it couldn't—"

His voice raised slightly. "I won't tell you again."

Morelli shut up.

"That's better. Your skepticism is understandable, but your boundless stupidity is not. If you still need more proof, look at the girl's neck. The marks there are small, but not invisible."

Escott's eyebrows went up and his mouth popped open and shut before he blanked out his face, wisely deciding that my love life was my own business.

Morelli was not quite as liberal minded and he pulled at the neck of her wrap. Bobbi tried to shrug him off, but he forced her to hold still. When he saw them he let her go and crossed the room to get away from her. He even wiped his hands on his clothes. Bobbi glared at him—no woman likes that kind of rejection—then her eyes glazed at Lebredo.

"You fat, stinking bastard." She got up and went to the door, stopping inches away from Gordy. Gordy looked at Lebredo for a cue, seemed relieved when he got one, and moved aside. She tore the door open and left. Morelli started to object, but Lebredo curtailed it.

"This is a boat, where can she go? Her faithlessness can be dealt with later, or need I remind you that you were the one to encourage it to start with? You have forgotten that women are very dangerous children and should not be trusted."

"Shut up!"

"For now, we'll consider how to deal with you. You and Paco betrayed me to get the list for yourselves—"

"And why'd you go to Paco for it, huh? You could have asked me."

"I'm not stupid enough to send an ape to look for a banana and expect to get it from him. I went to Paco because he obeyed orders as long as there was sufficient money, but he went to you, which was a very bad mistake. He found out exactly what he was looking for, then you both decided to keep it. I should have guessed at what was going on when you both disappeared for three days."

"We still didn't get it."

"That was very fortunate, or else I should have to take it back from you, perhaps even trying the same method you used with Fleming."

"Try it and see how long you live. New York wouldn't stand—"

"Your New York friends and I have an agreement. They understand how valuable I can be even if you do not. I made sure of that. They're running a business these days and have learned that hotheads like you are a liability. Don't rely on them to avenge your carcass, because your crude actions have put you in a very bad spot. Three times you had this man in your hands and you failed because you didn't take the trouble to look for his weak points and play on them."

Morelli shook his head and went over to the bar to pour out

a stiff one. He drank it down straight and poured another, then lit one of his cigars.

"Put that damned thing out," I said.

He seemed surprised that I spoke to him but wasn't about to douse it on my order, so he kept puffing. I slowly got to my feet so as not to startle Lebredo. My head was still bad, but not unbearable. I went to Morelli, yanked the cigar from his mouth, and crushed it.

"That is really a disgusting habit you got."

He hit me in the face with his fist, this time I didn't fake being hurt by the blow. It jarred my head a little, but for him it was like trying to punch out a tree. He yelped and clutched his hand. I grabbed the scruff of his neck and tossed him across the room. He smashed against the wall, sank to the floor, and didn't move. I went to the window seat and dropped onto it, tired. Lebredo and Gordy hadn't budged, which was fine with me.

"All right, let's go get your stinking list and clear this up."

"Where is it?" asked Lebredo.

"I hid it in the big library on Michigan Avenue, up on one of the shelves. I'd have to show you where."

Gordy shook his head. "He gave us that kind of story before."

"You weren't pointing a gun at my friend's head then."

"The library's closed now," said Lebredo.

"I have a way to get in. Let's go get it if it's still there."

"It had better be."

Morelli groaned and rolled over. That decided Lebredo, he didn't want to stick around for any debates. He took Gordy's gun in one hand, leaving Gordy free to find some rope. They had Escott stand and his hands were tied behind him and a gag was forced into his mouth.

"Gordy . . ." It was Morelli, looking groggy. "For Chrissake, kill Lebredo."

Gordy paused, not turning to look at him. "I can't, Slick, you know I can't."

Morelli got unsteadily to his feet, leaning on the table.

"I'm not going to forget you said that, Slick," Lebredo told him. "Gordy knows better than to cross me. He knows what defenses I have arranged if anything happens to me, and so do you."

"Damn you . . . Goddamn you—" There was a soft click

and Morelli threw his knife. It was the last thing he said and
did. Lebredo ducked and fired twice. Morelli twitched back from
the impact and lay still. He stared at us and we stared at him.
Lebredo gave the gun back to Gordy and we all filed out.

Lebredo either had control of Morelli's crew or replaced them
with his own men; either way they got a rowboat ready for us
without questions on the gunplay below. Gordy and Escott got
in it first, along with a man to handle the oars. They reached
the pier and their figures left the boat and slowly climbed the
steps. They waited for us just outside the cone of light from the
streetlamp. The boat returned and I got in, clutching the sides
and trying not to think about the black water all around and the
crossbow behind me. It took forever to row to the pier. My
presence made the passage difficult for the oarsman. He was
puffing and covered with sweat from the effort when we finally
got there. I thankfully climbed up the steps. All I wanted was
plenty of land between me and the water.

Morelli's big car was waiting for us on the road. Escott and
Gordy got in the front seat, Lebredo in the back. They put me
behind the wheel and the first thing I felt was the crossbow
brushing my neck. I could have whipped around and grabbed it,
but that would have left Escott with a stomach full of lead and
a convenient lake to sink him in. Lebredo, poker player that he
was, held all the cards. I started the car, worked the gears as
smoothly as I could, and drove to the big library.

As directed, I parked on an empty side street in between the
glow of the two streetlights. Lebredo told me to get out. I got
out.

"No tricks, no funny stuff. You get it and come straight back
here and I'll tell you where your trunkful of earth is."

"You took it?"

"Ask your friend."

Escott nodded in confirmation, his shoulders drooping. He
was feeling responsible for the mess and could do nothing to
make things right again.

Lebredo went on. "You wouldn't have had it if you didn't
need it. I put it in a very safe place, just in case Escott wasn't
enough of a lever."

A lot of things to call him came to mind as I glared at his
impassive face. I might have been able to take him out, but was

in a tactically poor position to take care of Gordy as well, and he was looking nervous.

I pushed away from the car and walked around to the front of the library. It was well after two, but there were still a few lonely cars cruising up and down the street on their own business. A block away a beat cop was rattling doorknobs, but I couldn't ask him for help. Explanations would take too long and Gordy could cut him down easily enough if Lebredo told him to. The cop might even be one of his blackmailing victims, Benny O'Hara had made that much clear. For the moment I was stuck.

I went inside and re-formed, climbing the stairs quietly to the right floor and keeping a look out for a night watchman. I was still dressed in what was left of my haunting clothes, odds were the guy would either shoot or have a heart attack at the sight of me.

It was a big place; my steps echoed loud in my ears, the quality of sound giving me the creeps. I found the right section and went to the very back to the correct shelf. Raising a hand, I felt along the top, but my fingers scrabbled over smooth bare surface. Nothing was there.

Partially dematerialized I let myself float up. The shelf was clean. Of all the lousy times to dust the joint . . .

I forgot to concentrate, went solid, and dropped to the floor with a jolt.

Damnation. And a lot of other useless words.

Lebredo would never buy it. Escott was a goner. I fumed and cursed and accomplished little in the way of coherent thought, wanting to tear the place apart, especially the jerk who had been cleaning. The papers could have gotten anywhere after all this time, most likely they were long lost to the garbage.

I sulked past the main desk. The wastebaskets were empty. Just for the hell of it, I rooted around. Some of the drawers were locked, but after seeing the handles were strong enough, I broke them open anyway and discovered the lost-and-found box.

Envelopes, magazines, a purse, eyeglasses, and a sheaf of loose papers. The two sheets I wanted were mixed in with them. If I'd been breathing I'd have sighed with relief.

Lebredo's flat eyes took on a kind of gleam as he watched me return and get back in the car. Escott gave me a questioning look, I nodded, hoping Lebredo would keep his word and knowing that that was a long shot at best. Feeling naked, I turned my back on him and watched him in the mirror.

"Hand them over."

He took them and leaned back to examine them in the dim light. Escott's eyes were closed and the air hissed softly from his compressed nostrils. He wanted me to do something, but I was stuck until the situation changed. I was hoping Lebredo would not make his final move in the car.

"Very good," he said, folding them into his pocket with one hand. "Now you will drive where I tell you."

This was it, the kind of one-way ride that Chicago had made famous, only I was the chauffeur.

"You got your stuff, let him go."

"No." A simple, unarguable denial. "Start the car and drive. I can kill you both now or later, I think even you would prefer a little more time."

His undisguised disgust for me was reciprocated, but I did start the car. Teeth and gears grinding in frustration, I followed his directions. The route was familiar. Escott and I exchanged puzzled looks as I completed the last order and turned the car into the driveway that led to Frank Paco's big house.

I braked next to the front door. Gordy got out and pulled Escott with him. Lebredo heaved his way from the back and held the crossbow on me as I emerged. The place was dark and quiet except for the sound of crickets and our feet crunching on the white gravel.

"Is my trunk here?"

"Open the door."

It was unlocked, the others followed me into a marble-lined entry hall. The air still had a sharp, smoky tang to it and the ceiling showed signs of discoloration from soot. The electricity had been fixed. Lebredo hit the lights. I blinked in the sudden brightness. He wasted no time, planting his broad feet carefully and taking aim.

I tried to buy more time. "Why here?"

"Why not? Paco's men found you here the night of the fire. They've been squealing that often enough to save their skins from the arson charge, so the police know it, too. You've been connected with Paco and Morelli, the police will jump to the easy and obvious conclusion that Paco's men killed you out of revenge."

"In an all-too-obvious location, don't you think?"

"A thin case for the district attorney's office, but a suggestion or two from me and the investigation will go no further."

"They're on your list, too?"

"A few key people."

"You don't ask them for money, do you? You don't really need it; it's being able to tell people what to do, to make them sweat."

"No doubt."

"But you don't have to do this. You must know I can be very useful to you."

"But the only way I have of controlling you is with Escott and possibly Miss Smythe, and such an arrangement would be complicated and clumsy. If I can't have complete control over someone, I don't bother; my present arrangement is satisfactory. It's much simpler to kill you, you're too much of a threat to me and everyone else."

"I can't see you doing this for the sake of saving humanity from my kind."

"That's right, I'm doing it for myself." He pulled the trigger.

I wasn't over running water this time, the second his finger tightened past the halfway point I vanished. The wooden bolt cut through the space where I'd been and imbedded in the wall beyond. At the same time a gun went off.

Escott.

I hurtled past Lebredo, materialized in front of Gordy, and grabbed the gun from him. He offered no resistance even when I shoved him hard into Lebredo. Both men staggered and Lebredo's hard-to-balance body went down.

I expected to see Escott dead or wounded because of my delay and Gordy's speed, but he was standing, white faced, looking out the open front door. Gordy did, too, then glanced down at the grunting man on the marble.

"Hey—somebody got Lucky."

I truly believe he never meant it as a joke, but outside someone laughed. Bobbi walked stiffly into the room, both her small hands held together clutching a gun. Her lips were knife thin, her face hard with hate. We all stepped away from her, except for Lebredo, who was gaping and glaring in sheer disbelief. He'd forgotten to take his own advice about women.

Gordy made a helpless gesture. "Bobbi, why'dya do that for? You know what'll happen to me?"

"I know how to take care of it," she finally said. She was having trouble talking. Her breath was uneven as she tried to hold back the tears.

Escott made an impatient noise. I pulled the gag out. It took a moment for him to work the saliva into his mouth to talk. I unknotted the ropes on his wrists. He thanked me and went to check Lebredo.

"*Keep away from him!*" Bobbi's voice went up to a near-shriek. Escott stepped hastily back and looked at me.

"Bobbi . . ." I said.

"I heard him in the car. I heard him telling Gordy what they were going to do with you and how they were going to get rid of Slick's body."

Lebredo twisted himself upright with some difficulty. "Gordy, take the gun from her. You know what will happen to you if I die."

"Oh, do be quiet," Escott said irritably. He had the right idea. The more Lebredo opened his mouth, the worse he made things for himself.

"Gordy—"

Bobbi made a short, sharp noise, like she wanted to call him a name but couldn't think of one bad enough. Instead, she pulled the trigger. Lebredo yelled and grabbed his shoulder.

"For Godsake, Gordy!"

She fired again, clipping him in the side. Her eyes squinted slightly as some of the gun smoke drifted into her face.

Lebredo bared his short, blunt teeth. "You dirty little whore, I'll make sure you—"

She gave out a strangled half-scream of rage and fired again, hitting him square in the face. He flopped back spread-eagled, his big stomach jiggling a little, then going still.

No one moved for quite a while. Bobbi's face took on more normal lines. She seemed smaller in some way. Without looking at us, she carefully wiped the gun down with the hem of her black wrap, placed it on the floor, and walked outside.

Gordy chewed the inside of his lower lip and looked worried.

Escott heaved a sigh, then calmly picked up his crossbow and clucked over some scratches on the stock. He went through bredo's pockets, fastidiously avoiding the silent red explosions, and pulled out the list, offering it to me.

I shook my head. "You keep it, I don't even want to see the damn thing." I gave him Gordy's gun and went outside.

Bobbi was leaning back against the car, her arms crossed with one heel resting on the running board. Her hair was a tangled, damp mess and her makeup had been smeared by a good cry. She was just beautiful.

I was hesitant to approach her, but she looked up and smiled wanly.

"I was afraid I'd be too late, I thought he'd gotten you."

"How did you get here?"

"The minute I was out of the cabin I rolled my shoes up in this robe and went overboard. It's not a long swim to the pier, and a person swims better naked." Feeling modest now, she pulled the wrapper more tightly around her shoulders. "I knew he'd use the car sometime, so I hid in the trunk."

"Are you all right?"

She nodded. "Now I am. I didn't think I could do anything . . . but when I heard him talking—it doesn't seem like I did it now, it's like it happened to someone else."

"He made it easy."

"I wanted to help you and to get back for Slick. He was a roughhouse, but sometimes he was good to me. I guess it's not just bodies after all."

"Where'd the gun come from?"

"It's Slick's. He always kept a spare in the glove compartment. The cops'll think he did it." She looked at the open door of the house.

"He couldn't do it and be dead on the yacht."

"He can if we get Gordy to help."

"Gordy? But—"

"Lebredo's got some stuff on him, that's why Gordy had to play the stooge. I figure it's with his lawyer. You can imagine what kind of lawyer Lebredo had. We just offer him more money and buy it from him."

"And if he doesn't sell?"

"Then you can burgle the place. From what I heard you've got a real talent for it."

"You don't mind what I am?"

"I don't care about that. You are what you are. You don't

judge me, I don't judge you. But could you tell me how you got this way?''

"Because of a woman."

She shook her head and laughed a little. "I guess we're starting even. I'm the way I am because of a man." She went tiptoe and kissed me. "Come on, let's get this mess out of the way. I'm tired."

With Bobbi's persuasion, we called a truce with Gordy. He drove us back to the yacht while she explained what she could do about Lebredo's lawyer. All Gordy had to do was transport Morelli's body to Paco's house so it'd look like they shot each other. I guess in a remote way they had.

"With any luck," she said, "no one's going to know they're dead for a couple of days at least, and by that time we'll have found your stuff."

Gordy nodded agreeably, he trusted her. He set the brakes and started out of the car, and I grabbed his shoulder.

"Where's my trunk?"

"Trunk?" He winced. I eased my grip.

"Lebredo took it," said Escott. "Where is it?"

"But he didn't, said it was too much trouble. He told me to go along with him on that. He just let it drop to keep you both in line."

I shook my head. "A bluff."

Gordy shrugged. "Poker was his game." We all got out and watched him walk down the pier to the rowboat. He started talking to the oarsman, telling him about the change of situation.

"I hope he remembers to leave his gun with Lebredo so the bullets match up," I said.

"He might also wish to clean the clip and the unspent bullets left in it of any prints as well," Escott suggested.

"I'll make sure," said Bobbi. "We may need the car. Will you be able to get home all right?"

"Yeah, I'll call you tomorrow night. Promise."

She kissed me again and went to join Gordy.

"What a very remarkable girl," Escott commented as we walked slowly away, headed for my car that I'd parked near the club.

"I think so."

"You know this makes us all accessories after the fact?"

"Yeah, but do you think she should go to jail?"

"Not for a single hour." He looked like he wanted to say more, but he was tired and it was a long walk for him. He eased into the passenger seat with a grateful sigh, then pulled out the list and squinted at the figure-covered pages.

"Benny said something about substitution." I started the motor.

"Then it shouldn't be too difficult to solve." He nodded at the eastern sky. "You'll have to hurry, the dawn does not wait."

"*I* should be the one to say things like that."

"Yes, but you're not as melodramatic as I am."

"That's a shame. Considering what I've become, I really ought to go in for it."

His eyebrows twitched. "You're not seriously thinking of acquiring a black opera cape?"

I chuckled. "Don't be ridiculous. It's the wrong season and they cost too much anyway."

He looked relieved.